Volume I

Captivity

Mike pointed. His mouth opened and closed, but no sound came. Wade turned. Something stood in the dark shadow of the trees, only glimpsed in the flickering firelight, except for the glowing red eyes. Eyes too high off the ground to be a raccoon. Wade scrambled to his feet and backed away until he ran into Mike, now also standing.

"What's the matter with you guys?" Josh asked drunkenly, looking around.

It stepped from the shadows into the firelight, short, maybe five foot four inches, and female, although that was only an impression. All that was really visible in the firelight was a white face surrounded by black. The eyes stopped glowing red and became black, piercing, hypnotizing. Scarlet lips were a slash across the white face.

"Oh, Wade." The soft voice was lyrical and seductive. The mouth smiled, red lips stretched back and parted, and Wade saw sharp, pointed fangs. A pink tongue licked lips hungrily. "Come here, Wade."

Wade's heart raced with fear.

What They Are Saying About
Captivity

"Not a vampire devotee, I had no preconceived notions when I began reading Captivity by Linda Suzane. Am I glad I started it on a weekend, because I simply HAD to finish it RIGHT AWAY. In a word, Wow! The power of Ms. Suzane's writing propels you into the story with vivid images, strong characterization, and totally believable scenario. An unequivocal thumbs-up!"

--Christine Janssen,
author of Dark Legacy

"I'm awaiting the next book in what promises to be an entertaining new series. I'm looking forward to more about the past, present, and future of Linda Suzane's vampire world. I would recommend Captivity to fans of the vampire genre."

--Kate Hill,
author of the God of Grim.

Linda Suzane pulls off this vampires' tale with finesse and flair. She has an uncanny way in Captivity of combining two plot lines into one incredible story. If vampirish stories are right up your alley, then you won't want to miss this one!

--Patricia A. Rasey,
author of Deadly Obsession
and the Hour Before Dawn

A fast-moving "good vampire vs. evil vampire" adventure, with the two sides fighting over a kidnapped teenage boy, CAPTIVITY has rich characterization as well as sustained suspense. The "evil" vampire is sometimes almost pitiable in her madness, and the "good" vampire has enough of a dangerous edge to make him believable as a centuries-old creature of the night. Linda Suzane achieves a fresh approach to the familiar vampire problem of tension between living ethically in the human world and protecting the secret of the immortal blood-drinkers' existence.

--Margaret L. Carter,
author of Dark Changeling (www.hardshell.com),
winner of the 2000 Eppie Award for Horror

Wings

Darkhour Vampires

Volume I

Captivity

by

Linda Suzane

A Wings ePress, Inc.

General Fiction Paranormal Novel

Wings ePress, Inc.

Edited by: Marilyn Kapp
Copy Edited by: Dianne Hamilton
Senior Editor: Marilyn Kapp
Managing Editor: Dianne Hamilton
Executive Editor: Lorraine Stephens
Cover Artist: Pat Casey

Wings ePress Books
http://www.wings-press.com

ISBN 1-59088-904-5

Published In the United States Of America

July 2002

Wings ePress Inc.
403 Wallace Court
Richmond, KY 40475

Dedication

This book is dedicated to my husband, Jerry, who has always supported my dream to be a writer. Married over 30 years, I couldn't have asked for a better or more loving husband. I got a real winner.

I would also like to say a great big thank you to my favorite writing comrade, Walt Kleine, whose keen eyes and flaming red pen improved this book immensely. Thanks for being my editor as well as my friend.

And finally to my grandson, Draven, whom I hope will someday grow up to think it is neat to have a grandmother who writes about vampires.

One

Wade dropped his backpack and stood looking around the glade. The late afternoon sun slanted through the pine trees to spotlight soft green ferns. In the still quiet, the murmur of the stream rushing past the campsite and the mingled song of several birds, counter-pointed by the high bright voice of another, seemed almost deafening. Wade looked up into the forest canopy, trying to spot the songster. He couldn't, but neither could he get rid of the feeling that something was watching. Then he heard the chattering scold of a squirrel and spotted him, staring down from a tree branch, gray tail twitching. Wade smiled and let the woods fill him with the peace and sense of belonging he always got when he went camping.

"Wow, what a great spot!" Mike exclaimed, effectively silencing the sounds of the woods.

For an instant, Wade resented the intrusion, then he turned to his friend. "I told you it was. My dad and I used to come here a lot, but we haven't been here since Mount St. Helen's erupted last year." Wade looked around. The Santiam Wilderness, seventy-five miles south of Portland, had been too far from the eruption to get more than a light dusting of ash. The woods looked as he had always remembered them--rich with that fresh, May spring green.

It had been Mike's idea to go camping to celebrate Wade's birthday. Just the guys--Mike and his big brother, Josh, who was twenty-one and supposedly a responsible adult. A weekend alone in the woods. Mike planned it for weeks. No, they had planned it. The only thing better would have been to bring a couple of chicks, but they had a hard enough time convincing Wade's parents they were old enough to go camping on their own to even tackle the girl thing. But he was old enough, an adult. Next month, when school ended, he would graduate, class of 1981. If he was still going to his old school, graduation would have meant something, but he had been going to school in Portland for less than a year. He felt lost among a class of seniors larger than all the students from his old high school put together. Mike, who lived in the same apartment complex, was his first, and sometimes Wade felt, his only friend in Portland.

Josh straggled in, unloaded his pack, and collapsed onto the ground, back against a log. "You guys didn't tell me it was going to be such a hike."

Josh had quit school at sixteen, had a child he never saw or cared to see, and worked as a gas jockey. He'd been recruited to give the trip the appearance of adult supervision. Mike had laughed and said it was a good thing that Wade's parents really didn't know his brother.

"Hey," Mike said, "let's go skinny dipping."

"That water's like ice," Wade protested.

"Yeah, I know. I like it when my balls pull up so tight, they like disappear. Come on. It's time that you started to live."

Wade laughed and started pulling off his jacket. "Race you." Both boys ran, leaving clothes in a scattered path across the rocky bank. At the stream's edge, Wade pulled off his hiking boots and pants. "Follow me." He leaped naked onto a large rock, then rock-hopped across the stream to the fishing hole, a spot where the stream had scoured out a deep pool. The water was smooth and dark. They stood staring into the depths, the sun hot against their naked bodies.

"Now!"

They jumped into the water together. There was a great splash, and both boys screamed, half with the abrupt shock of the cold and half with glee. They splashed each other. Mike tried to push Wade's head under, but Wade flipped him off and climbed, shivering, onto the rock. He reached out his hand and pulled Mike up. They lay shivering, trying to soak up warmth from the sun and the stone.

"This is the life," Mike said. "I'd stay here forever if I could."

"Not me," Wade replied. "I got dreams. I'm going into the army when I graduate, or maybe the navy. I want to learn to take care of myself. I don't want to spend my life in one place."

"What about Wanda?"

Wade laughed. "You mean Want'ta Wanda?"

"Yeah." Mike licked his lips. "She's really got the hots for you. She wants to get in those pants of yours and see what you got." Mike made a close inspection. "Not that it's much."

Wade laughed and made a mock grab for Mike's genitals. "Yours ain't any bigger."

"But it gets bigger, much bigger."

"Well, so does mine, when it's not cold and lonely," said Wade.

"The only friend yours has is your hand," Mike shot back.

"I'm saving myself for the right girl."

"Man, if I had your looks, I'd have so many chicks."

Wade found it hard to think of himself as good looking, but more than one girl had told him so. They liked his black hair. Once, a girl told him it was so thick and shiny, so soft looking that it just begged to have a girl's fingers run through it. But most of all they liked his eyes. His mother called his eyes bedroom eyes and told him they'd get him into trouble if he wasn't careful.

Wade supposed he should have done "it" before now. He'd had chances. He wasn't sure why he hadn't taken them, except, maybe, his mother and father. They were happily married, about the only parents he knew who had never been divorced. When he was thirteen, he and his dad had that "father-son" talk. His father told him how his mother had been a virgin, but he hadn't, and how much he regretted it.

"When you find the right person," his father said, "it's so much better, it's worth the wait." His dad had gotten the silliest grin on his face after that. He had even blushed. Wade had known it wasn't just something his father felt he had to say. The regret was real when his father warned him not to let his friends tease him into doing "it."

He knew his parents expected him to wait, but it was also the fact that the only girls who seemed to go for him were like Want'ta Wanda. He couldn't imagine going through life remembering her as his first. He really liked Sue. She was petite, blonde, and on the cheerleading squad, but she was also already going steady with the captain of the football team.

He flipped over on his stomach to let the last afternoon rays warm his back. "You want to go in again?"

"No way!" Mike said. "I'm still shivering."

Wade looked over the edge of the rock into the stream. "Too bad we scared away all the fish. I could've caught dinner."

"Really?"

"Sure. My dad and I do it all the time. Let's go back. I'm getting hungry, and we have to make camp before it gets dark."

They put on their pants and boots, picked up the rest of their clothes, and made their way back up the shale to the camp. Josh sat just where they had left him, although now he had a cigarette in one hand and a beer in the other.

Mike grabbed the beer out of his brother's hand and took a big swallow, then passed the can to Wade. Wade hesitated for a moment, then took a drink.

Previous campers had built a nice fire pit, even left some firewood behind, but Wade gathered more. It was still May, and the woods would be cold tonight. They hadn't brought a tent, only sleeping bags. They were roughing it, this time.

Later, as they sat around the roaring fire, Wade wasn't surprised that Josh had complained about the hike. He had two six-packs of beer and a bottle of tequila in his backpack. After they finished dinner, Josh produced a joint of marijuana, which he generously shared. Almost solemnly, they passed the joint around. Wade took the can of beer Mike handed him. He thought about what his dad would say if he knew about the beer and the marijuana. Wade had already heard the lecture on the dangers of drugs, but marijuana didn't do anything more than give him a gentle buzz. He wondered what was so bad about that.

"Hey, what's that?" Mike demanded. "Did you hear something?"

Wade shook his head. "It's probably just an animal. You know the woods are full of them. They live here."

"Oh, sure."

"Or maybe it's the demon," Wade said, getting into the spirit of the darkness and the roaring campfire.

"The demon?"

"Yeah, didn't I tell you? About three years ago, a young couple came out here to camp. I'm not sure, this might even be the very spot where they pitched their tent. Then something happened. No one knows for sure, cause they didn't find their bodies for a long time and what was left wasn't pretty. Most people say the demon got them."

"Yeah, sure," Mike said scornfully.

"No, it's true. People have seen the demon for years. Red glowing eyes peering out of the darkness. Sometimes they hear it growl. Others, they say they've heard it howl when it makes its kill. Some people say it's just an old wolf or a mountain lion, but others, they say it's human, but not human. What's really scary--this guy told me, he said it was a suc--suc-something, I can't remember the word. Anyway, it's a demon who appears in the shape of a beautiful woman. She seduces you and then kills you."

"I wouldn't mind if she was pretty enough. Would you, Wade?"

"Yes, I would. I don't want to die. Not yet."

They were quiet for a while.

Mike started. "There! I saw something."

Wade looked where Mike was pointing and saw nothing.

"Red glowing eyes," said Mike.

"Sure you did," Wade answered sarcastically, certain Mike was just trying to scare him.

"Yeah, I did. Josh, did you see that?"

Josh looked around, his eyes glazed, "What'd you say?"

"He wouldn't know if the demon came up and bit him, he's so out of it," Wade said, with a laugh.

Mike kept staring out into the woods, nervously jerking his head from side to side trying to see all around him.

"Come on, Mike, it was probably just a raccoon. Their eyes glow when light hits them, just like a cat or a dog. Relax."

"What if it's the demon?"

Now Wade really laughed. "That's just a story. Me and my dad have been coming here for years. Never saw any demons. A skunk or two, a raccoon, but demons, no. Relax, man."

Mike lay back against the log. “I know I’m being silly, but I can’t help feeling we’re being watched. I don’t know why, but it just feels that way.”

It felt that way to Wade, too, but he wasn’t about to admit it. It was just Mike’s nerves. An animal, nothing more. “What’s your favorite movie monster? Frankenstein or Dracula?”

“Frankenstein? Dracula? That’s kid stuff. Nothing scary about vampires. That last Dracula movie, that Langella guy, ugh, all mush and lovey-dovey. My mother actually likes *Love at First Bite*. Vampires--no way! Now if you want to be really scared, *Friday the 13th Part 2* is opening next week.”

“With an R rating, my folks won’t let me see it.”

Mike grinned. “Hey, you’re eighteen. They can’t stop you.”

“Right!” Wade returned the grin.

“Did you hear that?” Mike sat up and looked around. “I could’ve sworn I heard someone call my name.”

Wade laughed. “I’m not going to fall for that. You’re just trying to scare me.”

“Wade.” It was a whisper, almost a sigh of the wind. Wade wasn’t even sure he had heard it. The sound came again. “Wade.” He looked at Mike, then realized the sound had come from behind him, not from Mike.

Mike pointed. His mouth opened and closed, but no sound came. Wade turned. Something stood in the dark shadow of the trees, only glimpsed in the flickering firelight, except for the glowing red eyes. Eyes too high off the ground to be a raccoon. Wade scrambled to his feet and backed away until he ran into Mike, now also standing.

“What’s the matter with you guys?” Josh asked drunkenly, looking around.

It stepped from the shadows into the firelight, short, maybe five foot four inches, and female, although that was only an impression. All that was really visible in the firelight was a white face surrounded by black. The eyes stopped glowing red and became black, piercing, hypnotizing. Scarlet lips were a slash across the white face.

"Oh, Wade." The soft voice was lyrical and seductive. The mouth smiled, red lips stretched back and parted, and Wade saw sharp, pointed fangs. A pink tongue licked lips hungrily. "Come here, Wade."

Wade's heart raced with fear. Something inside him wanted to obey her command, yet he couldn't move.

Two others emerged from the shadows. Taller than she. Ordinary. A white man with dark hair, wearing a red flannel shirt and jeans, and a skinny black man, young, wearing an Oregon University sweatshirt and black pants. Ordinary, except their lips curled back in hungry grins over long fangs.

Then the white one fell on Josh.

Josh's bewildered "What's up" changed to a scream.

Mike grabbed Wade's arm. "Run, man, run."

Wade ran.

He heard the tinkle of laughter behind him. Then he was out into the darkness, blinded, stumbling, running. He hit the stream, his feet splashing in the cold water, and he turned and ran along the stream bank. He heard Mike stumbling after him; at least he hoped it was Mike. What were those things? What were they doing to Josh? Josh! He should go back, but he kept running.

"Oh, Wade," the voice called. Close to his left. Wade ran harder.

He heard Mike fall and cry out and turned to go back. It was there, in front of him, the white face.

"Run, Wade," it said. Wade turned and ran, leaving Mike behind.

A branch whipped his face, stinging, making his eyes water in pain. Now he really was running blind. He wiped his sleeve across his eyes trying to clear them. He took a deep breath. The trail, the trail that led back to the road. If he could find that and go for help. He took another deep breath and stood still, trying to get his bearings, but in the darkness, it all looked so unfamiliar. He knew the trail went down the mountain to the road, so if he followed the slope downward, maybe he would cross the trail. He pushed through the bushes, hurrying, tripping over rocks and stumps.

"Oh, Wade," the voice called. "I'm coming for you."

Wade's whole body trembled with fear. He tripped over a log and fell hard, knocking the breath out of him. He gasped for air. He knew he had to get up, to run, but he couldn't make himself. Then he knew it was too late. *It--she* was there.

Touching him.

He tried to roll away, but she followed, straddled him. "Be still, I won't hurt you," the voice said. He couldn't see the fangs, only the suggestive blur of her white face in the darkness. He felt her touch, stroking his cheek. "Relax. Don't be afraid. Just come with me quietly. Everything will be all right. I promise you."

A scream sounded through the woods, full of fear and anguish. He knew the voice. Mike's voice. Mike's death cry.

He pushed the thing off of him and struggled to his feet. She grabbed his arm. He tried to break away, but the creature's grip was too strong. She slapped him, so hard he saw stars, the pain radiated up his jaw.

"Enough fun and games, boy. I'm tired of the hunt." She yanked him by the arm. He tried to dig in his heels. She slapped him again. He tasted his own blood from a split lip. "Behave yourself," she commanded. "Or I will be forced to punish you." He could see her dark lips move and knew she was smiling. She dragged him after her; the hand encircling his wrist imprisoned him like an iron manacle. Though she was a good six inches shorter than he was, he felt as though he was no more than a small child being dragged by his angry mother. He was so afraid of that anger.

She pulled him back to the campsite, into the firelight.

The other creature hunched over Josh. He looked up. Blood covered his white face and spotted the bright red of his flannel shirt with a darker red. When the creature stood, Wade looked down at what had been Josh. His white tee shirt was soaked in red, above that, what had been a throat was torn open, red flesh, gaping like an obscene mouth. Josh's own mouth was open in a silent scream. His eyes stared--vacant, dead eyes. Wade bent over and vomited. He couldn't help himself, couldn't stop himself. He knelt on the ground and puked his insides out. The acids burned his mouth, the taste sour. He gagged as he began to have the dry heaves, having no more to give.

Hands pulled him up, lifting him by his collar, holding him so his feet barely touched the ground. He stared into demonic eyes, hungry eyes.

"Wolf," she commanded. "Let him go. He's mine."

Wolf licked his lips hungrily. Wade stared at the fangs, sharp, thin, pointed fangs that sprang from high in the gums, over other teeth, between the canines. Needle sharp. Ready to pierce his neck.

She had her hand on Wolf's arm. "You shouldn't have bolted your dinner, you bad boy. Let him go. He's mine, Wolf!"

Wolf let go and stepped back, hanging his head like a dog, which had disobeyed its master. "Yes, Cassandra."

Wade wasn't sure his legs would support him, but her hand gripped his arm and held him up. Her free hand caressed him. "Don't worry, I'll protect you. You're mine now."

For the first time, Wade got a good look at her. Hooded deep dark-brown, almost black eyes grabbed and held his attention. The face was smooth and wrinkle free, although if he'd been asked to guess, he would have called her middle-aged. The wide mouth distended by the fangs. Not the distorted, evil monster face of the movies, yet a frightening face--cold, predatory, inhuman.

The other one came into the firelight. "Panther, how was it?" she asked.

The one she called Wolf was, maybe, thirty-five. The other one, Panther, was in his early twenties, a black man, with deep dark black-black skin. Wade couldn't see any blood against the black skin, but Panther was licking his fingers clean.

"Oh, Cassandra." He looked at her with eyes of adoration. "His blood was so hot and sweet. And he was so frightened. So very frightened."

Wolf laughed. "This one was too stoned to be frightened." He laughed again. "I think I'm drunk."

"That happens," the woman said. "Now, be good little boys, and let's go home."

Panther looked at Wade. "What about him?"

"He's mine. You will not touch him. Do you understand?"

Panther looked at her. "You're going to keep him, aren't you?"

"Yes."

"But Cassandra," Panther whined.

She patted his cheek. "Don't worry. I will still love my Panther, but I'm bored. You wouldn't deny me a new play toy?"

Panther looked at Wade, a look so full of jealous anger and hatred that Wade found himself trembling.

As Cassandra pulled Wade out into the darkness, Wade glanced back at Josh, lying dead beside the campfire. Somewhere in the woods, Mike lay dead.

"Where are you taking me?" Wade asked. No one answered.

~ * ~

Wade followed Cassandra blindly through the darkness, tripping and stumbling, her hand wrapped tightly around his wrist, his only guide. None of the three stumbled, but walked confidently through the night. They were climbing now, a narrow trail, no more than a track. Then they rounded a rock and slipped behind it. What little illumination the stars had provided was gone, and he was in the cold, dank darkness of a cave. The perfect black, black. Still, they moved unerringly. Finally, a grating sound, stone against stone, and a dim light appeared as a door opened and they entered a tunnel lit by a smoky torch.

Wade looked back as he was pulled down the tunnel and saw the door sealing itself. Irregular, jagged-edged like rock. A secret entrance, into where?

A second door, this one heavy wood, banded with metal, then they were inside a building. Plastered walls, tile floors. Oil lamps, hung from an arched ceiling, cast a soft yellow glow.

"Now, boys," Cassandra said, "Go entertain yourselves. I want to get to know our guest better."

Wolf grabbed Panther's arm and started pulling him down the corridor. Panther went unwillingly, his eyes pinning Wade with hatred.

"Don't mind Panther," Cassandra said, as she led Wade in the opposite direction. "He used to be my favorite, but he'll get used to it." She opened a door and pulled him in. "Welcome to my lair, Wade. I know you're going to enjoy your stay."

Wade felt like Alice in Wonderland having fallen down the rabbit's hole. Or perhaps he had gone back in time. Candles and a fire lighted a room filled with Victorian furniture. He had an aunt who collected Victorian antiques, and there was enough here to make her very happy. The walls were draped in red brocade. Oil paintings hung from thick gold cords. The pictures were nudes, some women, some men, some of couples making love. Statues adorned pedestals and end tables, again nudes.

A man rose from placing a log on the fire. He wore a black, old-fashioned suit and looked like a butler, an old, gray-haired butler.

"Mistress, was it a pleasant evening?"

"Yes, Stanos, a very pleasant evening."

Stanos looked at Wade and smiled. "I see the mistress has found something of interest."

"Yes. Didn't I? Wade, wait here, I won't be but a moment. I want to get out of these clothes and into something comfortable."

Wade looked at her. She wore black pants, a jacket, and high boots. Her hair was black and long, worn in a thick braid that hung over one shoulder. She smiled at him. There were no fangs. She looked human. Wade shook his head, had he only imagined the fangs? No, they had been real.

She left him with Stanos.

"Please, you have to help me," Wade pleaded.

The old man looked at him sternly. "I would suggest, young man, that you do everything possible to please the mistress, or you will not like the consequences."

Wade's heart pounded. He shivered with fear and hopelessness. If he tried to escape, Wolf and Panther would get him. He was trapped. Even the blazing fire couldn't warm the cold chill of fear. To keep himself from thinking about her and what she might do to him, he forced himself to look around the room.

Soon he became uncomfortably aware there was no place that he could look where there weren't erotic statues or paintings. Not pornography. Not like the Playboy magazines the guys hid in their gym lockers. Old oils, old-fashioned women, plump and not particularly attractive, lying seductively on chaises or making love in a stylized countryside. The statues were anatomically correct, reminding him of the pictures of Greek statues in his history book. The beginnings of a boner shocked and disgusted him. He forced himself to stare into the flames of the fire and think of nothing.

He heard her return. Unable to help himself, he turned to look. She wore a black velvet dress that swept the floor; at her throat and cuffs were swirls of red lace. She had combed out her hair. It curled about her shoulders and down her back. She was attractive, in an old sort of way. He guessed she was his mother's age.

She grabbed his hand. He tried to pull away, but her grip was too strong. She tugged him over to the sofa, pulling him down next to her.

Intense dark brown eyes captured his, holding him prisoner in their gaze. When he tried to look away, she grabbed his jaw, forcing him to look at her, holding him still. He heard his heart pounding loud in his ears.

"You find me beautiful, don't you Wade," she whispered. "Very beautiful."

Beautiful. Yes, she was very beautiful.

"You want to be with me, don't you Wade! To stay with me!"

Wade wasn't sure what had happened. The fear he had felt was gone. No, not gone, suppressed. He felt heavy, tired, unable to move. But why should he want to move? He wanted to be with her, to stay with her. She let go of his face.

She looked down at the hand she held. "My poor boy, you've injured yourself." She gently licked away the blood from a gash. She had Stanos bring a basin of water and she began to wash away the dirt and clean Wade's wounds. Where there was blood, she licked the skin clean then washed it.

"Your jacket is dirty and torn. Take it off. It is warm enough in here." Wade suddenly felt hot, the jacket too warm, so he took off his jacket.

She reached for the top button of his shirt. He wanted to stop her, but he couldn't move. He could only stare into her dark eyes.

"Have you ever been with a woman?"

Wade stared at her, not comprehending what she was asking him. She unbuttoned another button on his shirt.

"Have you ever made love to a woman? Tell me the truth, Wade."

"No," he said.

She smiled. "Such a sweet boy you are." His shirt was unbuttoned. She pulled it off his shoulders and down his arms. "You ran so hard, you're positively sweaty. Take off that tee-shirt."

He obeyed.

"But it was such a delicious chase." She stared at his naked chest, and he felt his cheeks grow hot. Taking the wet cloth, she began to wipe down his body, taking her time. He felt himself grow hard within the tight confines of his jeans. When she finished washing him, she looked down at his boots. "Bad boy," she scolded. "You've tracked mud on my beautiful carpet. Take those boots off and Stanos will take them away."

Wade unlaced the boots and took them off. Stanos carried them away as though they were something disgusting, shutting the door behind him, leaving them alone.

"When I saw you in the firelight," Cassandra said, stroking his bare chest, "I knew I had to have you."

She rose and pulled him to his feet. She smiled seductively. "Come, Wade, let me be your first, the first one to teach you about love." She pulled gently on his hand. Without will, he followed.

~ * ~

Wade groaned, his pleasure so intense he thought he might die. Never had he imagined that having sex could feel the way it did.

Cassandra bent her face to his neck and bit. He cried out against the sharp pain then shivered in delight as she began to suck. He felt himself engorging again, still inside her. His face was smothered in the heavy silkiness of her hair. Frenetically, his hands roved up and down the smooth skin of her back and arms.

Her sucking made him arch against her. There was a rhythm he had no will to resist until he exploded inside her. She too arched, lifting her face from his neck and crying out in pleasure.

She rolled off of him, licked his neck another time, and lay curled up next to him, her hand gently resting on his spent penis.

"You were absolutely wonderful, Wade."

Wade found himself touching Cassandra in awe. She was the most beautiful creature he had ever seen, and what she had done, what they had done...he felt himself grow hard beneath her gentle fondling.

"Oh, the resiliency of youth," she whispered, with a slight chuckle. "Well, my love, are you ready for your next lesson?" Without waiting for his answer, she began to teach him.

~ * ~

The city, smelling dirty and crowded, pressed against Donovan. He was alone in the dark street, yet felt the weight of all those lives that inhabited this place, their presence inescapable, hammering against his senses. He longed for the quiet of the clinic, the tranquility of life in Fillmore Grove, where all he had to do was climb the hill behind the clinic to slip away, to slip into the past.

He remembered the first time he had come here, to San Francisco. The flood of gold fever was ebbing, funneling waves of humanity back into the then tiny city. It had been the beginning of winter, and he had come out of the hills, down river on the crowded riverboat, his pockets heavy with gold. He had, as so many like him, never struck it rich, a nugget picked up here and there, a small claim soon cleared. Mostly his gold came from others, won at the gambling tables or earned by providing meat for miners too busy to hunt for themselves. As the snows came to the higher elevations, he found himself wealthy, for unlike most miners, he spent none of his gold on outrageously priced necessities or riotous living. He craved gold, not with the gold fever that burned in most, but as a means to an end.

He burned for knowledge and understanding. What *was* he? Why hadn't he died from the Spanish bullet? Why had everyone at the Alamo died, except for him? Why had he become a monster? But more than understanding, he craved to once again be like other men--to be free of this curse.

He found hope in modern science that was finding cures for all sorts of diseases. With money, he could travel to Europe, seek out specialists, find a cure, and end his suffering. So he had set out to make himself rich, and he had found himself in San Francisco.

Its energy had been just as frenetic then as now. Not as many people, but after his years of isolation, it had been overwhelming. He found the temptation of all the beating hearts and the rich scent of blood too much to bear. He had almost fled in fear of himself and what he might do, when he had felt her pass by. A gaily laughing woman surrounded by men. She stopped, turned around, and came back.

She stood looking at him, and he knew she was like him.

"I'm Amanda."

"Donovan." His voice choked on the one word.

"It's a pleasure to met you. Come, we will go to my place and visit."

The males around her grumbled.

She laughed. "He is a distant cousin, I'm sure."

Amanda had saved him. She told him what he was, a vampire. There was no cure, no end to the nightmare, but at least, he was no longer alone.

Now, Donovan studied the dark empty street in frustration. He knew what he sought must be hiding nearby, but where? Every second that passed moved the newborn closer to killing again. It would be tonight. The last body had been discovered three days ago. The newborn couldn't resist the hunger another night. Donovan walked briskly down the street and turned into the next alley, searching all the time for that which had drawn Amanda to him--the sense of knowing when another of his kind was near. He kept moving. A dark shadow dressed in black. Hunting. Then he caught the trace of feeling, tingling at the edge of his consciousness. He stopped, stood absolutely still, trying to pinpoint the direction. In the distance, he heard something, too faint perhaps for normal hearing, but he heard a fearful whimpering, then a metallic noise, maybe a trash-can falling. He ran toward the sounds, running hard, knowing he was already too late to stop what was happening.

The newborn had an old woman down on the ground behind a garbage dumpster. He crouched over her, his teeth sunk into her throat.

Donovan reached down and ripped the newborn from the woman and threw him hard against the brick wall. The newborn wore a white lab coat, filthy with dirt and blood, and pants he'd stolen from somewhere, or maybe they had been his own. Maybe he hadn't walked out of the morgue naked. His face had been torn in the crash that killed him. Bones broken. It had healed in a fashion, solidified into the face of a nightmare monster.

Damn. This is going to be a hard one.

There was no intelligence in the eyes, only the blind blood lust, the overwhelming need to feed that had driven this creature out of the hole in which he had been hiding. Now he turned on Donovan, as any starving animal would, to protect what was his. Growling and snarling, he leaped.

Donovan put up an arm to protect himself and felt the newborn's teeth sink into his flesh. The force of the charge knocked him backward, hard. His head hit the pavement. The newborn pinned him against the cold, damp concrete. Pain stabbed through him.

Two

The newborn's fangs sank deep into Donovan's flesh. The pain shot up his arm, paralyzing him for a moment. He tried to pull free, but he couldn't loosen the jaws' rabid grip. Donovan forced himself to relax, to let the newborn feed, while his free hand reached for the pistol in his pocket. He found no touch of cold metal. The gun was gone. Blindly his hand groped the ground around him. Nothing but cold, wet, flat pavement. He felt something. It crumbled softly beneath his fingers--paper--trash. His fingers moved on. Something hard, it moved under his hand. Carefully he reached out, afraid he would send it further out of reach.

As his fingers clasped the gun, relief surged through him. Slowly and deliberately, he placed the pistol against the newborn's side and pulled the trigger.

The body above him jerked, then relaxed against him. He pushed it to one side, rose, and hurried over to the victim, who lay in a heap, blood oozing from the neck wound.

"Damn." Donovan went down on one knee, picking up her limp body, his own lips fastening over the wound, the sweet fresh blood spurting into his mouth. He swallowed. He couldn't help himself. God, he wanted to keep drinking, but the poor old woman was still alive. She could be saved if he acted quickly.

Donovan forced himself to stop drinking and began to lick the wound. The healing properties of his salvia slowed the bleeding. He licked the skin around the wound clean of blood then licked the wound again. The bleeding had almost stopped.

But his hunger hadn't. The taste of blood had sent his ever-present need raging, like a burst of oxygen on a smoldering fire. He laid the woman gently on the ground and returned to the newborn. He picked up the man's wrist and bit it neatly, drinking deep, as much for the control it would give him over the newborn as to ease his clamorous hunger.

Donovan drank until almost sated, stopping as he felt the effects of the newborn's tranquilized blood steal over him. The newborn's eyes opened, he writhed under Donovan. Donovan captured the newborn's eyes with his gaze, commanding, but the newborn's blood craze was too powerful. Before the newborn could break free, Donovan took the pistol and shot another tranquilizer dart into the man. Then he carefully licked the blood from his lips. Hiding both bodies behind the dumpster, he went to get the van. On the way back he stopped at a pay phone to call Edmund.

"I've got him. He's in bad shape. I've also got a victim. Alive but severe loss of blood."

"Bring them on in."

Donovan drove into the alley, quickly loaded the bodies into the van, and drove to Edmund's Nob Hill mansion. The lower floors had been converted into a research laboratory, clinic, and operating room.

He carried the old woman in first and laid her on the examining table. Edmund looked at her, took her pulse. "Maybe it would be kinder to let her go. She's been living on the streets."

"Give her the blood."

Edmund had been a large man when alive, tall, broad of shoulder and wide of girth, whose body and attitude reflected the strange combination of hardworking, shrewd businessman and pampered, self-indulgent plantation owner, first in the West Indies and later in the South. He had been middle-aged when he became a vampire. Too much food and drink and self-indulgence had marked his body. Put him in a powdered wig and he would remind one of Ben Franklin. Or maybe he had consciously chosen to model himself after a man he greatly admired.

As Edmund hung a pint of whole blood, O positive, from the stand and worked to insert the IV needle in the woman's arm, Donovan wondered if all vampires created themselves to look like someone else--put on costumes of others' lives, assumed roles that were played out, not on the stage, but in real life. He knew he did. Usually it was the role of the kindly doctor. Tonight it was the hunter. Dress in black. Only his sandy hair and clear blue eyes kept him from appearing sinister.

He went back out to the van for the newborn, hauled him out, and tossed him awkwardly over his shoulder. When Donovan died, he had been considered a tall, strapping young man. Now he was just average.

The newborn hung limp, still under the power of the sedative, but not for much longer. Vampires metabolized drugs rapidly.

He placed the newborn on the second examining table.

Edmund turned his attention from the woman to the newborn. "What's his name again?"

"Thom Barber. He died in a car wreck five days ago. The morgue was backed up. They hadn't gotten around to him when he got up and walked out."

"You didn't stop his first kill did you?"

"No, he's already done that."

Edmund looked down at the grotesque face. "Let's get him to x-ray and see what we need to re-break to get it to heal correctly."

Vampires healed quickly. Sometimes if a bone was broken, it would heal crooked, necessitating breaking it again to bring it back into alignment. A painful process.

Once Edmund had the x-rays, he set up a constant IV drip to kept Thom under sedation while he worked, then he added another pint of blood to the woman's IV.

"You have any to spare?" Donovan asked.

"You hungry?"

The woman's living blood had set up a clamorous need that kept intruding on Donovan's consciousness.

Edmund looked hard at Donovan. "You drank from her?"

"It was the only way to stop the bleeding."

"If you weren't so stubborn, you wouldn't find yourself having problems."

If he drank regularly from humans--Donovan knew that was what Edmund meant. Living blood. If he gave in and satisfied his craving regularly, then it wouldn't hit him like he was a damn alcoholic who finally went off the wagon, but he refused to use humans as merely a food source.

Edmund took a bag out of the refrigerator and stuck it in the microwave to warm. Edmund was the director of the Franklin Blood Bank. Most people assumed it was connected with the Red Cross, but much of the blood went to satisfy vampire needs under the guise of research.

Donovan took the bag and poured the blood into a cup. He sipped, grimacing at the taste, flat, dull, and bitter. He forced himself to keep drinking. Only overindulgence could calm the clamorous need and sooth the hungry beast that was his constant companion.

Edmund turned back to Thom. He cut open the man's face and delicately manipulated bone and muscle. When he finished, he sutured the skin back in place.

"He'll probably have some scarring, but at least he won't look like a Frankenstein monster." After Edmund bandaged Thom's face, he called Willie.

"Yes, master," Willie said, with the deep southern slave accent he'd never lost.

"I need you and Ruby. I've got a hungry newborn who is going to need to feed."

Donovan almost offered his own arm as one of the hosts, but he knew the loss of his blood would only start the vicious cycle of hunger and need again.

"You'll take him back to Oregon?" Edmund asked.

"That's the best place for him for now. Did you get a blood sample so we can figure out his parent?"

"Yes. When are you going to leave?"

"As soon as possible. If you loan me John, we can drive straight through and be there by afternoon."

"When are you going to make your own servant?"

"I've gotten along without one for all these years. I really don't want to bind anyone to me. Besides I can always borrow yours," Donovan said, with a grin.

Grumbling, Edmund went to find his servant.

~ * ~

Thom yanked at the handcuffs attached to the bolt in the floor in the back of the panel truck, snarling like an animal caught in a trap. Donovan let him exhaust himself in the frenzy of fear, waiting for the moment when the rational part would assert itself over the instinctual animal.

"Where are you taking me?" Thom asked in a hoarse voice.

"To a safe place where you won't have to kill to survive."

"Who are you?" Was the next question.

Donovan turned to face Thom and smiled, letting his fangs show. “A friend, someone, just like you.”

The sun was rising; Donovan felt the edge steal over the horizon. Thom felt it too and panicked; above the bandages, fear clouded his eyes--fear of the sun, of being exposed, of being helpless. The same fear echoed through Donovan, though he countered it with his rational mind. He knew he was perfectly safe. The van had been custom designed to protect him. The windows of the car reflected 95% of the sun’s rays. The body of the car was made of special polymers, with layers of insulation, double reinforced, as heavy and strong as a tank, to keep him safe from the weakening and damaging power of the sun. The sun could not harm him. Still, he cringed and felt a pang of sympathy as terror consumed Thom. Whimpering, Thom curled tightly into the fetal position, trying to protect himself against his own fear and the sun. Then the whimpering ceased as the power of the sun claimed its victim, forcing him into the darkness of the daily death.

Despite all the protection, Donovan felt the sun’s power boring into him. He fought to ignore it, to resist its siren’s call to sleep, but it had been a long night and he couldn’t. He turned himself over to the uncertain fate of the day, trusting in Edmund’s servant John to protect him.

~ * ~

Wade was dreaming. He was in a dark place. Sue was there, and they were naked. They had done it. When he looked down at her, he saw she was covered in blood, lying in an ever-widening pool of blood. It glistened beneath her, red, crimson, shining fresh blood. He was shaken awake.

At first Wade didn’t remember where he was--then he saw Cassandra.

“Get up and come with me.” Her voice was harsh. He hurried to obey. She handed him his jeans, and he pulled them on while she waited impatiently. He followed her out of her rooms, down the corridor, to another door, which she unlocked. When he entered, he saw it wasn't a room, but a small cave. The walls were bare rock and the floor dirt and rock. There was a hole in the cave roof, and he could see the sky, soft gray, through it. On the dirt floor was a pile of animal pelts as bedding.

She pushed him over to the pile, bent down and snapped a shackle around his ankle.

The shackle was attached to a long chain that ran through a heavy iron ring embedded in the rock. At the other end was another shackle, too large to pull through the ring. He yanked the chain and then looked at Cassandra.

"Why?"

"It's for your protection, my love. You'll be safe here. And I do want you safe." She kissed him again, long and hard. "Go to sleep. I will see you tonight."

Wade heard her lock the door behind her and he was alone. He lay down on the pile of furs, pulling one over him. They were soft and sensual against his skin. He thought about what had happened, how Cassandra made him feel, how wonderful she was, but he couldn't keep his eyes open.

He awoke with sun shining in his face, warm and comforting, and snuggled deeper into the soft furs. Then came the abrupt jerk of knowing he had awakened in a strange place. It all came flooding back. Last night. Cassandra stepping into the firelight. His terror as he ran through the woods. Josh's body. Images came as though he were watching a horror movie. His fear faded as he found himself thinking of Cassandra and getting a boner. Cassandra loved him. That was all that mattered.

He touched the wound on his neck. He couldn't deny it. She was a vampire. They were all vampires.

~ * ~

Donovan woke. He was alone in the parked van in the clinic's darkened garage.

Obviously Rose and John had taken Thom down to the basement, but had wisely left Donovan to awaken on his own. They could have aroused him, pain could awaken Donovan from even the deepest sleep, but he would have reacted instinctively to the threat. Not worth the risk and the two servants knew it.

Donovan climbed out of the van, stretching the kinks from his body. Without having to see, Donovan knew the sun was still a hand-span above the horizon, a good hour and more until sunset. Over the years Donovan had trained himself to awaken before sunset, to be active, to appear normal.

He winced as he stepped from the garage's darkness into the clinic's bright fluorescent-lighted hallway. The corridor had that hospital smell, antiseptic and clean, a smell he had long grown accustomed to and now spoke of home and comfort. As he approached the nurse's station, Rose looked up and smiled.

Rose was officially his head nurse. She ran the clinic during the day, while Sandy worked as the chief night nurse. Sandy was one of Donovan's blood-daughters, a vampire. Rose was her servant. Rose was a tiny thing, who hardly looked big enough to lift a patient. She was always smiling and joking, her countenance perpetually happy.

"So sleeping beauty awakens."

Donovan grimaced. "Where's the new patient?"

"Where do you think?" Since Rose was Sandy's servant, she made sure that he knew he had no control over her or maybe she just enjoyed giving him a hard time. "There's a reporter waiting for you."

"A reporter?" Alarm coursed through Donovan.

"A Miss Cordova. She said she had an appointment with you, something about an article for *Psychiatry Today*."

Now Donovan remembered. "Didn't you call and cancel?"

"Yes, I called her and told her you had been called out of town on a case and didn't know when you would be back, but she stopped by anyway. Wanted to look around, maybe take some pictures, do some research. Since you were here, I told her to wait."

He didn't feel like talking to a reporter, but he'd agreed to the interview. Since both he and Miss Cordova were here, it didn't make sense to postpone it. With heavy resignation, he asked, "Where is she?"

"In the common room."

"Tell her I'll be with her as soon as I clean up and change my clothes."

Fifteen minutes later, Doctor Donovan Reed had replaced the Dark Hunter. Donovan, now dressed in a tweed jacket, brown slacks, white shirt, and dark tie, walked into the common room. It was a large room where the clinic's patients gathered. A TV stood in one corner, a cluster of chairs in front of it. A couple of patients were watched a game show.

The reporter sat at one of the long tables, helping a patient put together a jigsaw puzzle and trying to talk to the woman. Leeann was psychotic with delusions that she was the Virgin Mary. Donovan wondered what the reporter was learning.

She looked up and saw him. She was young, early twenties, bright-eyed.

She got to her feet as he approached.

"Dr. Reed?"

"Yes." He smiled cordially. "I'm afraid I've forgotten your name."

"Amanda Cordova."

Amanda. Probably that was why he'd agreed to the interview. Her name reminded him of his Amanda. This woman looked nothing like Amanda, who had been blonde, flirtatious, but every inch a lady. This Amanda had dark brown hair and eyes that were half hidden behind glasses with tinted lenses. Studious, serious, that was the image she tried hard to portray.

"It's a pleasure to meet you," he said. "We'll talk in my office." He turned away and led her down the corridor. "Have you been a reporter long?"

"I'm a journalism senior at Willamette University."

He held the office door open for her. As she walked past, he smelled her perfume, the heavy warmth of her body, and the sweet scent of her blood. Clean blood. A pang of hunger shot through him. He tried to ignore it.

He took a seat behind his desk, to put distance between them.

She took the chair opposite and rummaged through her purse, extracting a small tape recorder.

"Do you mind if I record this? I want to be sure to get everything right."

"Fine." He found himself studying her neck, sensing the blood coursing beneath the surface.

She took out a steno pad and a pen.

Donovan leaned back in his chair, forcing his attention away from her. He stared a little over her shoulder at the framed diplomas that graced his wall as a way of focusing his attention away from himself as a vampire, to once again assume the persona he'd so carefully built.

His office, his appearance, his attitude, all reflected what he was, a trained psychologist, almost to the point of being stereotypical. Dr. Donovan Reed.

"Now, Dr. Reed, yours is a very exclusive clinic. Can you give me a little background information?"

"The clinic was built in 1930 by my father. I became director in the late sixties."

"And the name The Edmund Horn Clinic?"

"It was named after a friend of my father's whom he admired." He found himself distracted, staring once again at the white column of her throat. Temptation rang through him, making him shiver. He could take her here in this room, just a taste, a sweet taste. He could make her forget that it happened. No one would know. It would be easy. But he would know. He had vowed never to use a patient that way. *She isn't a patient, the voice of temptation argued.*

She was young, innocent, trusting. *No!* He told himself firmly, meaning it.

"And your training?" she asked.

"Classical Freudian, then Jung," he answered her question, not bothering to mention that he had studied with both men personally. "But I'm much more interested in new directions. Not so much the causes, but how the mind works--how our beliefs can be manipulated."

"What made you interested in the study of vampirism as a psychosis?"

Donovan motioned around the room. "You may have noticed that there are no windows in my office."

The reporter nodded.

"That isn't just to make my patients feel more comfortable. I suffer from a rare affliction. I'm allergic to sunlight. I can be out in the sun for only short periods. When I venture out, I must be protected from head to toe. This medical problem has forced me to live as a creature of the night."

"There's no cure for your condition?"

"No. It is a genetic disease. So like the vampire of legend, I must hide from the sunlight."

"It certainly would give you an interesting perspective." After a moment, she asked, "Do you currently have any patients?"

"Two, and," Donovan raised his hand, "before you ask, no, you may not meet them."

"Can you describe your method of treatment?"

"Usually the psychosis is very strong when they first arrive. I've found I get the best results by making them feel safe. That is, we treat them as though they really were vampires. They sleep during the day in special underground rooms."

"In coffins?"

"If that's what truly makes the patient comfortable, but most of our patients prefer a bed." Donovan gave her a warm smile. "There are no mirrors or crucifixes. No food is prepared with garlic. I have even forbidden the staff to eat garlic before they come to work."

"And the drinking of blood?"

"Ah, yes, the all-important blood. Of course, human beings can't survive by drinking blood, although there are some African tribes who regularly drink blood from their cattle. We've devised a special drink that is very nutritious, red, just the color of blood. At first, our patients believe they are drinking the real thing. Perhaps you would like to try it?"

"I think I'll pass. It doesn't sound all that appetizing."

Donovan grinned conspiratorially. "It isn't. But it does give all the essential nutrients."

"How long do your patients stay in treatment? What is your success rate?"

"Our success rate is very good. It depends, of course, on the individual patient and the depth of the psychosis. Most can be restored to their family fairly quickly."

"But surely this is a rare psychosis."

"Not as rare as you think. Ever since Bram Stoker's *Dracula* was published in 1897, there has been a continuing fascination. Witness all the books and movies. There is something very seductive about the darkness and the vampire."

"What do you think it is?"

"It's a combination of ultimate power and absolute submission. Dracula has the power to bend anyone to his will, to make them his, to control them. We all hunger for that power. To be the one who is in control. Yet there is a side of ourselves that wants to be the helpless victim, to give in to our fantasies, to pleasure, to do the unspeakable, to be dominated. So we have created this creature of ultimate power, which will live forever and yet is forced into absolute submission. At sunrise, he becomes the helpless victim."

She finished writing down what he had said. "One last question. Do you believe in vampires? Do they really exist?"

"They are creatures of our imagination. Sometimes, what we imagine can be very real. But no, I don't sleep with a cross over my bed and garlic wreathed around my door."

She turned off her tape recorder, stuffed it and her notebook into her bag, and stood, putting out her hand to shake his. "This has been very interesting. Thank you very much for taking the time."

"Thank you for agreeing to having this interview so late in the day, but of course, for me and my patients, our day is about to begin."

He showed her out of the office and through the clinic. The reporter commented, "This is quite a large place for just two patients."

"But you already know I take patients with other problems. Leeann, the woman you were talking to, her problems are quite different. In addition, since this is such a small community, we handle most of the emergencies, a few medical convalescences, and we have an M.D. on staff who sees regular patients during the day."

He opened the front door and stepped out onto the covered veranda, wincing at the brightness of the setting sun. "I'll say good-bye here, if you don't mind."

The reporter glanced at the sun. "I've never thought what it would be like to think of the sun as an enemy. Not to enjoy its warmth. To live mostly in the darkness."

"Oh, but the night has its own pleasures and rewards."

"Such as?" she asked curiously.

"Life moves at a much slower pace than during the day. It is quieter, more peaceful, for one thing. For another, can you honestly tell me that you haven't found a moonlight night just as beautiful as the bright noontime, maybe even more beautiful?"

"I hadn't thought of that. You have given me much to think about. Thank you."

He stood for a moment watching her go down the stairs and out to her car. Then he went inside. The exposed skin of his hands and face itched and burned where the sun had kissed his flesh. He shut the stout wooden doors. He had built this place so that if he wanted to, he never had to see the sun. Oh, he hadn't built a windowless box. There were windows, but there were also stout wooden shutters that could be closed during the day and opened to let in the night.

He crossed the entry hall to the nurses' station. Sandy and Rose were talking to the new orderly. Sandy gave Donovan a maternal smile as she handed him a pile of patient charts in their covered metal clipboards.

Donovan asked, "Did John leave?"

"Yes," Sandy said. "Rose found one of the locals to drive him to the airport in Eugene," Where Rose was small, Sandy was taller, thick through the shoulders and hips. She wore her white uniform with comfort and ease, and she made patients feel that way.

Donovan began going through the charts. He was pleased to see that Mr. Todd's kidney stone had finally passed. "Anyone Doc wants me to keep an eye on tonight?"

"No. And no new patients, except the one downstairs."

The orderly, Frank, glanced at the clock. "Well, it's about feeding time at the zoo." Donovan stared at him, until he looked away nervously. Then he looked back, his eyes belligerent and yet afraid. "It's just not normal. Keeping him locked up down there. And what he eats."

Donovan put on his best doctor's persona. "Rat and our new patient are troubled souls who need our help, not our ridicule."

"Yeah, right. But it still gives me the creeps."

"Then it's a good thing that your duties don't take you down there too often. Speaking of duties?"

Sandy broke in. "Frank was just going to see if he could get Mrs. Mashek out of bed for dinner."

Frank took the hint and headed down the corridor. He was a young Hispanic. His employment record said he had worked in several nursing homes. When Donovan checked his references, he'd been told the man's work was no more than adequate, but since they had needed the help, Donovan had hired him. Now that Frank was showing an interest in the patients in the basement, it presented a problem Donovan would have to solve.

He looked at Sandy, and she nodded her agreement. "It's either do a quick wipe and fire him or bind him, your call."

"Let me think about it," said Donovan. "Well, as Frank said, 'it's feeding time at the zoo'."

Donovan headed through the clinic, thinking about Rat. He hadn't mentioned to the reporter that he had his failures as well as his successes. Rat was one of his failures. Not really his. They didn't know his real name or how long he had existed in the sewers, living on rats, but it had driven him insane, completely unreachable.

Donovan stepped outside into the flaming sunset. He walked across to the barn and around to the bunny hutch.

They kept a variety of animals for live blood, a couple of cows, rabbits, and chickens. Donovan preferred to hunt his own food in the woods beyond the clinic, but that wasn't always possible.

He reached into the hutch and grabbed a rabbit by the scruff of its neck and walked back to the clinic.

He felt the rabbit's fear. Its natural instinct told the creature here was a dangerous predator. He held the animal tightly so that it wouldn't have a chance to escape. Inside the back door, he took the stairway down to the basement. Sandy was waiting at the bottom. She quickly injected the rabbit, then unlocked the door, pulling it open just far enough for Donovan to push the rabbit inside. Rat needed to hunt. That was the only way he would eat. They'd tried everything, but only this had worked. They both looked at their watches. The hypo contained a sedative. Once in the rabbit's bloodstream, it would enter Rat as he fed. Later, when he was calmer, more relaxed, they would make sure that he was bathed and cared for. It wasn't much of a life, but it was better than sewers.

"You'll have to handle Rat tonight by yourself," said Donovan. "You'll be all right?"

Sandy laughed. "Of course, I'll be all right." They had learned early on, not to turn their backs on Rat. "Go see your new patient." Sandy handed him a tray. It held a bottle and two glasses.

Donovan unlocked the door and made his way through the suite's living room to the bedroom.

Thom lay on the hospital bed, restraints strapped to his wrists and ankles, a wide band across his chest and another across his legs, immobilizing him. He could have been a corpse lying on a morgue table, a dead thing. No movement, no breath.

Donovan felt the sun set. He didn't need to see it to know when it slipped beyond the rim of the earth. His whole being awoke; it was as though he'd been half-dead and now was alive.

Thom's eyes blinked and opened. For a moment they were clear. Then the terror returned.

Three

Wade heard the key in the lock, and the door opened. Cassandra's two vampires entered, both laughing and grinning. There were no fangs. They looked perfectly normal, which frightened Wade even more than if they had looked like creatures out of a nightmare.

Wolf unlocked the shackle around Wade's ankle; Panther pulled him to his feet.

"Where are you taking me?" Wade demanded, fear hammering at him, making his voice tremble.

Panther grinned. Now his fangs showed.

Wade started to struggle, but Wolf and Panther dragged him from the chamber.

Wade's struggles died and his fear faded when he saw Cassandra.

Cassandra sat like a queen on a throne. She looked like a queen. The deep red burgundy dress was off the shoulders, revealing an expanse of white skin broken only by a large cameo with a black velvet ribbon tied at her throat. Wade longed to touch those white shoulders. Masses of fabric swirled about her, the fullest long skirt he had ever seen.

She gently waved an antique lace fan held in a white-gloved hand. The glove went clear up past her elbow.

He'd seen the re-release of *Gone with the Wind.* The dress looked like something Scarlet would have worn to a fancy ball.

"Let him go, boys," she said, and they obeyed her. "Wade, come sit next to me."

Wade hurriedly took his place beside her on the love seat. Panther glared at him, but Wade wasn't afraid as long as he was next to Cassandra.

"How did you sleep?" Cassandra asked.

"Ok."

"Are you all right?"

He glanced around. "I sure could use a bathroom."

"Of course, how quickly I have forgotten what it is like to have a mortal. I'm sure you're hungry, too."

Wade nodded.

She picked up a silver bell from the table next to her and rang it. It had a surprisingly loud, deep tone. Stanos appeared in the doorway.

"Yes, Mistress?"

"You will take care of Wade, see to his needs and that he is fed."

"Yes. Come this way, young man."

Reluctantly, Wade followed Stanos out of the room, glancing back longingly at Cassandra, but he did have to go to the bathroom bad.

At the end of the hall was a stairway, blocked by a heavy wrought iron gate. Stanos unlocked it and climbed the stairs. At the top was another locked door, which he unlocked, and beyond that, another door. This one he slid open and showed Wade into a small bedroom. Well, at least it had a bed, although nothing else. "In there." Stanos pointed to an open door. Wade went through the door and found an old-fashioned bathroom. He glanced around. There was a small window, high up and way too small to climb through. He took care of his business, and when he came out, Stanos was waiting for him.

"Come this way." He opened the bedroom door and led Wade down a dark hall, paneled in knotty pine, to a small kitchen, lit by one dim light. The only thing modern was the refrigerator. There was a small table with two wooden chairs. "Sit," he commanded, and Wade sat.

Stanos soon brought Wade a cheese sandwich on thick, home-baked bread, and something that looked like a milkshake, but didn't taste like it. Wade put down the glass.

"No," Stanos said, pushing the glass across the chipped painted surface of the table. "You must drink it. You must be strong for Cassandra."

Wade drank.

There were no windows in the kitchen. He didn't know whether he was beneath or above ground, except he thought because of the window in the bathroom, he was above ground. A cabin.

"Where are we?" he asked.

"That should not concern you, young man. You should only be concerned with making my mistress happy."

Wade thought of Cassandra and was suddenly eager to get back to her. He finished the sandwich quickly and drained the last of the drink.

"I will go to town tomorrow," Stanos said, "and get proper food. You must keep up your strength, so that you may serve the mistress for a long time. We'll go back now, but, young man, though I may look old, I assure you I'm very strong. Even if you thought to overpower me, you could not escape. Everything is locked up tight. If you did try to escape, Wolf and Panther would drag you back and Cassandra would punish you."

Stanos led Wade back down the hall and into the bedroom. The door was gone, hidden behind paneling. Wade realized with both entrances carefully disguised, Cassandra's lair was safely hidden. No one would know it even existed. No one would know where he was, where to find him. Stanos touched a knot among the many in the knotty pine paneling and the door slid open.

Wade was alone and his despair crashed over him in an agonizing wave.

"After you boy," Stanos said, motioning to the stairs.

Wade hesitated, tears burned his eyes, but he had no choice, he was trapped. He went down. Stanos carefully locking each door and gate behind him.

"Hurry, boy, she's waiting," Stanos urged him forward.

Wade entered the parlor. When he saw Cassandra, suddenly his fear and despair disappeared. She was the most beautiful creature in the world and he belonged with her, belonged to her.

Panther sat next to Cassandra, kissing her. Wade felt white-hot jealousy burn through him. Cassandra looked at Wade, her eyes teasing. She let Panther continue to kiss her, sometimes her lips, or her white shoulders, or the soft mound of her breast that rose above the tight line of her bodice. The only thing Wade could do was watch, wishing she would send them away. Finally she did, but not without protests from Panther.

As he walked by Wade, Panther whispered. "You're dead meat, boy."

~ * ~

Thom saw the man from last night standing next to the bed. He tried to sit up and realized he couldn't. He was strapped down. Fear coursed through him. He pulled against the restraints, twisting, jerking, but his struggles were futile, the restraints held. He was helpless--a captive, a prisoner.

"What do you want with me?" he demanded.

"I'm sorry about the restraints. They're for your own protection."

Thom didn't believe him. "Where am I?"

"My clinic. I'm Donovan. Dr. Donovan Reed."

"Am I insane?" Yes, that was it. Memories of what he had done came rushing back. He had experienced some kind of horrible mental breakdown. He was insane. That was what this place was, an insane asylum. It was a relief to know what was happening to him. Insane, yes. He relaxed. Insanity was curable, wasn't it? Didn't it mean he was getting better if he knew he was insane? The man's next words shattered the brief illusion that he understood what was happening to him.

"No, you aren't insane. Do you remember the accident?"

Fragments of memory, bright flashes. "I think so." Thom shook his head hoping to make the images come clear. "No, not really, bits and pieces. I was in an accident?" He realized his face was bandaged. A head injury? Maybe he wasn't crazy after all, maybe it was all a hallucination caused by a brain injury. The thought frightened him. He had heard terrible things about people with brain injuries, paralyzed, unable to speak. No, he could speak, think, and move, but the nightmares, the hallucinations.

"You were in a car crash. It's normal not to remember exactly what happened. The important thing is not only were you in a car accident, but you died in that accident."

Died? What was the doctor trying to say? Had he died and been brought back? He didn't remember any bright light, long tunnel, or long dead family and friends waiting for him, not any of the things he read about near death experiences.

The doctor placed his hand over Thom's imprisoned one.

"I know this will be difficult to understand. You died, but your body didn't stay dead. It changed into something different. You changed. You became a vampire."

Another surge of fear coursed through Thom. Yes, he was in an insane asylum! This man was a patient, not a doctor!

"Are you crazy?" Thom could think of nothing better to say. Crazy, insane, it was all insane, but the picture flashed through his mind of himself bending over a man, tearing at him with his teeth, drinking the blood that gushed from the ghastly wound. No! That couldn't be real. It was a delusion. Just a delusion.

"No, I'm not insane, and neither are you. We are both vampires. We need blood to survive."

Last night--Thom assumed it was last night, no, that felt right. It was night. He was sure of it. He looked around the room and noticed there were no windows. It might be noon, instead of night, but he couldn't explain it, it felt like night.

He had to think. The last thing he remembered was being in a truck, chained. He remembered the sun rising, then nothing until he woke up here.

Before that, they had been in a hospital somewhere. He remembered two blacks. The man had cut his wrist and given it to Thom to suck. Yes, he remembered drinking the blood, lips fastened to the wrist, first the man, then the woman. The thought of the blood woke a hunger in him. No. He couldn't want blood. That was an illusion, but the more he tried to deny it, the more the hunger grew.

The doctor, if he really was a doctor, picked up a bottle and poured something into a glass. It was the deep rich color of blood, almost maroon, a bright mesmerizing red.

He held the glass under Thom's nose. The smell twisted Thom's gut into a burning knot of hunger. The blood was like nothing he had ever smelled before, a complex blend of odors, sweet, bitter, home, joy. It was like being in his Grandma Barber's kitchen on Christmas morning, the delicious smells mingling into one, the smell of cinnamon the strongest, always bringing back those memories. This smell was different and yet just as powerful to evoke memories. It wasn't a memory of a time or a place, but a feeling and a need. It was blood, and he knew it.

The doctor put the glass on the table, and Thom groaned in frustration. Thom wanted, needed, what was in the glass. He yanked at the restraints.

"Let me undo that and raise the bed. Then you can drink." One wrist restraint was undone and the bed rose. Thom reached out a hand shaking with need. He took the glass and gulped down the thick fluid. It flowed through him like 110 proof rum, hitting his stomach and spreading warmth through his whole being. He felt himself relax as the gnawing pain eased. He held the glass out to be refilled. He drained that too, this time more aware of the flavor of what he was drinking. It was different from what he had consumed from the black couple last night, and their blood was different from the woman in the alley, from the man before that. He looked at the doctor who had said his name was Donovan Reed. His blood had tasted different, more like the black couple, but still different. Thom was amazed that he could taste the differences--like various vintages of wine.

"What is this?" he asked.

"Blood. Cow's blood."

"It's different."

Donovan nodded. "First, it's not living blood. I get it from a local butcher. But it will meet your body's needs. Are you ready to accept that you are a vampire?" He refilled the glass; Thom drank it more slowly. His body began to feel warm, alive. He hadn't realized how cold he felt, almost wooden, until the sensations began to fade. There was also clarity to his thinking. A high. From his Haight Ashbury days, he knew highs. He knew drugs. He had never felt this good on any of the drugs. He felt invincible, full of confidence, a sense of well being that made him smile. It was the blood. He knew it. He didn't feel like a thirty-eight-year-old IBM engineer, with a receding hairline, and a slight paunch.

Still, he didn't want to believe that he was a--what--a monster--a vampire.

"It's called newborn shock," said Donovan. "It's one thing when you know what's happening, when you are properly initiated, but quite another when you wake up changed, craving blood, and not knowing why."

"What happened to me? Why?"

"As I said, there was a car crash. You died. Your heart stopped beating, but you regained consciousness pretty quickly. Since a vampire's heart doesn't seem to beat, no one noticed. According to the report, you were pronounced dead at the scene and taken directly to the morgue. The morgue was backed up that day so they hadn't gotten to you."

"I remember I kept trying to tell people, but I couldn't seem to move or speak. They put me in this plastic bag and took me somewhere. I guess to the morgue. I just lay there for a long time. Finally, I rolled off the cart and staggered out of there."

"You were lucky. The modern autopsy is today's version of a stake. Embalming or a quick cremation will also do the job. In fact, American funeral practices don't particularly favor the vampire."

Thom suddenly got the image of a coroner cutting into his body as he lay helpless. Yes, he had been lucky. "All I could think of was blood. I found this homeless drunk passed out in a doorway. I broke an empty wine bottle and cut him and sucked up the blood. Then I found an abandoned building and crawled inside."

"A vampire's instinct for survival and its hunger are two things that can't be resisted. When we change, the first thing we need is blood, the second is a safe hiding place."

Thom nodded his agreement. "It was like there was another person inside of me doing all this while I watched. I tried to stop, but I couldn't. It was like a horrible nightmare."

Thom shuddered, remembering the man, the man he had killed.

Donovan reached out and patted Thom's arm. "I know. I know just how hard you tried."

"But I killed a man."

"It's called the first kill. We all have to do it. Your fangs came in then, right?"

Thom nodded. "What about the woman last night, did I kill her too?"

"No. I dropped her off at an emergency hospital. She got a transfusion."

"How did you find me?"

"I use a clipping service. Every day they check newspapers, police, hospital, and morgue reports. When a body goes missing from a morgue, it's a good clue. The man you killed was the next clue. It gave me a place to start looking. Instinct is if you've found a good hiding place to stick to it for a while. So I cruised the area until I sensed you."

"You sensed me?"

"Yes. When you're older, you'll acquire a sense that tells you when another vampire is near--and a few other skills."

"But that still doesn't explain why I didn't just die."

Donovan smiled at him. The corners of his blue eyes crinkled. It was a warm smile, except for the glimpse of fangs. He poured himself a glass of blood and sat down in the chair next to the bed. "You think you're ready for Dr. Donovan's how-to-make-a-vampire in one easy lesson routine?"

Thom nodded slowly.

"Four things are required to make a vampire. First, you have to have been bitten by a vampire. But just biting won't do it.

You have to drink some of his or her blood. This has to happen on at least three separate occasions. It could happen in one night, but usually it occurs over a space of time. Finally, you have to have the right genetic make-up. That's why there aren't more vampires running around. Less than five percent of the population has the genetic disposition to become a vampire."

"But I wasn't bitten."

"There are two possibilities. You are a spontaneous mutation. They're rare, but they do occur. There had to be a first vampire. The second is much more likely. You were bitten but told to forget. It could have happened at any time during your life, not just recently. Your death triggered a mutation, if you will. We've been doing research to clearly identify what happens, but we still don't know. We cross over. Or we say that we survive the change. Reborn, if you prefer, as a vampire, a creature of the night, the undead. I wouldn't call us *undead* though. Our hearts beat, at a much slower rate. We breathe, but our need for oxygen is much less. We think, our brain waves show on a brain scan. So we aren't dead or undead, just changed. As to whether we are cursed or damned, I don't know. It's what you believe yourself to be that seems to make the difference."

"Am I immortal?"

"We aren't immortal, but we do live a long time. We merely age at a much slower rate than the average human."

"And sunlight? Will it kill me?"

"No, you aren't going to burst into flames and dissolve into dust at the touch of the first ray of sunlight, but you will get a severe sunburn. As for the rest of the vampire mythology, it seems to have a lot to do with your beliefs and how strongly you hold them. I've seen vampires who couldn't see themselves in mirrors, who have been burnt by crosses or holy water, who couldn't step on holy ground or enter a house unless invited, and who were repulsed by garlic. But no vampire I've known has been able to turn himself into a bat or fade away in a wisp of smoke. Most wouldn't be caught dead sleeping in a coffin, although we tend to rest more comfortably underground. You're in the basement of the clinic. The soil protects us from the rays of the sun, grounds us, and gives us strength, but it isn't necessary to have your home soil. As for the other stuff, you will be stronger than you were, you will heal faster. In fact, if you like we can take off the bandages."

Thom touched the bandages.

"What happened?"

"In the accident, your face was badly mangled, skin cut by broken glass, bones shattered. We heal fast. I'm afraid that your face looked like a movie monster's. Edmund did some reconstructive surgery, repositioned the bones and sutured the skin, but there may be some scarring. If you aren't up to it, we can look tomorrow."

Suddenly Thom wanted to see, to know. "Now."

"Let me get some supplies. I'll be right back.

Thom lay back against the pillow. A part of him kept hoping he would wake up and find it was all a hideous nightmare or that the real doctor would come and take Dr. Donovan Reed away. He knew it wasn't going to happen.

The blood. The way he felt.

He was a vampire.

Dr. Reed returned with a tray, covered with one of those blue paper towels seen in doctor's offices to keep things sterile. He removed the towel to reveal scissors, a hypodermic needle, a mirror, and more gauze.

He carefully cut away the bandages and then smiled. He handed the mirror to Thom.

Thom looked at his reflection. Same receding hairline, same washed-out blue eyes, same lines at the corner of his mouth.

But his face was different. The fangs stretched his mouth in a funny way. Needle sharp fangs that came from above the gum line, over his other teeth. It wasn't just the fangs. His face was a bit more asymmetrical, and there were several faint white scars, whiter than his pale skin. Yes, he looked paler than normal.

"No movie monster," said Dr. Reed. "Edmund did a superb job. The scars may fade; they may not."

Thom turned his head to the right and then the left. The scars actually added character to his face. The thing he couldn't believe was that they were so healed. He wondered if he had been kept drugged, unconscious for a long time, long enough for the wounds to mend. Why would anyone do that? Why would anyone try to convince him he was a vampire?

"What happens now?"

"You'll stay here until your body adjusts. You'll be provided with all the blood you need. I'll come every night and talk to you and answer all your questions."

"Where's here? You said clinic earlier?"

"I have a small private clinic. It's in Oregon, a little town near Eugene. Now that's more than enough for you to digest for one night. I think it's safe to remove the restraints, but you'll have to stay here, under lock and key."

"I'm a prisoner?"

"For a time. It's really to protect you. Your fangs won't retract for a while yet. Eventually they do. For now, you look like a vampire, and this clinic is open to the public. There are only three vampires here, myself, my head nurse, Sandy, and one other patient like yourself. Also it's for the protection of my other patients, the humans. Newborns have been known to lose control. I don't think you will, but I don't want to take the chance. In about a week, I'll give you the key and you can start locking yourself in. After your fangs retract, you'll have free run of the place. There's TV with lousy reception and a stereo.

Just let me know what kind of music you like, and I'll get you some tapes. And books to read. Again, any favorite authors, just ask." He went to the desk and opened the drawer. "Pen and paper. Some of my patients have found it helpful to keep a journal or at least write down their questions. I can tell that I've overwhelmed you, so I'll leave and give you some time to absorb all of this. One more thing. That's an intercom." He pointed to the phone. "It connects with my office or the nurses' station. Anything you want, need, or you just want to talk. Call. I'll check on you before sunrise."

Dr. Reed left and locked the door behind him. Thom got up and wandered around. As prisons went this was rather nice. Comfortable furnishings, more like an apartment than a hospital room or a prison cell.

He was a vampire! He didn't want to believe it, but he picked up the mirror again and stared at his face. It was true. He was a vampire. If Donovan was correct, another vampire had bitten him three times. Surely he would remember that. Why didn't he?

~ * ~

Wade and Cassandra were alone.

"Do you know what I am?" she asked.

Wade nodded.

"Then say it."

"You're a vampire."

"That means we live for a long time. When I became a vampire, this is what women wore." She did a slow turn, the hoop skirt swaying gently. "I was only sixteen when I became a vampire. Of course, Brandon had taken me into his bed when I was only twelve, almost thirteen. He taught me all the arts of pleasure. He was a gambler. We worked together. Sometimes I would play, having only my clothes to bet. I would lose, not too fast, but eventually I would be naked. The other players were so distracted, they weren't aware that Brandon was winning. Other times he would offer me to cover his bet. I would disrobe so the gamblers could see what they were getting." Her eyes got a far away look. "Sometimes when his friends liked it that way, he would tie me up and leave me helpless to wait the pleasure of the winner. That was the way it was the night they killed him. Those filthy carpetbaggers! Somehow they learned what he was. They shot him, then cut off his head. As his life-blood poured onto the carpet, they each had me. The leader, his name was Travis, took me with him. He enjoyed inflicting pain, he liked to use a whip or a riding crop." She was now lost in reliving the horror. "I knew the only way out was to die. I broke a chair that was the only piece of furniture beside the bed in the little room he kept me locked in. One of the legs splintered with a sharp point. I wedged it solid in a crack in the rock wall. Then I ran at it, impaling myself on the point. I didn't die. I became a vampire. My first taste of blood was Travis. I didn't kill him, not that night. Later, I went back and drained his body dry, drinking until there was no more to be sucked from his dry flesh. Then I killed each of his friends." She seemed to shake herself out of the past.

"But I dressed this way to please you," Cassandra told Wade. "Do you like it?"

"Very much. You're beautiful," he said, meaning every word.

She preened like a young girl. "Tell me more, Wade, surely you can do better than just I'm beautiful."

"Your eyes are like limpid pools, your lips are like red ripe cherries," he said, quoting something he had read or heard, being unable to think of anything else to say.

She laughed and swatted him lightly with her fan. "I can see I will have to teach you how to tell a woman she is beautiful. But come," she held out her gloved hand, "we have a full night of pleasure ahead of us." She led him into the bedroom. "I dressed especially this way so that you and I might have the pleasure of undressing me."

There was a small alcove, surrounded by mirrors. She stood in the middle of the platform and held out a gloved hand. "Come here and kneel in front of me. You may remove my glove."

Wade knelt. Cassandra's glove wasn't cloth but soft white leather. It reach past her elbow, ending just below the rounded puff of her sleeve. There were tiny pearl buttons at the wrist. He carefully undid them and tried to pull the glove from her fingers. It wouldn't move, so he gently rolled it down her arm to her wrist and then removed it.

"You may place the glove on the top of the dresser, making sure to smooth out every wrinkle and crease." He did as he was told, repeating the process with the other glove. Then he unlaced her boots, one at a time and put them away. When he tried to hurry the process, she chided him about the impatience of youth. He finally realized that the careful folding and putting away of each item of clothing allowed her to watch him. His shirt and his shoes had disappeared, so all he wore were jeans. Bare-chested--somehow made him feel, well...seductive. Then he realized there was another facet to the experience. She was enjoying ordering him around, having him playing her maid-servant, and so was he. A moment of guilt flashed through him, then he was kneeling in front of her, looking into her eyes, and all else faded, except his need to do as she wanted.

She turned around, presenting her back to him. "You may undo my bodice." Tiny buttons again, a long row of them, his fingers fumbled with them. Finally the bodice was open and he pulled it off, realizing with acute dismay just how many articles of clothing a woman could wear. "We have all night, my love," she said. "Enjoy it."

He untied the hoop skirt, which collapsed at her feet in a series of rings. Then he carefully unlaced the corset, which had made her waist no larger than the span of his hands. Her breasts were round, full globes above the lace of her camisole. Carefully he removed the camisole, pantaloons, and finally stockings, until at last, she stood before him naked, except for the velvet ribbon with the cameo around her neck

Wade could wait no longer. Picking her up in his arms, he carried her to the bed and laid her down reverently. He struggled briefly with his jeans, then he was free. She spread herself wide in invitation. Without hesitation, he thrust himself into her, his pent-up frustrations making him come quickly.

He relaxed in relief against her. As they lay together, she stroked his back, then she pushed him off of her and onto his back.

Leaning on one elbow, she said, "Last night I drank your blood. Tonight, you will drink mine." Arousing him slowly, she finally bit his neck. As it had last night, the bite only intensified the experience, until she was the only thing that existed for him. She twisted her ring, then rubbed her hand across her breast, leaving a long bleeding gash. She pressed her bloody bosom against his lips. "Drink."

Wade licked the dripping blood from her skin, then his mouth closed over the wound and he began to suck. Her lips returned to the bleeding wound on his neck, clinging to it. Later, he couldn't remember exactly what happened afterward, but he knew that it had been good--good beyond belief. He loved Cassandra, needed her. He couldn't exist without her.

~ * ~

Upstairs, Donovan went into the common room. A cluster of patients sat watching TV.

Yolanda sat in the corner of the room. When she saw him, her eyes came alight. She raised an old, arthritic hand. "Where's Amanda?" she asked. "I'm waiting for Amanda."

Donovan patted the frail white head. "I know. Amanda will be along. You just wait for her." Though Amanda had died fifty years ago, Yolanda still lived only to serve her. Sometimes Donovan thought it would be a kindness to ease her way out of this world, but Yolanda was one of his last links to Amanda and to his and Amanda's child, Clare, so he clung to her. Yolanda was ninety-two. He wondered how much longer she would be with him.

He sat down next to her and gently took her hand in his. "We'll wait for Amanda together."

Yolanda nodded and smiled.

The news was on, the announcer said, "President Reagan met today with members of Congress regarding the worsening economic situation. The search has been called off for the night for Wade Kain." A picture of a boy appeared on the screen, obviously a school photograph of a handsome, dark-haired boy, with a strong face and an air of innocence. "The mutilated bodies of his two friends, brothers Mike and Josh Torra, were discovered by hikers today in an isolated part of the Santiam Wilderness area. The bodies of both boys had been badly mauled in a wild animal attack, possibly a mountain lion or wolf."

"Please," Yolanda whimpered. "You're hurting me."

Donovan looked down and saw he was gripping Yolanda's hand so tightly he was pinching her fingers. He let go immediately. "I'm sorry." He picked up the frail hand gently. "Are you all right?"

She nodded. He kissed her hand and laid it on her lap.

"No sign of the boy has been discovered," the newscaster continued. "Hikers and campers are warned to be extra cautious. Now on to sports."

"You wait here for Amanda," he told Yolanda. "I have something I must do."

"Yes, Donovan."

Donovan glanced back as he left the common room and saw her head nodding, already drifting off to sleep.

He went into his office, picked up the phone, and dialed a number from memory. When it was answered, he said, "This is Donovan. I need everything you have on those two boys found in the Santiam Wilderness." When he hung up, he went to the filing cabinet and pulled out a folder full of clippings. Some were yellow with age, the paper brittle. But he was only interested in the more recent, going back five years or so. There was a pattern.

It was Cassandra. Cassandra had killed those boys.

He didn't have enough to go to the Directors yet, but he would.

Four

Sunset, Thom woke.

Donovan had explained that, as a newborn, Thom would sleep from sunrise to sunset. Sleep wasn't the right word. There were no dreams. Nothing. He died to the day, only to awaken to the night. Thom called it "sleep" because he could think of no other word he preferred. Unconsciousness, death, suspended animation, oblivion--none sounded right.

Thom tried to fool himself into believing that everything was as it had been, that nothing had changed. He got up, took a shower, shaved, brushed his teeth, all those human, normal things. Then he would catch his reflection in the mirror. The fangs. No, he was no longer human.

He heard the sound of a key in the lock. As much as he might pretend, things were not normal. His room might look like an upscale apartment, Donovan Reed might be an extremely likeable man, but he was still a jailer and this was still a prison.

The rattle of glasses as Donovan put the tray on the table, the soft sigh of a seat cushion as he made himself comfortable. Thom's hearing had improved.

Thom finished dressing and came out of the bedroom.

"Good evening," said Donovan, pouring a glass full of blood and handing it to Thom.

The blood's smell made Thom's insides burned with a gnawing hunger and twisted his whole being with craving. He gulped eagerly and held the glass out for more. Donovan filled it. "Does it get any easier, this raging hunger?" Thom asked.

"Yes. I told you, you're still a newborn. Your body is adjusting to its new state."

"Undead," Thom said flatly. They sat in silence for a while, then Thom said, "I have a question." He hesitated for a moment. "I'm not sure if it's proper etiquette to ask, but just how did you become a vampire?"

"The Alamo."

"The Alamo?"

"Yes. 1836. The Alamo. There was a vampire among the defenders. His name was Charles. I remember him, but I don't remember being bitten nor did I, or anyone else, know he was a vampire. Sometimes I wonder if he was attracted to the war because of the easy pickings and just became trapped or whether he was really a patriot and when he knew we must suffer certain defeat, he envisioned us rising up from death to take our revenge on the Spanish. Anyway, in the early hours of March sixth, Colonel Travis sent myself and James Allen out as couriers. We went separately, hoping that one of us would make it through. Just before dawn, Santa Ana attacked. The fighting was fierce, and by 6:30 a.m. everyone was dead. I didn't know that, not until later. I just wanted to deliver my messages and get back. It was late afternoon when I had the misfortune to run into a squad of Spanish soldiers. Their marksman was a good shot. I didn't realize what had happened to me, that I had changed. I just knew I craved blood and I hated the Spanish. When I made it back to San Antonio, the funeral pyres were still smoldering, after two days. Charles would have probably survived his wounds, but Santa Ana ordered all the bodies burnt and so he died, without ever telling me what I was. I was alone and frightened, but determined to make the Spanish suffer."

He paused and poured himself a glass a blood. He took a sip. "I followed the Spanish, haunting their ranks at night, hiding during the day. I drank and I killed. I swam in Spanish blood. The continuing battles helped to hide my atrocities. I have no idea how many I killed, but I became a monster. When it was over and Santa Ana defeated, I returned home. It was then I discovered that everyone assumed I was dead." Donovan's voice turned bitter. It was obviously a painful memory. "My father met me and told me it was better that all thought I had died a hero, rather than live as a traitorous coward. Since I died before I could deliver my messages, he refused to believe that Colonel Travis had sent me out as a courier. He turned his back on me. I left, but I decided I would not go alone. There was this girl, a pretty thing, from before the war."

He became still, staring down into his glass, memories playing across his face, unpleasant memories. After a few minutes, he continued his story. "By that time I had come into my powers, though I didn't understand them. I went to Sophia and asked her to come away with me. She came. She couldn't help herself. That night, when we made love, I bit her. In all those days, I had never once learned control. It was drink and kill. When I was through, she was dead. I swore to never touch another human being and fled into the mountains.

"I lived as a hunter and trapper, existing on the blood of animals and shunning human contact. Over time I learned control and no longer needed so much blood. But there was one thing I hungered for and that hunger grew with each passing year. I didn't know I was a vampire. I thought I was sick.

Desperately, I sought a cure. I tried Indian shamans, patent medicine, quack doctors, real doctors. Of course, I had to be careful how I described my problem. One doctor suggested a specialist in Europe, but I had no money for such a long journey. Then gold was discovered in California. If I was rich enough, I could travel to Europe. I could find a cure and once again be like normal men.

"One night in San Francisco, I met Amanda." Donovan smiled at the memory. "We passed on the street, and she knew I was just like her. If you could have seen Amanda, she was beautiful. Men flocked around her. She ran a very fashionable salon and high-class brothel, where only the wealthiest and most elite came. She taught me everything. It's called fledgling, when an older, more mature vampire takes a younger one under their wing. She helped me understand what had happened and even helped me track down who my parent was. She became my family."

"1836--" Thom struggled with the idea that the man before him had been at the Alamo and lived through the California Gold Rush. "You don't mind my saying you don't look a day over 100." Donovan smiled at Thom's small joke. "Actually," Thom said, "you don't look any older than me."

"I was seventeen when I became a vampire. As I told you, unlike the legends, we aren't immortal and we don't remain forever young. We age, but at a much slower rate. The oldest vampire I know of is around five hundred and fifty, and he does look over a hundred."

Five hundred years--Thom tried to imagine it and failed. He had never been very good at history. Was it 1492 or 1692 that Columbus sailed the ocean blue? He couldn't remember. The oldest vampire would have been witness to the founding of America. A witness to so much. What about him? In five hundred years, he would be alive to see if Star Trek's predictions of the future came true. Would mankind survive that long? Suddenly he felt the burden of knowing he would live, live and have to do something with his life. He'd planned for his retirement, although it had seemed a long way off. Someday he would have time to pursue those dreams of youth, to take up a hobby, maybe travel, after he got the kids through college. Now that those plans were nothing, where was he? What was he going to do with this expanse of life?

Donovan seemed to catch his thoughts. "You live, you learn. Obviously, I didn't start out as a psychologist. That is one of the benefits of long life, the opportunity to study and grow, to do and be things that you weren't before." Donovan put down his glass and stood. "Come with me, I want to show you something."

Thom hesitated in the doorway, suddenly afraid to leave his safe haven, afraid someone would see him, see him for the monster that he was. The grade-B movie image of people screaming and fleeing in terror flickered across his mind. He hurried after Donovan, down the corridor, up the stairs, and out into the night.

He was so focused on Donovan that Thom was maybe ten paces along the path before it hit him. He stumbled to a halt, staring wide-eyed at the world around him. It was night, he knew that, but this was not like any night he had ever known. It was dark, but the darkness was alive with the colors of black. How could he explain the colors in black?

There were colors in black, more than just tones or shades of gray. And something more. The tree before him glowed with a faint luminosity. He felt drawn forward. His hand reached out.

"Go ahead, touch it," said Donovan.

Thom softly touched the tree, feeling the rough bark beneath his fingers, fingers suddenly more sensitive than ever before. It was more than just bark. A strange tingling sensation move through his palms. Life. He could feel the tree's life, pulsating as though it was blood surging through veins. He turned slowly. Each blade of grass, each bush, each tree wore the luminous glow of life. He looked at Donovan; no glow outlined his form. Of course, Donovan was dead. He looked at his own hand, dark against the tree trunk. Dead. That was what he was--a dead thing. Death among all this life. As he stared at his hand, he realized it wasn't so. There was that same sense of something, a color, a glow, a presence. Not the light, but one of those rich colors of black. The life was there, but different, changed.

He heard a sound and looked up to see an owl peering down from its perch on a tree branch above him. The owl blinked once, then spread its wings and flew. Thom tracked its flight for a long time before he realized how clearly he could see. He had seen the individual feathers on the owl's spread wings, the curve of the sharp talons. He had tracked it farther in the darkness than he could have before, even in bright daylight.

"I didn't know," Thom whispered. "I didn't know." He gave a deep shuddering sigh.

"Come on." Thom followed Donovan up the path to the crest of the small hill behind the clinic. He stared across the wide, black expanse of the Willamette Valley, black, with its scattering of lights, and up into the star-filled heavens. What heavens! The multitude of stars were bright, brilliant diamonds of throbbing color against black velvet. A thin wedge of crescent moon hung on the horizon, so bright that Thom doubted he would have been able to look at a full moon, any more than he could look directly into the sun's blazing painful brilliance. Donovan said, "It's like trying to describe a Monet painting to a person blind from birth and expecting them to be able to see and understand it. Words can not express what the night is to a vampire."

"How come I didn't know before?"

"The blood craze of your newborn state kept you from truly seeing the night."

It was late, almost 3:00 a.m. The peaceful quiet was like a warm comforting blanket, and yet as Thom stood on the crest of the hill, he became increasingly aware of the aliveness around him. Animals, insects, even the plants had a life. He had always thought of the night as being absent. Everything asleep, at rest. Now he realized it wasn't so. There was a world that lived in the darkness, as vibrant as the daylight world, a world that he had not realized existed. He belonged to this world. *A creature of the night.* He had heard that term before. Now he accepted it.

They walked on through the darkness. It felt like velvet against Thom's skin, as though it had weight and substance. It had taste as well, and smell. He had this wild urge to tear off his clothes so that every inch of his body could feel the caress of the night, feel a oneness with it.

"It never loses it wonder," said Donovan. "In those first years, I often despaired, alone, and thought of ending my life, but I couldn't bear to leave the night."

Thom thought about Donovan's story, remembering the pain he had heard in the man's voice at his father's betrayal, even after all these years. Thom thought about his own family. They thought him dead, too.

"I was thinking about what happened with your family. I can't go home again, can I?"

"No." Donovan shook his head regretfully. "I know it's hard to accept. Your family and loved ones are still there, close by. You want to see them, be with them, but you can't. For them you must be truly dead. For their sakes, you must accept that they are lost to you forever." He seemed about to go on, but stopped. When he continued, Thom felt sure it was not what he had been about to say. His tone was different. "Don't worry about your kids, they're being taken care of. We've seen to it. They were the beneficiaries of a rather large insurance policy in your name. We'll continue to look after them. We can provide you periodic updates, if you'd like, let you know what's happening to them. Some find it comforting to know, to follow their families through the generations, while for others it hurts too much. That's certainly not something you must decide today."

Thom thought about his children. They were so young to be without a father, just eight and ten. Abandoned. He wanted to go back, but how could he? He was dead. By now his wife and kids were mourning him, maybe even had the funeral. What did they think about the fact that his body was missing? Did they hope he was alive? That it was a mistake? Maybe he could go back? But he wasn't the same. He was a monster. He thought about Donovan killing the girl. Would he lose control, kill his wife, his children? For their sakes, Donovan had said, for their sakes, he couldn't go back.

"It's hard, especially the first time," said Donovan, his voice full of sympathy. "But it's a fact of vampire life. We assume an identity, live it for maybe twenty or thirty years, then become someone new, before anyone notices that we aren't getting any older. It hurts to make a clean break, but believe me it hurts worse if you don't, if you try to watch from the shadows. Now, tell me where the sun is. Don't think with your mind or even look at the watch on your wrist. Feel it."

Thom turned and pointed, easterly, but downward. "It's coming. I can feel it. It frightens me."

"We are of the darkness and yet we are even more the creatures of the sun. It inscribes the arc of its being across our souls. Even in your oblivion, your daily death, your body and soul track the sun. We live by the sun. Perhaps it is appropriate that the sun can kill us. We'd better get back."

"Thank you," Thom said.

"You needed to see some of the advantages of being a vampire. Long life, that's hard to grasp, but the darkness, that's easy to understand."

They walked back to the clinic. Donovan said good night and locked Thom in.

~ * ~

Wade stared at the sunlight, high on the wall. Stanos would be coming for him soon. He moved, the chain rattled. He tried to think back to before Cassandra, but his mind refused to move past her. Beautiful Cassandra, whom he loved, who was his existence. He couldn't count the number of nights he'd spent with her, a few or many, he wasn't sure, but he did know that it seemed normal to be shackled and chained during the day while he waited for the night and for Cassandra. He drifted off to sleep again.

Stanos woke him. "Your dinner is ready." He unlocked the shackle.

"Why does Cassandra chain me like a dog? Even if I wanted to, I couldn't escape. The door's locked. There's no way I could climb out!" He pointed at the hole in the ceiling, a good six feet above his head. "What's that metal shutter thing?" He pointed to the series of grills that partially covered the hole. If it was to keep out the rain, it wouldn't work, for they were full of holes.

"You ask too many questions."

"And you answer too few!" Actually, if they were questions about Cassandra, Stanos would answer. He loved to talk about her. Each day, Wade listened to Stanos and pieced together more of Cassandra's story.

Stanos had come into Cassandra's service shortly after World War I. His father had served a royal household, but after the war that house no longer existed. Stanos wandered, another refuge of the war, until he had seen her advertisement. *Someone to do for a lady of quality*. They traveled all over Europe, she and her traveling companion, Stefan. She was accepted into the best houses. They spent a lot of time in Germany, where they met a young idealist named Hitler. Stefan had been quite taken with the man and his ideas, claiming a bond between the two of them because they were born in the same year. Wade couldn't reconcile Stanos' fond recollections of a man named Hitler with what Wade had read in his history books.

Then Cassandra and Stefan returned to the House in California. Wade was unsure what that was or where, for Stanos always became angry at that point. Cassandra's enemies had conspired against her; even Stefan deserted her. In the end, she had been exiled to this place in the mountains. Stanos had accompanied her and tried to make her life bearable, so he had told Wade.

Upstairs, Wade took a shower and changed into clean pants, an old pair of sweats that Stanos produced, from where Wade didn't know. A meal was laid out on the table--liver, again--spinach--a protein drink--and a handful of vitamin pills.

Stanos hung a bag from a small hook screwed into the wall above the table. The bag was clear, but the contents red. A tube came out of the bag.

"Give me your arm."

"What's that?" Wade asked, eyeing the bag fearfully.

"A transfusion. I don't like the way you're looking. You're too pale. You've been dizzy, right, and tired?" Wade nodded. "Then you will let me do this, so you will be strong for Cassandra."

Wade obediently held out his arm. Cassandra had been taking blood every night. Not much, but still, he grew weaker. He didn't want to grow so weak that she wouldn't want him anymore. That thought terrified him.

Stanos inserted the needle and taped it in place. He stood back. “Eat, boy. It won’t be long ‘til sundown, and she will be expecting you to be ready for her.”

Wade began to eat. Between bites, he said, “I’ve been thinking about what you said last night. You must be over eighty. Aren’t you going to retire?”

“No. I will die in my lady’s service.”

Wade accepted what the man said as truth. When he thought about it, he didn’t think vampires had retirement programs or pension funds. “How long have you been here?”

“Since 1930.”

“Fifty years? Will you be here forever?”

“No, only twenty-five more years. The Directors sanctioned her for seventy-five years.”

“I guess if you are going to live forever, seventy-five years isn’t much.” Wade knew Cassandra had become a vampire during the Civil War. If he remembered his history right, the Civil War had been sometime in the 1860’s. So she was over a hundred years old. He could think in those terms, but couldn’t make himself believe. She didn’t seem a hundred, maybe thirty-five, older yes, but it didn’t feel as though she was that much older than he. She was just the most beautiful woman he had ever seen, and he loved her. Not like a teenager, not like he had liked Sue, but as a man loves a woman.

When the bag was empty, Stanos pulled out the needle and had Wade hold a cotton ball over the wound until it stopped bleeding. Wade drained the last of the protein shake with a grimace. Stanos smiled, pleased with him. “She likes you, you know. You try to please her, you understand?” He led Wade downstairs, locking each door and gate as they went.

Please her, that was all Wade wanted, to please her. He never knew what mood she would be in. Playful, giggling like a young girl in love, or the demanding taskmaster? An imperialist queen and he her humble servant, or did she want to be his abject slave?

Her latest game was that he should be naked, in chains, waiting for her when she woke. He undressed at the door of her bedroom, went in quietly, and let Stanos fasten the manacles, which hung from a chain fastened in the ceiling, around his wrists. He stood on the little platform in the alcove of mirrors. Though Cassandra preferred candles or oil lamps, there was a spotlight here. Stanos adjusted the brightness of the light so that Wade stood in its glow, before quietly slipping from the dark room, leaving Wade to wait Cassandra's pleasure.

She expected him to be ready for her. The first time, he hadn't been and she had punished him. Now it was easy, once in the manacles, he couldn't seem to think about anything but Cassandra and what he wanted her to do to his body. He felt himself harden, eager for the night to begin.

In the dimness, Wade could see Cassandra's naked body lying on the bed, arms across her chest. Wade didn't know how, in this underground, windowless room, Cassandra knew when the sun set or rose, but she did. One moment she would appear asleep, lying with the stillness of death, the next wide-awake.

He felt her eyes on him, watching him from the bed. Then she came out of the darkness toward him, naked and smiling. A wave of relief surged through him, followed by eagerness.

Cassandra let her fingers trail across his chest. "Have you been a good boy?"

Wade nodded. "All I can think about is you, your beautiful creamy white body, your dark eyes, that silken shower of black hair, those hands softly caressing me."

"Much better, you are learning to compliment a lady."

"I think I've learned how to do other things well, too," he said boldly then held his breath, wondering how she would respond.

Today, she laughed. "I'm going to take the boys hunting tonight, so I don't have much time. Now, don't pout." She stroked his lips. "Or I will leave right now and you can wait until I get back."

"No, please don't leave me." He heard the fear in his voice.

"Then tell me precisely what you want these soft hands to do to you." She turned him around so he could see himself in the mirror; see her and what she did to him. "Tell me," she whispered. He told her.

She took her time, touching him gently, caressing him, rubbing her naked body against his back and legs.

Wade watched, but what he stared at was the stranger in the mirror. It didn't look like him. Almost as pale as she, gaunt body and darkly shadowed eyes. He tried to see who he had been, that boy who had jumped laughingly into the cold stream and lay on the warm rock with his best friend. With a shock, he remembered Mike. How long had it been since he had thought of Mike, or his parents? How long since the only thing he had known was Cassandra? He didn't know--days--weeks, maybe?

"Now come show me what you have learned." She snapped the release on the manacles and led him to the bed. Wade deliberately pushed his parents and Mike back into a corner of his mind and shut the door. He knew what Cassandra wanted and what would happen if he didn't please her.

Later, she kissed him good-bye. She was dressed in black as she had been the night she found him. Suddenly, he was afraid. "Are you going to...?" He couldn't bring himself to say the words, but she seemed to know.

"My beautiful boy, you don't need to worry. I won't be bringing anyone home to take your place. We don't hunt humans tonight. Probably a deer. It won't taste as sweet as you, but blood is blood, and my boys do have to feed. Wait here until I get back. I'm sure I will be hungry for things other than blood." She took a long look at his naked body, licked her lips, and Wade saw her fangs.

Then she was gone. He lay on the bed and let himself go back into his mind and open that door and let Mike out. He couldn't believe Mike was dead. Maybe Panther hadn't really killed him, but Wade remembered Josh and knew Mike was dead. Following Mike came his parents, and he found himself crying. Did they think he was dead? Had they stopped looking for him? He tried to figure out how long he had been here, but time blurred. At least a week, more like two, possibly three. He wasn't sure. They must have stopped searching for him. He was sure they had, or Cassandra wouldn't risk going out hunting. He thought of his mother grieving for her son.

He had to find a way out of here. Chained during the day, with Cassandra at night, his only chance was when Stanos fed him, but though old, Stanos was strong and watchful. Wade got out of bed. This was the first time he had been left alone. He hurried into the other room, hope dying, as he found Stanos dusting.

Stanos looked up. "Do you wish anything, young sir?"

Wade shook his head. He began to wander around the room, examining the art. It no longer embarrassed him as it had the first night. Nor that he was nude. Cassandra liked him that way. Looking at a statue of a couple in the throes of passion, he thought he was just one more of Cassandra's pieces of art, part of her collection. When he stopped pleasing her, would she throw him away as she had Panther? He was beginning to understand why Panther hated him. He didn't think he could bear to be out of Cassandra's arms.

He circled the room, but he felt uncomfortable with Stanos watching him, so he went back into the bedroom.

He had never really had time to examine this room. His attention had always been focused on Cassandra. The heavy four-poster canopied bed was high and old-fashioned. There were pillows but no blankets. Vampires didn't suffer the cold as humans did, and Cassandra thought they got in the way. Attached to each of the strong posts were chains and restraints. Another game he had learned to play.

Beside the bed, the mirrored alcove, was a fireplace and the same style of overstuffed Victorian furniture that decorated the other room. In front of the fireplace set a double-wide, velvet chaise lounge. Sometimes Cassandra would lie on it, looking very much like Cleopatra, and sometimes they made love on it, instead of on the bed.

He went through the other door into Cassandra's dressing room. Beyond was an enormous closet full of clothes. On a mannequin was the burgundy red dress she had worn the second night. He couldn't stop his mind from undressing her again. He wondered when she would return. It seemed so long.

Perfume bottles, brushes, make up, jewelry littered a mirrored vanity. He idly fingered the bottles and picked up a nail file, a long metal one, like his mother had, with that diamond coating. An idea began to form. What if he could use it to unlock the shackle? Then he could fashion a rope from the fur or his pants and hook it over the grill in the ceiling and climb out. Or he could use the nail file to unlock the door to his prison. During the day the vampires would be asleep. Maybe he could escape. He saw a pair of scissors, then thought better of it. A nail file, Cassandra might not miss, but a pair of scissors, she was sure to notice and question.

Stanos came in and began straightening the bedroom. Wade stood with the nail file in his hand, afraid to put it down, afraid

Stanos would notice the movement. Stanos picked up Wade's clothes, folded them neatly, and placed them on a chair, then added a log to the fire and carefully brushed the ashes off the hearth.

While Stanos concentrated on the fire, Wade moved to put the nail file back, but he stopped. He walked over to the pile of folded clothes and dropped the file next to his pants. He hoped he could hide the file when he put on his clothes.

"When do you think she'll be back?" he asked Stanos.

"Not for some time, I imagine."

Wade climbed onto the bed and lay down to wait.

~ * ~

Wade woke with a start as fingers trailed across his cheek. Cassandra leaned over him, smiling, but something was wrong with the smile, lips mis-shaped, then he realized blood, fresh bright red blood, smeared her face. Her finger touched his cheek. It felt moist as it painted a strip across his skin. He knew she had marked him with a bloody finger. The image of Josh, blood soaked tee shirt, gaping wound, flooded his consciousness. She bent closer, her bloodstained lips almost touching his. His heart pounded frantically. He screamed; his hands pushed the horror away, pushing hard, panic surging through him. He fought her, but her strength held him pinned. Fear washed over him, turning him inside out, then he could no longer contain it and it vomited out of him, spewing upward to hit her and then splash back on him. She let him go, and he rolled over, the convulsive heaving bringing up everything he had eaten long before. The bile burned his throat, but he couldn't stop.

"Stanos," she screamed.

The servant appeared in the doorway.

"Get this disgusting thing out of here and clean up this mess."

Wade stared at her, his whole body trembling with fear. “I’m sorry, Cassandra, I didn’t mean to. I couldn’t help it. I’m sorry.”

She turned her back on him, stalking toward the closet to change her vomit-splattered clothes.

Stanos grabbed his arm and dragged him to his feet. “Come with me, boy. Pick up those clothes.”

Wade bent over to pick up his pants and saw the long silver shape of the nail file.

Stanos yanked him.

Wade’s hand closed over the file, the sharp point stabbing into his palm.

Five

Wade followed Stanos, only too glad to return to his prison, to feel the heavy weight of the shackle around his ankle, and to hear the door lock. He huddled on the pile of furs, trembling. Finally, he pulled the nail file out of his pocket where he had managed to hide it as Stanos watched him don his pants.

The terror that had sent him running into the woods that first night had returned. All he had against that fear was a slender piece of metal and the hope of escape. He clutched the file and waited for the day and enough light to see the lock.

He had no idea how to go about picking a lock, but on TV it always looked easy. He twisted his leg around, jammed the point of the file into the manacle's lock, and wiggled it around, trying to turn it like a key. Then the tip of the file broke. Panic filled him. If Stanos came back and found the lock jammed, he would know what Wade had done and he would tell Cassandra and she would punish him. He worked frantically to pry the little piece of metal out of the lock. His eyes burned with tears of frustration and fear. Finally, the tip dislodged and fell to the ground.

Wade collapsed weakly, relief flooded his whole body, and in its wake, sleep. When he woke late that afternoon, the panic had subsided.

If he couldn't pick the lock, maybe he could saw through one of the links and free himself that way. He examined the chain carefully, looking for any weak spots. The chain wasn't heavy, but it was strong. Finally, he picked a link at the far end and began to file. He worked a long time before he saw a tiny ridge appear in the surface. Still that tiny indentation filled him with hope.

He heard Stanos' key in the door and quickly hid the nail file under the bedding, covering it with a layer of dirt. Wade's heart hammered against his chest. Would Stanos know? Would he suspect? But Stanos merely unchained Wade and motioned him out of the room.

Wade showered, dressed, and sat down to eat. Stanos was brisk and uncommunicative. His mistress was upset with Wade, therefore Stanos was as well. Remembering how angry Cassandra had been with him last night, Wade faced the night with dread.

When he was brought to Cassandra, Panther was there. Panther who hated him, who had killed Mike. The bloody image of Josh superimposed itself over Panther's dark face, and Wade imagined Mike, lying alone, broken and bloody, in the darkness. Cassandra reached out to Wade, and he couldn't stop himself from jerking away from her hand.

Wade stood, head bowed, body trembling, waiting for her anger, her punishment.

"What's this?" Cassandra asked, raising his head with a finger under the chin. "Surely my Wade isn't afraid of me?"

Wade forced himself to look at her, but last night and her blood-smeared face flashed across his mind and he shuddered. She frowned, her dark eyes glittering cold and hard. She walked around him slowly, fingers trailing, circling his neck, pausing on the spot where her fangs liked to sink into his throat.

Another shudder shook Wade, hard. She continued around him, until she was once again standing in front of him.

Her voice was sharp with anger. “You are mine, Wade. Do you understand? Whether you live or die is my decision, my choice. You cannot hope to escape me, no matter what you do.”

Fear coursed through him. Did she know about the nail file?

She picked up his wrist and brought it to her mouth, licking the inner surface slowly with her tongue, then she bit him. He cried out in pain and tried to jerk away, but she held him. As she drank, the sense of ecstasy flowed up his arm until he was cloaked with it. “Tonight Panther will have me, Wade. Tonight, you will think about Panther and me together and what he is doing to me, the pleasure he is giving me, pleasure that you could have given. You will think about it. You will want me. You will be consumed by desire for me, to hold me, to touch me. You will feel the burning rage of jealousy as you think of Panther’s dark hands against my white body. You will only think about me tonight. Of nothing but me. Stanos, take him away.”

She turned to Panther.

Panther’s look of triumph burned into Wade’s mind and stayed with him after he was returned to his prison. As Wade filed, he kept seeing Panther’s grin and other images--images of Cassandra and Panther together, naked in that big bed.

He hadn’t wanted Cassandra to touch him, but the thought of Panther touching her white skin with his black hands drove him nearly crazy. Burning jealousy filled him. He filed feverishly. He saw himself breaking free and dragging Panther off Cassandra, reclaiming what was his. Toward sunrise, he was certain that Cassandra had only done this to make him jealous. Tonight, it would be as it had been.

He fell asleep, until a dream woke him. Josh and Mike lay dead and Cassandra, her mouth and body covered with his friends' blood, came toward him. He wanted to run, to scream, but he was paralyzed with fear. The fear woke him, and he lay, beneath the blankets, shivering.

He thought about last night, his jealousy, his need to be with Cassandra, his feverish filing. Cassandra had told him to feel jealous. She had told him to think only of her last night. He had. The same thing happened when Stanos chained him to wait for her to awaken. Once the cuffs were around his wrists, he could think only of her.

God, what a fool he had been. She had hypnotized him, made him do exactly what she wanted. He didn't feel jealous any more. That was gone. The dream had wiped all that away.

Now that he knew what she was doing, he wouldn't let her do it again, wouldn't let her hypnotize him. *No more,* he vowed, *no more*.

~ * ~

Stanos woke Wade at nightfall. He was smiling. Wade followed him up the stairs. "Hurry and shower," Stanos said, "And put those on." He indicated the clothes hanging from the door of the bathroom. Wade did as he was told. The black leather pants were tight, almost too small. There was a black leather vest, but no shirt. He wondered what game Cassandra had in mind for tonight.

Stanos had another transfusion for him, besides his usual dinner. It had been two nights since Cassandra had fed on him, and he was beginning to recover a bit of his strength.

"Why the fancy outfit?" Wade asked.

Stanos just smiled. "My mistress has planned a special treat." That was all he would say.

With resignation, Wade finished his meal and followed Stanos down to a room he had never seen. It was a small room, dominated by a table and chairs. A dining room. The table was set for dinner, plates, crystal goblets, folded cloth napkins, and silverware. Not actually silver, but forks and sharp knives with gold handles. Candles in branched candelabra at each end of the table provided light. The chairs were heavy and ornately carved, one on each side of the table. The table was a strange size, long and not very wide.

Cassandra was awake and waiting for him, elegantly dressed in black. A wide pearl choker encircled and covered the column of her throat.

"Wade, I've been waiting for you," Cassandra said, with a smile. She slipped her hand through his arm. "My, you look so very handsome tonight."

"What's going on?" he asked cautiously.

She didn't answer him, but went to a sideboard and filled two glasses from a wine bottle. "I thought you would join me in a glass of wine." She held it out to him. The liquid was red, not the red of blood, but the deep red of wine. "Surely, you're old enough to enjoy a glass of wine."

He took the drink. "I thought vampires only drank blood."

"Another myth, like the one that we turn into bats." She took a sip, urging him with her eyes to drink as well.

He held the goblet, afraid to taste it.

"Drink!" she commanded, and he found himself raising the glass to his lips, even though he wanted to resist.

Just wine. He didn't have enough experience to know whether it was good or bad, but it was wine.

"See, I told you." She smiled. He took another sip and turned away so he wouldn't have to look into her hypnotic eyes. "What's the matter, Wade?" She touched his arm and he stepped away. "You're not afraid of me? I wouldn't hurt you. I love you. You've given me a reason to live, after all these long lonely years. You, and you alone, matter to me."

She sounded sincere. Maybe she did love him. He felt confused.

He moved as far away as the small room would allow. He took a swallow, then another. The wine helped.

"Am I to be dinner?" Wade asked, pointing to the table.

"No. Stanos has prepared us a feast. I just wanted you to join us. I frightened you the other night. I'm not usually like that. What happened?"

"I can't get the image of Josh out of my mind, all the blood."

Cassandra frowned slightly, then brought the wine bottle around the table and refilled Wade's glass.

"That was Wolf, he lost control. I would never do that. I could never hurt you. I love you. I want you with me, beside me, for all time. You can be, you know." She touched his neck, an old bite mark. He jerked at her touch.

"Last night, I only did that to make you jealous," she continued. "When Panther's dark hands were stroking my body, I was thinking of you, wanting you." In his mind, he saw Panther's hands touching her body, as he had seen it in his mind when he had been consumed with jealousy. No, he would not think about that. He gulped the wine.

"You thought of me last night, all the time Panther was touching me, didn't you, Wade?" Cassandra's hand fondled her own breast, moved slowly downward. Mesmerized, Wade nodded slowly.

"You wanted it to be you touching me, didn't you? Your jealousy was a flame that burned inside you. It hurt, didn't it? Doesn't it still? Doesn't the thought of Panther touching me, drive you insane with desire for me? Don't you want to touch me, to hold me, to kiss me?"

As she spoke, the need to do just that grew. He thought of Panther holding her and hated him, hated him with a passion. He wanted to be the one touching her, holding her, kissing her.

"You need me, Wade, I am your life, your whole being. You want me, don't you, Wade?"

She leaned forward, her lips touching his. His need made him tremble as he took her in his arms and returned her kiss with a hungry passion. His body burned for her, his longing blotted out everything else. The wine goblet fell from his fingers and broke with a sharp crash. He stepped back. Cassandra's spell was broken. She had been doing it again, hypnotizing him.

Cassandra looked at the shards of glass and the spilled wine soaking into the carpet. "Stanos will clean it up. Let me pour you another."

When she handed him the glass, he moved away. He took a swallow, then another. The wine helped to distance him from her. If he didn't look at her, then she couldn't hypnotize him.

"What's the matter, Wade?"

"You're trying to hypnotize me, make me do things, feel things. I don't like it."

"Why do you say that?"

"It's true. You told me to feel jealous and I did." He glanced at her, trying to judge her reaction, suddenly afraid of making her angry.

She poured herself more wine, glanced at him, her expression unfathomable.

"You are such a strong young man, Wade. Like no one I've ever known. Maybe that's why I find you so attractive. Yes, I tried to make you jealous, but control you, hypnotize you, as you call it...Do you love me, Wade?"

The sudden question confused him. Did he love her?

"Isn't that what we share--love? You are jealous because you love me, not because I hypnotized you."

Was it true? Maybe she hadn't hypnotized him. Doubt flickered across his mind. She moved toward him and he stepped back.

She turned away with a sob. "Oh, Wade!" Her voice quivered dramatically. "I don't know what I'll do if you don't love me. You've given me a reason to live, after all these long lonely years. You, and you alone, matter to me." In a small girl voice, hurt, she asked, "You do love me, don't you?"

Did he love her? She was so beautiful. Yes, he loved her. He must, mustn't he? He felt sorry for her. She was all alone, lonely, and she loved him. He felt himself weakening, wanting to go to her, to ease the pain in her voice.

"Of course I love you," he reassured her.

She smiled tentatively. "I was afraid you didn't love me." She took the wine goblet out of his hand and put it down on the table. "Please, could you just hold me?"

He opened his arms to comfort her, to hold her, to soothe her fears. He felt so confused. He didn't know what to think. He loved her. How could he think she had hypnotized him? But hadn't she? The wine made him dizzy, clouding his ability to think.

Her head rested on his shoulder, her lips nuzzled his neck then he felt the sharp piercing pain as she bit him, followed by the wave of ecstasy that flowed through his body as she began to suck. His head spun as though he had drunk the whole bottle of wine.

"Wade, you love me passionately. I am the only thing that exists in your life. Your life before, what happened to your friends, they are only dreams, dreams that grow hazy. You will not think of them, you will not remember them. You will only remember me, think only of me, think that you love me, need me, want to be with me always."

He nodded.

"Tell me you love me!" Suddenly there was cold steel beneath her words, a command, not a question.

"I love you," he said.

She kissed him, her lips were cold against his own burning hot ones. He loved her passionately. She was the only thing that existed in his life. Before, what happened to his friends, were only dreams. He would not think of them. He would only remember Cassandra, think only of her, think how much he loved her, needed her, wanted to be with her always. He did love this woman, completely. He could never leave her. "I am yours, Cassandra," Wade vowed, still dizzy, still wanting.

"For the moment, yes." She seemed to make up her mind about something. "Yes, you will be mine completely, even if I must risk losing you. Now, come." She took his hand and led him to a chair. "Sit." He sat. She sat across the table from him. At her left hand was a small bell. She rang it. Stanos appeared. "You may serve now."

"Yes, mistress," he said, with a formal bow.

"Panther and Wolf will be here," she said. "You have nothing to be jealous about. You will ignore them completely. You will think only about how much I love you and how much you want to be with me, to please me, to obey me." Wade nodded. "You will remember that only I exist. I am your future, your present, and your past." She handed the goblet to him. "Finish your wine." He did. It was the best thing he had ever tasted, except for Cassandra. She smiled at him. "Tonight you shall have me in all ways. You will taste me, as I have tasted you. You will want me. You will do anything to have me, to be with me."

Wolf and Panther came in and took their seats at the ends of the table. Wade looked at Panther and felt nothing.

Stanos carried in a large covered bowl. He offered it to Cassandra. She pulled out a rat, a large gray rat with a long whip-like tail and picked up the knife. Quickly she slashed its throat and as the blood poured out of the wound held it over the goblet. Stanos presented the bowl to Wolf and then Panther, each taking a rat, cutting its throat, and letting the blood drain into their goblets. Wade watched as the red liquid pooled in the bottom of the crystal glasses. Almost the color of the wine he had drunk. He should be horrified, but he wasn't.

When the rat no longer twitched or dripped blood, Cassandra casually dropped it to the floor and reached across the table for the goblet in front of Wade. "You must try this. You will find you like it very much." She poured some of the blood into his glass and passed it to him.

He put it to his lips. The blood was warm. It coated his tongue.

"Drink it all; you like it."

Wade drank. Cassandra drained her goblet and licked her lips with relish.

Stanos brought a covered plate, lifting the domed lid. In the center of the platter lay a live rabbit. It had been trussed with cord so that it couldn't move. Cassandra picked it up by the ears and neatly bit its neck. After a moment, it stopped its feeble struggles.

Wade watched Cassandra, fascinated by what she was doing. She sucked for a long time, then she put the rabbit down and wiped her mouth on the napkin.

The rabbit lay limp on the plate. Taking the knife, she turned the rabbit on its back and almost surgically made an incision down the animal's chest. She reached in and pulled out the heart, still faintly beating, and popped it into her mouth. As she chewed, she smiled. She quickly skinned the animal and cut slivers of its flesh. Some she gave to Panther and Wolf, the rest she placed on the plate in front of her and brought it around to his side of the table.

"Try this." She held out a piece of raw meat. His mouth remained closed. "Open and eat." It was a command. He found himself obeying. He'd had raw meat before, slicing slivers off a steak before barbecuing, but this was different. The flesh was still warm, bloody, and good. She fed him more, smiling with pleasure as he ate.

Wolf and Panther carved slices of raw meat from the rabbit carcass and ate hungrily.

"Excellent," she told Stanos as they finished the meat.

"It is a pleasure to please my lady," Stanos said.

Wolf asked, "Perhaps, dessert?"

"Why not, but not too much."

Wade didn't understand what she was talking about until Cassandra's teeth bit his neck again. He was paralyzed, unable to move, as Wolf and Panther came around the table, knelt, each taking a wrist.

Wade knew only a desire to give, as they sucked his life essence from him. After a short time, Cassandra called a halt. Each of them licked the wound, causing the blood to coagulate.

Panther and Wolf left.

Wade sat, unable to move, but when Cassandra told him to stand and follow her, he did.

In her bedroom, she undressed him and they made love. She cut her wrist and held it to his lips and he suckled. "You will soon be mine," Cassandra whispered. "All mine, forever."

Wade smiled at the thought, curling up next to her cold body.

Six

Donovan took the stack of mail and walked toward his office, sorting through the pile as he walked. Mostly advertisements, junk mail. There was one large manila envelope. That would be the reports on those boys killed in the Santiam Wilderness. The return address on a plain white envelope caught his attention. Franklin Blood Bank. The report on Thom's blood work. He tossed the rest of the mail on his desk and opened the envelope.

Donovan read the report and then read it again. He found it hard to believe, but there it was. Thom was Valentine's get. He picked up the phone and dialed the blood bank just to confirm. Yes, they had checked it twice.

"Oh, by the way," the man at the other end of the line said. "You wanted to know if anything unusual was happening with Cassandra."

Donovan's interest sparked. "Yes."

"She's been ordering a lot of blood lately, more than usual. When we inquired, Stanos told us a refrigerator had malfunctioned and a whole batch was lost. I guess that's a reasonable explanation, but I thought you'd like to know."

"You know I would."

"For what she did to Amanda and Clare, I thought she should've gotten more than a few years locked up. She's vicious and dangerous."

"You don't need to convince me," Donovan said. "It's the others who need convincing."

Donovan hung up and leaned back in his chair, thinking.

Cassandra, beautiful, vicious, warped. Donovan had discovered Cassandra after the Civil War. There had been others like her, casualties of the war, dead and yet undead. Some had been slaves whose masters had died in the confrontation that devastated the South. They had been reborn, as he had, not knowing what they were, not understanding. He had made it his job to find and help them.

Cassandra had seemed no more than a beautiful child, hardly innocent, and yet vulnerable. In her, Donovan had discovered a purpose, to help her as Amanda had helped him. He made her his fledgling. Cassandra had initiated the lovemaking and for a time Donovan fooled himself into believing it was love, but Cassandra didn't know the meaning of the word. To her, love was merely a tool or a weapon to be used. Something warped and evil.

For that Donovan blamed Brandon.

Brandon had bought a 12-year-old slave girl, a mulatto, almost able to pass for white, and molded her to fit his own warped sexual tastes. He'd used her shamelessly and pimped her for profit, but made her believe he loved her and that she loved him.

Today much was understood about what sexual abuse does to a child. Back then very little was known. Donovan hadn't understood Cassandra, her need for love, for domination. In his kindness and open-handedness, he thought to teach her how love should be. He only fed her fears. He had taken Cassandra to Amanda in the belief that Amanda could make it right, as she had done for him, but from the moment Cassandra met Amanda she had been insanely jealous. Donovan realized now there could have been no other outcome, for Amanda was everything that Cassandra longed to be and never could. To Cassandra, Amanda was a threat to the only thing that Cassandra thought she wanted, Donovan. Amanda had advised Donovan to take Cassandra away, and finally after one of her jealous rages in which Cassandra attacked Amanda with a knife, Donovan agreed.

They traveled through Europe, and in London, they met Sir Alfred. Sir Alfred was a sadistic product of a wealthy society, and from the very beginning Donovan hated him. Donovan didn't realize that Cassandra's interest in Sir Alfred was merely a ploy to make him jealous. When she declared she wanted to stay with Sir Alfred, what she really wanted was for Donovan to prove his love by reclaiming her. By that time, Donovan was tired of the continual fights and sexual rages. He willing let her go. He walked away and, forever in her mind, abandoned her for Amanda. Yes, he had abandoned Cassandra, not for Amanda, but to Sir Alfred. An action he still felt guilty about.

Under Sir Alfred tutelage, Cassandra learned to crave and need power. Sir Alfred's sexual tastes were even more depraved than Brandon's and Cassandra was a willing pupil. The abused child became the abuser.

Time and again, Cassandra pulled Donovan back into her life. She would beg for his help. Despite his misgivings, Donovan would go. He felt guilty that he had failed his fledgling, not that he had done something wrong, but that he hadn't been able to counteract all the wrongs that had gone on in her life.

His own interest in psychology had grown out of his need to understand Cassandra and his desire to help her. A part of Donovan had clung to the fantasy that he could somehow right the wrongs of the past. That hope died when Cassandra arranged for the murder of Amanda and her child, their child. Cassandra was beyond help, warped, unrepentant, evil.

It frustrated him that others couldn't see her as he saw her. Donovan wished nothing more than to see Cassandra dead, but the Directors in their wisdom decreed a seventy-five year banishment as punishment for her crime.

The manila envelope lay on top of the desk. He took out the police report and read it. Two mutilated bodies had been found within five miles of Cassandra's lair. The third had not been found, but Donovan had no doubt he was dead as well, his body carefully disposed of. Then he picked up the autopsy reports and read them through. His eyes stopped on the paragraph in the second report describing the teeth marks. He glanced back to the other report. The teeth marks were different. Two vampires? Who could be hunting with Cassandra?

When the killings started only a month after Cassandra was condemned to the mountain lair, Donovan had gone to the Directors. Not a single member saw anything wrong with the occasional murder of a human. Of course, to them it wasn't murder. The victims were merely a food source. No, they declared, just as long as it did not attract undue attention and Cassandra remained at the mountain lair, she could hunt as she desired. They couldn't expect her to live for seventy-five years on dead blood. None of them could.

They condoned Cassandra's actions, but Donovan couldn't. Through the years, he had kept track of stories of lost hikers, of the occasional animal attack, of a beautiful woman who crept into a camper's tent in the night, and of course, the persistent legend of the red-eyed demon. Cassandra had been very careful, spacing her attacks and changing her approach, so that indeed, there was no undue suspicion.

Over the last five years, there had been a steady increase, more missing campers, more animal attacks like the one of the two boys. But this--Two vampires hunting together. This might just be the information he needed to get the Directors to act, but he would need more evidence.

The sooner he made the call to Valentine, the sooner she could assume responsibility for her get and the sooner he could find out exactly what Cassandra was doing.

~ * ~

"Donovan," Valentine said with genuine pleasure in her voice.

"I just called to tell you, it's a boy."

"A boy? What do you mean?"

"I've got a newborn here who's your get."

"No way. They must be mistaken. I'm always careful."

"I know. But they checked it twice. He's yours."

"How is he?" Now there was concern in her voice.

"He's making a very good adjustment. I got to him before he'd made his second kill."

"That's good," Valentine sighed. "I just don't understand how he could be mine."

"His name is Thom Barber, thirty-eight." Donovan sketched in the details of Thom's life.

"Doesn't ring a bell. Maybe when I see him, it will."

"Well, maybe this will help. The blood also has trace markers for Byron and Judith, but only you had the necessary three exchanges. He's your get."

Valentine was silent for a long time. Donovan could tell she was thinking, finally she said, "Haight Ashbury. That's the only time it could have been."

"Haight Ashbury?"

"Remember the sixties, free love, the hippies? A group of us, maybe eight or so, went up to San Francisco. It was a wild time. Free love meant free blood. Half the time, they were high on acid, and so we were high, too. I don't remember exchanging blood with anyone, but obviously I did."

"I'll ask Thom if he was in the Haight. If so, you'd better make a list of who went with you and try to remember the names of the people you met."

"Donovan, it's impossible after all these years!"

"You've got to try. If there's one, there could be more, and maybe I won't be so lucky next time. Now, tell me the exact dates you were there."

"August, 1966, I think. I don't remember the dates. Check the initiation records. None of us were standing as blood parent, so we decided to go party instead of waiting around. But we were back for the first kill. When do you want me to come get him?" There was resignation in her voice. One of the cardinal rules was that a vampire was responsible for his or her get.

"The sooner the bonding process begins, the better."

"It couldn't come at a worse time."

"What's going on?"

"There's this rather handsome architect who is helping design my new lair. He isn't going to be too happy having another man tagging along after me like a puppy dog." She laughed. "That's what happens when you have unprotected sex."

Donovan laughed with her. "You have a few days. His fangs haven't retracted."

"I'll be there as soon as I can." They hung up.

As always, when he thought of Valentine, he thought of Amanda. Beautiful Amanda. He had loved her as much as Yolanda did. He missed her. And little Clare. Such a beautiful child, his child, as much as if she was his natural child rather than adopted. Donovan ached with the memories, even though the memories and the pain were fifty years old.

~ * ~

It was full dark. Wade could see the sky through the hole in the ceiling. He could see stars against the blackness. Stanos had not come to get him. In all the days he had been here, Stanos had always come. Now, no one. Wade was worried. There were no lights in his prison, so he sat in the darkness and waited. Finally the lock on the door clicked, the door open, and Cassandra stood silhouetted in the light from the hall.

"Cassandra, I was so afraid," said Wade, brushing the tears from his cheeks. "I thought you had left me."

She came in and knelt beside him, taking him into her arms, comforting him as a mother might comfort a child. "I'm here. I wouldn't leave you alone. Never. Very soon now, you will have me for all time. We will never be apart. Would you like that?"

"Oh, yes, more than anything," said Wade earnestly.

She unlocked the shackle and pulled Wade to his feet. "I sent them all away, Stanos, Wolf, Panther, so I could truly be alone with you for the night."

Joy filled Wade's heart, he was alone with his beloved. He kissed her passionately, touching her intimately.

She laughed. "Come, my pet, I do have a special evening planned for us."

~ * ~

Donovan picked out a bottle of wine and, carrying two glasses, went downstairs. Thom was reading, but looked glad to see him. He eyed the bottle.

"From our own special vintner." The label read V. Impaler Vineyards. Donovan uncorked it and poured. "I think you will appreciate it."

Thom took a sip. "It's wine," he said in amazement.

Donovan nodded. "Of course. What makes it special is just the right blending of blood with the wine."

Taking another sip, Thom motioned Donovan to sit. "Is this just a visit or something special?"

"I have a question. Were you in the Haight Ashbury, August 1966?"

Thom nodded.

"Mystery solved. Among the free loving hippies were some vampires out for a good time. Evidently, some of them had too much of a good time."

"I sure don't remember, but then I was high most of the time."

"Valentine said the same thing. What is in the blood affects the vampire just as much as a normal human. If the vampire drinks from someone who's drunk or high, then he usually gets drunk or high."

"Who's Valentine?"

"She's your parent. You're her offspring, what is called a get," Donovan said. "Sometime during that wild weekend, Valentine exchanged blood with you three times. She wasn't the only one. You have traces of two other vampires, but neither of them had the required three exchanges. If they had, then you would be a spawn. I think I'm getting ahead of myself. I guess it's time for Dr. Donovan's lecture on the history of vampires."

"Do begin, Professor," Thom said, settling back in his chair, with his glass of wine.

"Vampires have been around since the dawn of time. Vampire legends exist in almost every culture. The reason that the world isn't overrun by us is what we call our fatal flaw. It isn't that we are allergic to sunlight. It's what we call line stability.

"When our parent dies, we die. No one has figured out why, but we weaken and die. The reason we have vampires at all is due to what I talked about the first night, the rare spontaneous mutation, that and the curious fact that if you have been bitten, but aren't dead before your parent dies, their death doesn't affect you. You start a whole new bloodline. I'm a sire, because my parent died before I did or as we say before I experienced the change." Donovan paused for a moment, then launched into history.

"Until the Middle Ages, vampires were a short-lived local phenomena, but the feudal system provided the ideal situation for a vampire. As lord of the manor, you controlled the lives of your serfs. You had a ready and easy food source. If someone sickened, you would have them brought to you for healing. If they survived the change, the serfs believed you were a great healer and you had another loyal servant.

"The crusades brought an exchange of ideas, but also bloodlines. They discovered that if you had been bitten by more than one vampire, all your parents would have to die for you to weaken and die. So interbreeding became important.

"The last great bastion of feudalism was the South, where great plantation owners lived on the backs and blood of their slaves. No one questioned when a slave disappeared or died. There was quite a colony of vampires throughout the South. It is considered the true Golden Age of vampirism. Then came the Civil War and it all ended. Not just the end of the plantations and the freeing of slaves, but we were moving into the modern age of communication. No longer could we expect what happened in an isolated corner to remain unnoticed. Newspapers were reporting on all kinds of occurrences, all around the world. Then in 1897, Bram Stoker published *Dracula*. He wasn't the first to write about vampires, and it was clear, he wouldn't be the last. The interest in vampires was growing. We could no longer assume we were safe hiding in the shadows.

"A group of us met in London to discuss what to do. Quite a meeting, more vampires than had ever gathered in one place. Most were for retreating to isolated areas, living as they had done for centuries. Then into the fray came Sir Edmund Horn." Donovan smiled at the memory. "Sir Edmund has always been somewhat of a revolutionary. He is a brilliant scientist and quite an orator.

"He said it was irresponsible to leave a trail of possible vampires behind you, when all it would take was one to prove to the modern, scientific world that we exist. He purposed we stop exchanging blood every time we fed. Blood exchange is instinctual. It is the way we survived. Sort of like the sea turtle laying hundreds of eggs in the hopes that one turtle will live. You can feed as often as you liked. As long as you don't exchange blood, you can't make a vampire.

"While many agreed with Sir Edmund, they thought such a ban would cause our extinction, but Sir Edmund had an answer. In 1866, a monk, Mendall, had pioneered research into genetics. His work was basically ignored, lost, except by Sir Edmund. Sir Edmund was the first to theorize there was a genetic disposition toward vampirism. Vampires had long recognized that if one sibling became a vampire, another was highly likely to as well. Sir Edmund hypothesized that by identifying the genetic markers, he could accurately predict who was most likely to survive the change. Vampires could be more selective in whom they chose and yet be assured of success.

"Your parent Valentine is proof. She's one of the first of what we call second generation. She had been selected as someone with the genetic disposition to survive the change. She had been bitten by five sires, five different bloodlines. According to Sir Edmund, she would have no problem with line stability, even if one or more parents died. I'm rather proud of

Valentine, since I'm one of her five parents, along with Amanda and Sir Edmund himself.

"In the last eighty years, everything has changed. Mendall's work was rediscovered in the early 1900's, gently pushed by Sir Edmund. Research into genetics and DNA has made great strides. Vampire scientists can now identify markers in the blood that are specific to a bloodline. That is why I can say for certain you are Valentine's get."

Thom said, "There's one thing I'm confused about. You called me a get. You said if there was just one parent and that parent dies, the offspring dies as well. Does that mean if Valentine dies, I die?"

"Yes, because you are her get. As I said, although you exchanged blood with several other vampires, it is only Valentine who had three blood exchanges. Don't worry, Valentine isn't likely to die for centuries. Remember you asked if I was going to teach you everything you needed to know, like Amanda taught me?"

Thom nodded.

"That's Valentine's job. As Valentine's get, she's responsible for you."

"What if I don't like her, if we don't get along?"

Donovan smiled. "You will get along, I promise. I think you'll like her. After all, she's my daughter."

"How old is she?"

Donovan thought for a while. "Oh, she's young, just 105, I think. You really will get used to the fact that age doesn't matter to a vampire."

~*~

Wade rested his head upon Cassandra's lap. The only light in the room was the firelight reflected across his naked body.

"Open," she commanded. He obediently opened his mouth like a baby bird waiting to be fed by its mother and she dropped another sliver of raw meat into his mouth. The last time he had eaten raw meat, warm and bloody, Wolf and Panther had been there. He didn't like to think about them or about what they had done to him, drinking his blood. That didn't matter, she had sent them away so she might be alone with him.

He raised his head slightly so he could take a sip out of the goblet she held to his lips. Wine. He had never drunk more than a sip or two of wine, and now, it seemed normal, but he could tell he was a little more than a bit drunk. Cassandra raised the cup to her lips and drank from it as well.

"Tomorrow night you will become mine for all time. You do want that, don't you?"

"Oh, yes," he said reverently.

She smiled. "What will you do to become mine?"

"Anything you ask."

"If I asked you to put your hand in the fire?"

He got up and walked to the fireplace and put his hand out.

"Stop," she commanded.

He turned to look at her. "You don't wish me to do it?"

"And burn that beautiful flesh. No. Just that you would do it is enough." He started to return to her side, but she stopped him. "No, stand in the fire light and allow me to admire you. You do have the most exquisite body. You know, I'm quite infatuated with you, my dear Wade. More than anyone in a long time. I do want you with me for always."

She stood and began pacing. Wade watched her, becoming concerned as she grew more agitated.

"If only I could have your blood tested. If only I could know for certain."

"Know what?" Wade asked.

"Nothing. It's nothing." She stared at him. "I wanted a longer time to enjoy your so-human-body." She studied him. "You are my slave, aren't you?"

"Yes, Cassandra, I am your slave."

"Then come here, young man, and worship me with those hands and lips of yours."

He did as he was bidden.

When she finally ordered him to dress and took him back to his prison for the day, she told him, "When you are brought to me next, you will again do everything I ask, without hesitation. You will please me. If you do, then you will become mine. You want that, don't you?"

"More than life itself," he vowed, and Cassandra smiled.

Seven

When Wade woke much later in the day, he turned over and his hand touched something warm. He opened his eyes and sat up. A girl lay on the blankets, her eyes closed. He gave her a little shake, her head rolled side to side, loosely. She moaned softly.

She wore a yellow dress, like a waitress's uniform. She even had a nametag pinned to her bodice. Wade wondered how she had gotten here and why.

Her eyes opened. They were blue, to go with her blonde hair. She sat up quickly and looked around. "Where am I?" One of the shackles had been attached to her wrist. She tried yanking at the chain, but of course, it did no good. "Where am I?"

"I don't know for sure," Wade answered truthfully. "Somewhere in the Santiam Wilderness."

"Three men kidnapped me. Why?"

"I don't know." Again Wade answered truthfully.

She noticed the shackle around his ankle. "You're a prisoner too?"

A prisoner? He hadn't thought of that. He supposed he was, but that didn't seem right. He was Cassandra's. That was the extent of it. But he didn't tell the girl that, because she wouldn't understand. "I'm Wade."

"Sue."

Dimly he remembered another Sue, a cute blonde. It was only a dim memory without substance. From before. From before he had become Cassandra's. It didn't matter. He let it slip from his mind.

"What are they going to do with me?"

Wade wondered if Cassandra had gotten the girl for Wolf and Panther, so they would leave him and Cassandra alone. He couldn't imagine her coming to love them as he loved Cassandra. "I don't know," he answered, not wanting to tell her what he thought.

"How long have you been here?"

"I don't know. I'm just here, that's all."

"Are you all right?" she asked, concerned.

Wade nodded.

"I was at work," she started to talk about what happened, almost compulsively. "There was this old guy at one of my tables. He was really nice, and very polite. He asked when I got off work. Not in a way that I thought he meant anything by it, just that he was curious. He said a young woman like me shouldn't be out alone at night. I didn't think anything about it then, and definitely not later. I was walking to my car, when two men grabbed me. A black and a white."

"Wolf and Panther. They're Cassandra's get."

She looked questioningly.

Wade didn't explain. "The old one is Stanos. He's nice. He takes care of me. I suppose he will take care of you, too."

"I don't want to be taken care of." She yanked on the chain. "I want to get out of here." She looked upward. "If I stood on your shoulders, I could climb out and go for help."

"No." Wade didn't want to leave. He didn't want to leave Cassandra, not ever.

She gave the chain another yank. "I guess it wouldn't work." She shivered. "It's cold in here." Wade wrapped one of the fur blankets around her. She pulled his arm about her and came close. "Hold me."

Wade did as she asked. He was unsure how Cassandra would react if she knew he was touching another woman. She would probably punish him. But it was nothing, merely sharing body heat and comfort.

The sun had just touched the edge of the blanket, when she asked, "How long are they going to keep us here?"

"'Til almost sunset. Only Stanos can enter when the sun is up. The sun protects us. Try to get some rest." He curled up and went back to sleep. As he fell into a doze, he thought he heard her crying softly.

Wade awoke as Stanos entered.

Sue moved behind Wade. "That's the man, the man who kidnapped me."

"His name is Stanos; he's Cassandra's servant."

"I'm to ready you and take you to Cassandra," Stanos said to Wade, unlocking the shackle.

Wade rose eagerly. Tonight he was to become hers, completely hers. Then he looked down at Sue. "What about her?" Wade asked.

"She will be dealt with later."

Sue cried out in fear.

"Don't worry," said Wade. "It will be all right."

"Come," Stanos said. "You mustn't keep the mistress waiting."

Stanos locked the door behind Wade. "What's going to happen to her?" Wade asked.

"This the mistress will take care of. Now you must take care of your needs and bathe quickly."

Wade did. When he asked Stanos about dinner, he was told he would eat later.

When Wade was brought to Cassandra, she was awake and dressed in a long hooded robe, blood red, richly embroidered in gold and black and set with jewels among the embroidery so that she sparkled like a pagan goddess.

"Remove those clothes," she commanded. "They offend me."

Wade quickly divested himself of his clothes and stood naked before her.

"On your knees before your maker," Cassandra commanded. Wade fell to his knees. "Bow."

He bowed until his head touched the floor. "My beautiful lady."

"Tonight, boy, I am your God."

Wade looked up at her. "Then I worship at your feet."

Cassandra laughed delightedly.

"You may rise." Wade got to his feet, finding something else rising as well. Cassandra smiled in appreciation of his eagerness. Her fingers fondling him, making his penis grow longer with each touch.

His fingers pushed through the folds of her robe to find her naked beneath. Lightly he stroked her breasts, rubbing the nipples.

He had learned well what pleased his mistress.

"Oh, my boy," she sighed. "My beautiful boy." Abruptly she pulled away. "You must be very strong tonight and want to be with me."

"You know I do."

"For all eternity."

"For all eternity."

Her expression was sad. “If only I could be sure--sure you would not die, that you would survive the change. I would hate to lose you.”

Die? Wade wondered what Cassandra meant, but he was afraid to ask. If she asked him to risk death for her, then he would, for he was hers to do with as she wanted. Boldly he posed another question.

“What’s going to happen to Sue?”

“Sue?” Cassandra looked puzzled.

“The woman Wolf and Panther kidnapped. She’s very frightened.”

“Oh, her. She’s for you, Wade.”

“For me? I don’t want anyone but you!”

“No, she will be your first kill. When you become a vampire you will drink her blood.”

Cassandra’s words sent shock waves through Wade’s whole being. He shook his head and backed away from Cassandra in horror. “I won’t hurt her. I won’t hurt Sue! No, you can’t make me!”

“I won’t have to, boy. You won’t be able to stop. You will drink her rich, sweet blood, gulping at her life. You can’t imagine what a wonderful sensation it is to hold another, to drink their blood, to feel the life seeping out of them and into you. You will revel in it. You will be my king, my equal.”

Wade shook his head in mute denial, the image of Josh came to mind, and all too easily he could see himself tearing into Sue’s delicate white throat. “No! I don’t want to be a vampire. You can’t make me become one.”

“But you want to be mine, don’t you?”

“Yes! But not a vampire.” He would be just like Wolf and Panther, forgotten while Cassandra played with another like him. He couldn’t bear it. “I won’t be a vampire. I would rather die." He was breathing hard, his body tense, he felt ready to fly apart.

"Die?" Cassandra voiced her disbelief.

Wade looked at her. "Yes! Kill me now, Cassandra! I would rather die than become a monster like you." His voice was hard with determination. As much as he wanted Cassandra, he knew his words were true. He *would* rather die. "You can't make me hurt Sue. I won't drink her blood. I won't be a vampire."

Wade watched Cassandra's rage grow, moment by moment. His whole body trembled with fear. He bit his lips to keep from pleading, closed his eyes, and waited to die.

"Stanos!" Cassandra cried.

"Yes, my mistress?" Stanos answered.

"Take him away, until I decide what his punishment will be."

"Yes, my mistress." Stanos grabbed Wade's arm and pulled him toward the door.

"No, chain him in my bedchamber to wait my pleasure as he has so many times before."

Stanos dragged him toward the bedroom alcove. Wade fought being chained, but not hard for he knew there was no escape. Still, as the manacles closed about his wrists he knew a moment of stark terror and helplessness. Stanos frowned at him, and for an instant, Wade felt guilty at disappointing the old man.

Left alone, Wade pulled against the chains, but the manacles were tight. He knew each had a release button, rather than a key. He tried to make them work, but couldn't reach them. He sagged against the chains, hanging helpless.

No way he wanted to become a vampire! No way he wanted to kill Sue! If it meant losing his own life, then he would. His father had told him often enough that doing the right thing was sometimes very hard, but that doing the right thing was always worth the risk. Never take the easy way, just because it was easy. Had he just been taking the easy way? No, he loved Cassandra and she loved him. Hope flared. She loved him. She wouldn't kill him. As always when he was in the manacles, he began to think of Cassandra and felt himself grow hard. She would punish him, but she wouldn't kill him. He would make love to her, and she would drink his blood. It would be as it had always been.

~ * ~

After what seemed like a very long time, Cassandra entered. Her face was half-hidden in the shadow of the cloak's hood, and Wade couldn't judge if she was still angry. In her hands she carried a gold goblet.

"Drink," she commanded. Anger vibrated from her. Wade obediently opened his mouth and swallowed, then almost spit it back. *Blood!* Blood and wine mixed together.

"Drink all of it." One hand grabbed his hair and forced his head back, the other poured the liquid down his throat. He swallowed, choking, sputtering, gagging, but swallowed. The overflow ran down his chin, neck, and chest. He gasped for breath. She pulled his head further back and forced the remaining fluid down his throat.

A strange warmth filled his stomach, radiating outward, until it began to encompass his mind, clouding it, as he floated free, unable to help himself.

"You will not deny me, Wade."

"I won't be a vampire." His words sounded distant to his ears, as though he was not really speaking them.

"No, I have decided that you are not worthy to receive that gift. Not worthy of me."

Pain stabbed through Wade. He wanted to beg, but whatever was happening to him had already robbed him of his powers of speech.

"I was born in the South, Wade. My ancestors practiced Voodoo. There are ways, secret ways to make a man do what a woman wants. To make you do exactly what I want. You think you will not drink this girl's blood. You will! And you will relish it."

"*No!*" Wade's mind wailed in silent protest.

"I will make you drink her blood and much more. You won't be able to resist." She walked into her dressing room and returned with a small pot of cream. "I keep this to help the worn-out snake rise, not that has ever been a problem with you, Wade." She smiled grimly as she rubbed the cream into his penis. Then she left.

He struggled against the chains as his penis grew so hard that it hurt. He wanted, yearn to touch it, to sooth the aching need. Coherent thought faded until all that was left was burning desire.

Finally, Cassandra returned with Panther and Wolf. Wade cried in relief.

She ran her fingers down his chest to his throbbing organ. He thrust at her in desperation.

"I think you're ready." She laughed, a cold hard sound. Undoing the manacles, she ordered, "Bring him, boys."

Before Wade could move, Panther and Wolf grabbed him and dragged him through the lair to the dining room. This time the room wasn't set for dinner, no plates, goblets, or napkins. No gold-plated silverware. No candles glowing softly in graceful candelabra.

The only furniture was the table, which sat in the center of the floor, more like an altar than a dining table. The only light the red flickering flames of smokily burning torches.

Cassandra stood in front of the table, waiting.

The jewels on her robe and her eyes glowed red, reflecting the flames of torches. She was a high priestess presiding over a primitive ritual, ready to sacrifice upon the altar of a pagan god.

On the table lay Sue.

Naked and bound.

Her blue eyes were wide with fear.

Wade tried to resist, but there was no escaping Panther and Wolf's cruel grasp.

No escaping Cassandra's hypnotizing eyes. Or her voice.

"Yes, my love, you can't resist. You need it. You need to quench the raging fire." Cassandra touched him and his whole body seemed to burst into flames, as hot as the flame of the sputtering torches. He couldn't stand the pain, he moaned. "Mount her," Cassandra commanded.

Wade was pushed towards Sue.

Part of Wade knew it was wrong, but that part could no longer communicate with his body. He couldn't stop himself. He climbed up on the table. There was only one thing he could do, one way to stop the pain. Part of him cared that he was hurting Sue, that he was frightening her, but he was helpless to stop himself.

When he finally came, it brought no relief. His organ continued to throb and burn. He was no more than an animal now, a rutting beast, moved by instinct and need.

"Wolf, Panther, pull him off of her."

They pulled him off of Sue. He growled in frustration. They threw him down on the floor, holding him while Cassandra mounted him. He climaxed again, and again it brought him no relief.

It seemed to go on forever. Now Wade was so sore that he whimpered as Cassandra rode him, using him as brutally as he had used Sue. Finally, she screamed her own satisfaction.

She pulled him up, making him crawl to Sue. Sue's eyes were closed. Wade wondered if she was dead.

Cassandra took a knife and slashed Sue's wrist, pushing it toward Wade.

"Drink," she commanded. Wade sucked. His throat was so dry that the blood tasted good.

Sue moaned.

Cassandra came up behind Wade and pierced his neck as he knelt.

Wolf cut Sue's breast and Panther took the other wrist. The only sound was the slurping, sucking of blood.

Wade wanted to stop himself. He couldn't. He kept sucking until there was no more. Somewhere inside him, he knew that Sue was dead, and he wondered if he would be next.

Eight

Donovan came down the steps of the clinic to greet Valentine. She was tall and graceful, clad in a designer outfit that she herself had created. Her face was unlined, but the artful streaks of white among the black hair gave her the appearance of maturity.

"How's the fashion business?" Donovan asked.

"Terrible. No one has any taste anymore. Besides Valentine is about to suffer a fatal car accident."

"I'm sorry to hear that."

"That's life," Valentine said with a sigh. "But I'm really ready to move on and try something different."

Sandy came bustling down the stairs. "Valentine. Oh, Valentine!" She looked at the haute couture outfit. "You make me so envious. If only I had been given your body, instead of this rather frumpish one."

"I told you, when you decide on your next life, I'll make you over so even you won't recognize yourself."

"I like what I am, a nurse. I like looking the part, as well."

Instead of going inside, they moved to the end of the veranda and sat in the darkness.

"I thought you weren't going to be here for a while," said Donovan. "Something to do with an architect."

"Oh, he was merely a diversion. Nice, but it had to end. The house was almost finished, anyway. Now, he won't remember certain features of the house he designed." Such a memory loss would require a great deal of control, the kind that required a blood exchanging and bonding. Valentine sighed. "He was a rather handsome architect. Too bad his survival rating is so low."

"You reported him?" Donovan asked,

"Of course I did." Valentine looked at Donovan as though to say how dare he ask such a question. Then she looked embarrassed. "I assure you that one lost weekend was the only time."

"And Thom, the only one?"

"That I'm not sure about. I'm sorry, Donovan. I've talked to Judith and Byron. Their memories aren't much better than mine, although, they seem to remember one young man I was particularly enamored with. They're going to talk with the others who were at the party and see if we can put together a better profile."

"I've questioned Thom about that time. Got a few names. Not much to go on. He told me that a bunch of them got arrested at a protest. I've got Weber and Kleine doing a records search."

"What's he like?"

"I think you'll like him. It's a shame he's only a get. He's intelligent, rational. Maybe that's because he ended up working in computers for IBM."

"Computers. Edmund is convinced that's the way to go. Have you heard his latest? He's decided that our future lies in outer space. He's talking about how wonderful a colony on the dark side of the moon would be. No sun."

"Interesting idea."

"You know it's been years since I had any get. I'm not sure how to begin. Especially since it's been so long since that last bite."

"I've been priming him. No matter what you do, he's going to remain pretty independent."

"Sex?"

"That's up to you. He's not bad looking, a bit on the middle-age side, but not bad. It might be a good idea, since he hasn't had any experience along those lines yet. But don't start anything you aren't willing to continue."

"I don't see how Stefan does it. Since he's been elected to the Board of Directors, he decided he needs a whole army of get and servants to support his position. He just petitioned the Directors for two more get."

Donovan grimaced. He was glad that Valentine was Thom's parent. He could've done much worse. Stefan for one. Donovan knew Stefan's idea of get--indoctrination until the victims had no will of their own and became almost automatons. It was an all too common idea.

"Well, I suppose we'd better get started," Valentine said.

Donovan led the way downstairs and knocked at Thom's door, waiting until he opened it.

"Good evening, Thom. I'd like to introduce you to Valentine."

Thom stared at Valentine for a long time. "I remember you."

Valentine walked into the room, put out her hand to shake Thom's. He took it. She held onto his hand, staring into his eyes.

"Nice-to-meet-you..." Thom stammered, a bemused expression on his face.

Valentine smiled. Donovan was relieved to see that it was a smile of genuine pleasure.

"Donovan," Valentine said, "why don't you leave us alone to get better acquainted."

"Thom?" Donovan questioned.

Thom nodded absentmindedly. It certainly seemed that Thom remembered Valentine. Fifteen years, but he remembered.

"Now, Thom, tell me what you remember about me."

Donovan quietly shut the door behind him as he left.

He went upstairs since he was no longer needed. Valentine could handle it. He saw Yolanda asleep in her chair in the common room and went to sit next to her. The TV was on. One of those news updates. "Latest on the kidnapping of a Portland woman at ten. The police have a description of a possible suspect."

Only five minutes until the ten o'clock news, so Donovan stayed where he was.

"Police now have the description of someone sought for questioning in the kidnapping early Friday morning of Sue Jenkins, a waitress. She was last seen walking toward her car by Mr. Wallaby, owner of the restaurant. He reported seeing a couple of men grab her. Before Mr. Wallaby could respond, she was shoved into a van. He was unable to get a license plate but described the two assailants as a black man and a Caucasian. A van matching the general description of the vehicle was found abandoned two miles of the crime scene. The police are searching for this man..." A composite drawing flashed on the screen. The face looked vaguely familiar. An older man. White haired. "This man was seen talking to the victim inside the restaurant. He showed interest in when she got off work and whether she walked to her car alone. Anyone having information about this man should contact the Portland police."

Donovan stared at the picture. Something about the man bothered him. He couldn't grasp what, but he had an unsettling feeling that it was important. He sighed.

The new orderly came to take Yolanda to bed. Frank had been dismissed, given a good recommendation, and left without any memories of there being a basement at the clinic or any strange patients.

~ * ~

Thom and Valentine stood in awkward silence until Thom blurted out. "You look older than I expected."

Valentine patted the fashionable silver streaks in her dark hair. "Make-up. Artful aging. I've been Valentine of Hollywood for thirty years."

"Valentine of Hollywood?"

"Exclusive courtier to the stars. I'm a fashion designer, although not for much longer. I'm about to die."

"About to die?" Thom shook his head in confusion.

"Let's sit down." Valentine looked at the bottle of wine on the table. "And have some wine."

Thom poured her a glass, and they sat.

"Life as a vampire used to be much simpler," she said, "but harder as well. When most people lived only thirty-five to forty years, you could leave a place and return twenty or thirty years later. Everyone who might remember you would be dead or senile and you could safely take up your old life as your own descendent. Now, people live to be seventy, even a hundred. On the plus side, people are looking younger longer, with plastic surgery, good food and exercise. You can safely stay in one place longer before people begin to notice that you aren't getting older. But there's a limit, and I've reached mine. Besides, I am bored. Webber and Klein, a subsidiary of Darkhour, is preparing a new identity for me. They'll prepare one for you as well."

"Darkhour?"

"Hasn't Donovan told you about Darkhour?"

Thom shook his head.

"I suppose not. You might have turned out to belong to one of the other vampire groups. Do you know about Amanda?"

"She helped Donovan."

"She more than helped Donovan. She was the love of his life." For a moment Valentine looked sad, then she shook herself. "After the Civil War, some of the vampires, including Sir Edmund Horn, came west and took shelter with Amanda. She had a house in San Francisco. In 1875, those vampires wanted to make the arrangement more permanent. They decided to form something entirely new and modern. They created the Darkhour Corporation. One of Darkhour's first projects was to fund Sir Edmund Horn's genetic research."

"Donovan explained about second generations and the London conference. He said you were the first second generation."

"I was the guinea pig. A rather dubious distinction."

"I've heard of the Darkhour Corporation."

"Yes, we've become quite large and well diversified. While not all our companies support our vampire lifestyle, some do. I don't think it will surprised you to learn we own a number of Blood Banks, as well as testing and research facilities, a security company, a custom automobile manufacturer, whose specially built cars allow us to travel during the daylight hours. V. Impaler Vineyards is ours as well. Darkhour Corporation is one of the largest privately owned companies; all the stock is owned by vampires. As my get, you will be entitled to all the benefits of the corporation. You even own some of the voting stock, although as a get, it isn't much."

"So I've become part of a corporation." It struck Thom as funny. It seemed, well, so mundane.

"Darkhour is an excellent cover and it provides us with structure. The company's Board of Directors governs not only the company, but serves as our ruling body."

"How many vampires are there?"

"A few hundred--sires, second generations, spawns, get, servants."

"Do most vampires work, like you and Donovan?"

"Many hold jobs within one of Darkhour's companies. The secret to staying hidden as a vampire is to live a relatively normal life, which doesn't attract attention. Still sleeping during the day does limit the jobs we can do. If you don't want to work, you can draw an income from Darkhour. Does that make sense?"

"It does. I'm having difficulty understanding what it means to be your get?"

"Didn't Donovan explain it to you?"

"Oh yes. He explained. You have five parents. I have one. I will die when you die. But it was sort of like a father trying to explain the birds and the bees to a son without ever mentioning the word sex. I understand the relationship, but what does it mean in practical terms? What is our relationship exactly? He seemed to hint that we were linked somehow, more than just the fact that you are my parent."

"I see. I suppose Donovan has a hard time explaining the relationship because he's never experienced it. He's a sire. His parent died before he did so he's not bound to anyone. He's never made a servant or a get. He's stood as parent for those like me, but that makes him only one of five. When he tries to explain the bond between a get and his or her parent, he's rather like a priest trying to explain sex. He understands the principle, but he lacks the experience."

Thom grinned. "Just like that."

Valentine grinned back at him. "Vampires possess the power to influence minds and emotions, we use it to captivate and hold the interest of our chosen victim and then to make people forget what we are. When you and I made love, I made sure your mind had an explanation about my being a vampire and biting you that it could accept. I told you that all you would remember was that we had great sex. Your own feelings and beliefs reinforced my command, strengthened by the intimate connection that came when I consumed your blood. If it had gone no further, you would have remembered me fondly, nothing more. But you drank some of my blood. That created a much stronger connection between us. It gives me greater power over you."

She stared into his eyes, capturing his mind. The world seemed shift. "Thom, come here and kneel at my feet," she said.

Thom found himself kneeling in front of her.

"Kiss me," she said.

Her lips were soft on his. Memories of making love to her flooded his mind, as fresh as though it had been yesterday.

"Stop," Valentine commanded. Thom stopped kissing her abruptly. "Any of my five parents can command me just as I commanded you, because they are my parent. I could make you stand in front of me and undress or make silly barnyard noises. You would do it, and then convince yourself that it was what you wanted to do in the first place."

Thom backed away from her. "Then I'm nothing more than your puppet, your plaything?" His voice was angry.

"Until you mature into your powers, yes. Afterward, it will depend on how strong you are and how capable you are of resisting. A stronger vampire, and sires are usually the strongest, can command a weaker vampire. The closer the relationship or link, the harder to resist. Donovan, as a sire would have quite a bit of control over you. The fact that he is one of my parents would strengthen the bond."

Thom sat down, shaken. Had Donovan been controlling him without him even realizing it? Thom didn't think so, but now he wasn't sure.

"Don't worry," Valentine said. "Donovan wouldn't take advantage of his power. For a vampire he is extremely ethical. It has to do with his concept of personal freedom, the same idealism that made him take a stand at the Alamo. I think that's why he's never made a servant or a get. I know he has never once used his power on me, even though he is one of my parents and a very strong vampire." She smiled at Thom.

"What's a servant?"

"A servant is completely human, but is bound to a vampire by an exchange of blood and a special ritual which basically reprograms their minds. Servants are absolutely devoted to their masters. They're the only humans who may know vampires exist. They are so conditioned that they are unable to reveal or betray their master. The bond is virtually unbreakable. Almost all vampires have at least one servant, someone who takes care of the details of life during the daylight hours and protects the vampire. The relationship between a vampire and the servant is very intimate. The bond for both is very strong, although stronger for the servant than for the vampire."

"I won't have to have a servant, will I?" Thom asked, thinking that it smacked of slavery. The idea of forcing someone into unwilling servitude turned him cold.

"Of course not. I know it sounds harsh, even cruel, but it really isn't that way. Most servants are human friends, lovers, people the vampire wants to truly share their lives with, but the law is that no one may know of our existence who isn't bound to us, so that they can't threaten our safety. You know Rose?"

Thom nodded.

"She's Sandy's human servant. I don't think she's regretted for one moment the choice she made."

"I wasn't your servant, before I died?"

"No. I wasn't looking for a servant. For us, it was casual sex, casual blood-letting. You were no worse off. In fact I'm sure you enjoyed it very much. I know I did. Taking blood from a human, especially during sex, is highly satisfying. So is sharing blood. Very erotic."

Thom wondered what it would be like to bite someone during sex. It certainly would add an interesting aspect to love making.

"Especially between two vampires," Valentine said seeming to read his mind. Thom felt a stirring low in his belly.

With a seductive smile, Valentine rose from her seat. "I think that it's time you and I explored that aspect a little, see if we can rekindle some of what we felt all those years ago."

Uncomfortably, Thom followed Valentine into the bedroom. Valentine was a very beautiful woman and he was no twenty-year-old kid. Doubts assailed him. Doubts that were soon forgotten in the passion of the moment. When she bit his throat, his body flooded with ecstasy. He realized that all his life he had been searching to recreate what they had shared, not remembering it, but somehow knowing that sex could be more, wanting it to be more. Then it was his turn and he bit her. Her blood tasted incredible, salty, sweet, potent. Its power flowed through him as if an electric current, making every cell tingle in response. Valentine moaned, caught in her own passion. He felt her pleasure echoing through his mind. She spread herself wide in welcome and he entered, plunging deep within her. His penis was sensitized beyond anything he had ever experienced. The intensity was too much and he climaxed with a shuddering burst of release. She followed in her own spiral of ecstasy. They held tightly to each other, slowly spiraling downward.

She licked blood from his neck. He returned the favor, his tongue licking her cool flesh. Her wound was already healed, invisible. He touched his neck and found no mark.

They lay side by side.

Valentine sighed. "It has been a long time since I had a vampire lover. It's so freeing not to have to worry about how much blood I'm taking or to make sure you don't remember." She turned over and looked at Thom. "You were a good lover back then, but I think you are an even better one now."

Thom grinned at her foolishly, at least he felt as though the grin plastered on his face must look rather idiotic. "I think I will definitely enjoy being a vampire, being your get."

"There's so much to teach you, I can hardly wait."

~ * ~

Donovan was working in his office just before dawn when Valentine entered. Her hair was loose about her shoulders, her suit jacket gone, and she was smiling.

"I think I'm really going to enjoy Thom. He is, as you said, intelligent. Eager to learn and a good lover. He remembered me with great pleasure and enthusiasm."

"I'm glad," Donovan said dryly.

"Well, how long has it been since you had a good lay?"

"Probably too long."

"See." Valentine stuck her tongue out at him. "Don't knock it until you try it."

"Oh, I have," Donovan said. An uncomfortable silence followed as they remembered Amanda.

Valentine broke the silence, chattering on. "After all this time, I think I'm going to enjoy introducing Thom to the pleasures of being a vampire. At first, I thought it couldn't be a worse time. Now I think it is the best. Valentine, the designer, has to die! I wasn't quite sure what I wanted to do next, but I think travel. Yes, Thom and I are going to travel. Visit all the spots where the hunting is easy, where pleasure can be had for a song. Maybe we will join the swinging singles and party. Recreate a little bit of the Haight Ashbury. Indulge ourselves."

"Not too much, I hope."

Valentine laughed. "That's your problem, Donovan. You never just indulge yourself."

"How long are you staying?"

"Just a few days, this time. Have you started Weber and Kleine working on Thom's new identity?"

"Yes. They said a couple of weeks. While you're here, be sure to visit Yolanda."

"How's she doing?"

"Getting old. Most of the time she thinks Amanda is still alive. Sometimes, I pretend with her. Then I remember." He sighed. "I know Cassandra hated me, but why did she have to kill Amanda?"

"You know why. She thought she could assume Amanda's position. She saw that Amanda had the power she craved, power and your love. She thought she could have both, if Amanda was out of the way. It almost worked. She would have at least had the power, if you hadn't proven that she was behind the attack."

Donovan pushed the fat file folder across the desk.

"What's this?" Valentine picked it up.

"Cassandra. The latest was three young boys, brutally murdered while on a camping trip." Donovan remembered the autopsy report. "Is there any chance someone could be hunting with her? The autopsy reports two different bite marks. Two bodies, each with a different bite mark pattern."

"Two? I thought you said there were three?"

"They found two mutilated bodies. They didn't find the other one."

Valentine frowned. "I suppose it could have been Stefan hunting with her."

"He would risk being associated with her?"

"Stefan is a lot more confident lately. I've heard some talk about reducing Cassandra's sentence, that she has been punished enough. I'm sure Stefan's behind it, although I can't prove it."

Donovan's stomach knotted. "Don't they know that they will be letting a wanton killer loose? She ran the boys down and tore their throats out. The autopsies describe the deaths as "Savage attacks." Then she left them practically on her doorstep. Cassandra doesn't care! She's lost all caution. Surely the Directors can understand she is evil and a danger to us."

Valentine didn't answer him. There was nothing to answer and they both knew it.

"Damn it!" Donovan pounded the desk. Valentine looked alarmed at his sudden outburst. "That's why the picture was so familiar."

"What picture?"

"There was a young woman kidnapped in Portland. They have a composite of a man who might be involved. It looks like Stanos."

"Cassandra's servant?"

"I haven't seen him in years, but aged, yes, it looked like him."

"Aren't you jumping to conclusions?"

Donovan sighed. "You're right. But...maybe not. When I called the Blood Bank about the report on Thom, they mentioned that Cassandra's been using a lot of blood lately. Maybe she isn't alone."

"What do you mean?"

"Maybe Cassandra has some get. If it was Stanos who kidnapped the woman, the police report said there where three men involved. That would also explain the increased frequency of attacks in the last few years." Donovan smiled. "The Directors would have to act since, as part of her punishment, they specifically forbade her to have any get."

"What are you going to do?"

"I'm going to go up there and find out who has been hunting with her."

"Oh, Donovan, that could be dangerous."

Nine

Wade woke the next day so sick he crawled to the farthest length of the chain and vomited. Then he crawled back and huddled in the blankets. He tried to remember what had happened the night before. He couldn't; it was a blur.

When Stanos came in, Wade moaned, too weak to rise. Stanos pulled the blanket off him. Wade realized he was naked and covered with dry blood.

Stanos helped him to his feet. "Come on, young man."

"What happened to me? What's wrong?"

"You drank too much last night and have a bad hangover." He dragged Wade out. Wade was certain if Stanos hadn't been holding his arm tightly and supporting him, he would have had to crawl down the hall, he was so weak. He fell three times trying to mount the stairs. When he reached the top, he headed for the bathroom and vomited into the toilet.

"Blood first," Stanos said, dragging him from the bathroom to the kitchen, where he sat him down at the table and gave him two pints of blood, intravenously.

"I don't know what she's thinking of," Stanos muttered. "Blood supplies are low. Instead of letting you die, she wants life pumped back into you. She isn't through with you yet, she says."

Wade sat with his head hanging down, drifting in and out of consciousness. When the bags of blood were emptied, Stanos pulled Wade to his feet and shoved him under the shower. He roughly towel-dried Wade, then supported him back down the stairs. Wade noticed the sun was at the far end of the room, as Stanos fastened the shackle around his ankle, then unconsciousness took him.

He vaguely remembered Cassandra holding him, stroking his cheek, murmuring something about being sorry, not wanting to hurt him. Then she left him alone. Wade didn't know whether it was one or two days before he fully regained consciousness. The sun was shining on his face, warming his naked body.

An overwhelming lassitude filled him; he couldn't bring himself to move. His memory was all bits and pieces, vague images. They were going to be joined, Cassandra and he, for all time. Had it happened? He didn't know.

At sunset, Cassandra and Stanos entered.

She touched Wade's forehead. "He's feverish."

Stanos nodded.

"More blood?" she asked.

"There isn't any more, mistress. If I order more, they'll question it. We've used so much lately."

"Tell them something."

"I already told them our refrigerator broke down and a whole batch spoiled. They won't accept that again. They'll send someone to check."

She frowned. "If they send someone, they will take my beautiful Wade away from me, and Panther and Wolf. Maybe even you, my loyal servant. You must stop them."

"I will be ready for them," Stanos said grimly. "I will protect you."

She gave him a kiss upon his old, wrinkled forehead. "What would I have done all these years without you?"

She looked down at Wade. "I made a mistake, Stanos. I should have forced the change. Oh, I was angry with him, but down deep I was afraid I would lose him. He's so beautiful. I don't want to lose him, ever."

"I will take care of him, mistress. He will recover and be with you for a long time. He can be your servant as I have been your servant."

"Why would I need two servants?"

"Mistress, I'm growing old."

She frowned, looking at him as though she was really seeing him for the first time. "Oh Stanos, what would I ever do without you?"

"Don't worry. I'm still strong. It will be many years."

She smiled and patted his cheek, then looked down at Wade. "It will be as it was before. Wade will love me, and I will take care of him."

"Give him time to recover, and all will be as you wish."

"Oh Wade, if only you hadn't called me a monster. If only you wanted to be a vampire. Stanos, he told me he would rather die than be like me." Her voice broke in a sob. "How can I forgive him? My beautiful Wade, how can I forgive you?"

Wade wanted her to forgive him. He still wanted her, still needed her. He tried to tell her so, but his mouth was so dry he couldn't form the words. His body burned and his head ached so that he couldn't think. He closed his eyes, drifting away.

~ * ~

Thom followed Valentine with puppy dog eyes.

"Thank you," Thom said to Donovan. "Thank you. I never thought such a beautiful woman could love me."

Donovan knew he had to warn Thom that Valentine would soon tire and he would be relegated to the background as a new interest took his place. For now, she was enjoying playing the role of teacher and seductress. "Thom, you're thinking in human terms. Love is a human concept."

Thom looked inquiringly. "What are you trying to tell me? That Valentine doesn't love me?"

"Not in the way you think. You two are connected, but not as a man and a woman who love each other."

Thom waited for him to continue.

Donovan said, "You remember the old vampire movies, where the vampire looks into the eyes of the helpless victim, hypnotizing her?"

"Sure. Valentine explained all that."

"She did?"

"Yes. She gave me quite a graphic demonstration of her power over me."

"Oh," was all Donovan could think to say.

"I tried it, this hypnotizing bit, but I don't seem to have it or maybe I'm just stupid and can't get the hang of it." Thom looked worried.

"You have it. You just haven't needed to use it, since you haven't needed to hunt. It's instinct, but the conscious control, the finesse, comes with age and experience. For example, if I choose something that goes along with a person's natural inclinations, I can make anyone, with whom I have direct eye contact, believe what I want. The ideas would seem to pop into their head. No one really believes in vampires so when I tell them to forget that I'm a vampire, it matches their own belief system, and they tend to forget. Not always, but it usually works."

"Valentine explained about how the consumption of blood creates a connection."

"Did she explain the emotional echo?"

Thom shook his head.

"A vampire not only projects thoughts, but emotions. We pick up on the general emotional aura, amplify it, feed it back. Basic emotions, fear, anger, sexual arousal, especially sexual arousal, work best. We use the emotional echo to capture and hold a human's interest. We can be endlessly fascinating if we so desire."

"So you are saying that Valentine doesn't love me? She's using this emotional echo thing?"

"When there's an exchange of blood, a physical and psychic connection form. It's strongest between a parent and a get. What Valentine did was re-establish the connection that already existed."

"You mean she doesn't love me?" Thom demanded.

"Human terms again. As long as you live, which will be a very long time, you two will be connected, bonded." Donovan sighed. "I'm trying to say that Valentine has a rather short attention span."

"You're trying to warn me not to get too attached, because it isn't going to last."

Donovan nodded.

Thom grinned at him. "Well, I guess I'd better enjoy it while it does last."

"That's right." Donovan grinned. "There's a lot there to enjoy. You're very lucky that Valentine's your parent. She'll take good care of you."

Thom gave him a sideways glance, and Donovan realized something in his tone must have alerted Thom. Yes, the man was intelligent and perceptive.

"I think it's time for another one of Dr. Donovan's lectures. I'd better warn you that we vampires can be as prejudiced as any Ku Klux Klan member. Remember, I told you that the Southern plantations were the last great stronghold of vampirism. There are those vampires who regard their get with no more consideration than they had for their slaves. For some that is exactly what a get is, a slave."

"What are you two talking so seriously about?" Valentine came and sat on the arm of Thom's chair, putting her hand on his shoulder.

"Donovan's telling me the facts of life."

Valentine looked at Donovan with a question in her eyes.

"Vampire society."

"Oh, that," Valentine said with a laugh. "That's not hard. At the top you have the sires, like Donovan. They are usually the strongest. The source of a bloodline. Then you have the second generations. Second generation have sires among their five bloodparents. Some like me have only sires, while others may have one or two sires. A third generation has five bloodparents but no sires, usually second generations or spawns. No one knows why, but the further away from the source, the sire, the weaker the vampire.

"Now, Donovan here is considered by many to be one of the strongest vampires. Not all sires are as strong as he is, but most are stronger than we second generation are. We second generations are usually stronger than a third generation or a spawn. Finally there are the get. Many vampires consider a get as nothing more than extensions of themselves, slaves, servants."

"Donovan was explaining that."

"Any vampire who is not a get will consider himself above you in rank. He will believe he is more powerful than you. It isn't necessarily so. You are the get of a very strong vampire. But don't become involved in a pushing contest. You might win. Unfortunately, in vampire society, a get has no standing. So," she grinned, "let me do all the fighting. Thom, as far as I'm concerned, it doesn't matter if you are a get or another sire, the same goes for Donovan and Sandy, but you'll encounter others who are not so enlightened, even among the other get. Now, have I told him enough depressing news?" Valentine looked at Donovan.

Donovan looked at Thom.

"Let me get this straight," Thom said, "if I stick with Valentine, I'll be all right."

Donovan smiled. "You've got it. And I'm here if you need help or just to talk."

Valentine looked at Donovan. "Are you leaving tonight?"

"Yes."

"Do you want me to come with you?"

Donovan shook his head. "No. Stay and get better acquainted with Thom."

"All right, but be careful."

"I will. Thanks."

"If Cassandra has get, I'll go with you to the Board. They will have to listen."

Maybe this time, Donovan thought. He was doubtful. They'd never listened in the past.

~ * ~

Thom watched Donovan drive away. "Where's he going?" he asked Valentine.

"Hunting," Valentine answered softly.

"Who is Cassandra?"

"Cassandra is the vampire responsible for the death of Amanda and their child." She turned and walked away. Thom stared at her retreating back, the implications of what she had said echoing through his mind. He hurried after her and grabbed her arm.

"Wait a minute! You can't just walk away like that. You have some explaining to do. There are a couple of things I don't understand, like the word 'child.' I thought vampires couldn't have children. And just what do you mean 'responsible for Amanda's death'?"

Valentine sighed. "It's a long story."

"And we have all night."

Ten

"Let's go for a walk," Valentine said. She and Thom took the path up to the crest of the hill and sat on the bench that overlooked the Willamette Valley. Thom waited patiently for Valentine to start her story.

"You know who Amanda is?" she said finally. "Of course, I explained about her and the founding of Darkhour."

"Donovan talked about her, too. He was her fledgling, like I'm yours."

Valentine smiled at him. "At first, but they were both sires, so it was a bit different than it is between you and me. Donovan forgets that it was not always so perfect between them. They frequently disagreed. Amanda was a very independent woman for her time. Though she was from the South, she disagreed about the war, the Civil War, that is. They were in the South with Edmund and the others at the time, and Donovan wanted to stay and fight. Amanda didn't; she was a pacifist at heart. With the war looming on the horizon, she retreated to California and Donovan joined the Confederate army. Later, other things kept them apart.

"You asked about Amanda and the child. Whatever makes us vampires does make us sterile, but we are still human with human wants and needs--the need for love, to belong to something, a desire for a family. Maybe it took longer for

Amanda, but eventually she wanted those traditional things, a husband, a family, even if only for a while. She had come to love Donovan for his kindness and his understanding. He had always been crazy about her.

"Historically, when a female vampire wanted a child, the vampire stole a child at birth, killed its mother, and let the baby's first nourishment be the vampire's own blood. It was believed a bond would be formed between vampire and child, a maternal bond, and the child was more likely to survive the change to become a vampire. There are those who still follow the old ways, but now that we understand genetics, it is more usual to adopt a child with the right genetic make-up to raise as our own.

"A young descendant of Amanda's got pregnant at fifteen and was putting the baby up for adoption. Amanda wanted the child. She and Donovan adopted the baby, a beautiful little girl they named Clare. Donovan had just started the clinic, and they settled down in Fillmore Grove. I'd never seen Amanda so happy. Motherhood suited her. Clare was just three when Cassandra and Stefan returned to California. It was about 1935. Cassandra had always been jealous of Amanda. Now she couldn't stand the happiness Donovan and Amanda shared."

"Just who is Cassandra?"

"I told you that Donovan stayed in the South during the war. During that time of upheaval Donovan started on the path he is still on, rescuing newborns. Shortly after the war, he found a young girl. Cassandra had been the servant of a sadistic vampire named Brandon, a gambler and a pimp. Some carpetbaggers did us a great favor and beheaded the bastard. As I understand it, Cassandra killed herself to escape them. Unfortunately, she didn't stay dead." Valentine's tone became bitter.

She continued, "We don't like to believe that the blood of our parents determines what kind of vampire we become, but in

Cassandra's case she came from bad blood. It was clear from the very beginning that she was tainted with evil, but Donovan was too much of a rescuer to let go."

The moon crested the mountaintop, casting light across the dark valley. "Cassandra was there at the beginning of Darkhour. She was one of the founding sires, and over the years she continued to return, always making trouble when she did. One of the times she returned was during World War I. Her protector, Lord Alfred, was dead, and she told Donovan she wanted to return home. Donovan welcomed her back. For a while it seemed that she had changed. She was even nice to Amanda. Of course it didn't last.

"Stefan was the son of my-nephew. When was nine, he was orphaned and I took over his care and raised him for the next ten years. When he turned nineteen, he was initiated. Cassandra asked if she could serve as one of his blood-mothers. Foolishly, I agreed. Before we knew it, Stefan was Cassandra's fledgling and the two of them left for Europe. She did it deliberately to hurt Amanda and me.

"I didn't particularly like the man who returned almost fifteen years later. Stefan had always had a cruel streak. Under Cassandra's tutelage, it had blossomed. Nor did I like his new politics. Cassandra and Stefan had become friendly with Adolf Hitler. It was 1935. The Third Reich was just in its infancy. Stefan and Cassandra wanted the Darkhour Corporation to aid the Third Reich. Hitler was going to be the future, the future for the vampires, as well as the Germans. Stefan started talking about vampires as the master race. Amanda was their main opponent. She was on the Darkhour Board then, highly respected, with a lot of power. She believed in neutrality, in peace."

Valentine paused for a moment.

Thom was finding Valentine's story fascinating. He didn't want her to stop. "Go on," he urged.

Valentine resumed. "Donovan was away hunting rumors of a newborn. When he returned home, Amanda and Clare were dead, their home destroyed by fire. A terrible, 'tragic accident.' Donovan was devastated; we all were. Suddenly, there was Cassandra, getting herself elected to fill Amanda's place on the Board, continually at Donovan's side to comfort and support him. I tried to warned Donovan, but at first he wouldn't listen. He was in too much pain. Gradually, Cassandra's true face emerged. Donovan began to question what had happened.

"First, there was the newborn Donovan had been tracking. After the fire, the killings just stopped. There was no sign of a newborn. Donovan began to wonder if he had been deliberately lured away. Then there was the fire itself. It had burned so quickly and so hot that the house was totally consumed. He hired an expert to determine whether the fire was arson. It was.

"It was also murder. You see, it was night. Amanda was awake, in a house specially designed by a vampire. There were bolt holes, ways she and Clare could have escaped, should have escaped. The only possible explanation was that Amanda was hurt or dead before the fire started. Then there was Yolanda's claim that another vampire had been there that night. Yolanda was Amanda's servant and Clare's nanny. Clare had been running a fever, so Yolanda was sent to the clinic for medicine. When Yolanda returned, the house was already engulfed. Only the firemen kept Yolanda from throwing herself into the flames.

"Yolanda swore that she sensed another vampire that night, watching. No one believed her. Servants usually don't have our ability to sense our kind, and with Amanda's death, the bond between them had been broken brutally. Yolanda was never quite right after that night, but she never swerved from her story about the other vampire.

"Donovan started looking for proof. His search for the newborn or a vampire faking newborn attacks turned up nothing, but he had better luck finding the arsonist. According to his expert, the arsonist had left an unmistakable signature. Donovan tracked the man down. The man confessed and that led Donovan to the rest of the assassins. Donovan's not proud of what he did, but his grief and need for revenge were too great. He took a blowtorch to them and made sure it took them a long time to die.

"The only thing the assassins gave him was the arranger. There he got lucky again, since the arranger believed in keeping records. Donovan had his proof that Cassandra was behind Amanda's murder. He made a mistake. Instead of killing her, he took the matter to the Darkhour Board. On general principle, we avoid killing other vampires, especially sires. When you kill a sire, you damage or destroy more than just one vampire. You destroy their get and weaken the seconds, thirds, and spawn that might be linked to them. You may even be harming yourself. Vampire blood relationships are very complex.

"Stefan spoke in Cassandra's favor. He was eloquent. He claimed he was worried what killing two of his sires so close together would do to him. There were others who had both Amanda and Cassandra as blood-mothers. Not many, but enough. It was easy to believe that Stefan's fear was real, because so many of us were already weakened by Amanda's death. The Board of Directors voted that because Cassandra was a sire and it would affect so many others, they wouldn't kill her. They wanted to punish her, so they exiled her for seventy-five years. They let Donovan chose the place. He picked an isolated lair in the mountains. Imprisonment and isolation were deemed enough punishment. It wasn't enough for Donovan. It will never be enough for him."

"Why is Donovan going after Cassandra now?"

"She's been killing humans."

"Is that allowed?" The image of the man he had killed flashed across Thom's memory. Donovan had explained the necessity of the first kill, but had assured Thom he wouldn't have to kill, ever again.

"Never forget what you are, Thom. While we may look human and act human, we aren't. There is a beast inside us that can overcome reason, sanity. That beast inside owns us. It makes us all killers."

Thom shuddered, remembering those first days, the awful things he had done, his sense of helplessness in the face of his hunger and his instinct for survival.

"Most vampires don't kill, but some do. Some enjoy the taste of fear, the bitterness of death. Just as some humans enjoy killing. The vampire community as a whole condones it, as long as it doesn't draw attention to us. I wish that wasn't the case, but it is." Abruptly Valentine stood. "I'm going for a walk."

"Can I come?

"Not this time. Besides being one of my blood-mothers, Amanda was my best friend, the closest thing I had to a mother and a sister, all rolled into one. When Cassandra killed her, she killed something in me. I felt her death and it weakened me. It was as though an important part of me had gone missing. I keep searching, but it isn't there to find. I have recovered my strength, but never that missing piece. No, Thom, I think tonight I want to be alone."

She disappeared into the darkness of the surrounding woods, becoming part of the night. Thom was left alone, alone to think. Just like humans, there were good vampires and bad vampires. Becoming a vampire didn't change that. Valentine, Donovan, Sandy, they were the good ones. He didn't think he wanted to meet any of the bad ones, not Cassandra or Stefan. Slowly, he walked down the hill.

~ * ~

Stanos brought Wade soup and fed him spoonfuls. He cared for him as he would a sick child, and gradually Wade began to feel better.

"Where's Sue?" Wade asked, remembering the blonde-haired girl.

"She's gone," Stanos said. "Don't think about her."

But Wade did. He had nothing better to do. Gradually it began to come back to him--the room, Sue's naked body, and what he had done to her. Wade crawled to the length of his chain and vomited. He saw himself clearly. He had murdered a woman, worse than that, he had brutally used her, raped her. The words turned him cold. Rapist! That was something he would never do, not in a million years, never! Was it only a bad dream? A nightmare? No, something told him it was real.

When he told Cassandra he didn't want to become a vampire, that he didn't want to kill, she had forced him. He remembered Cassandra compelling him to drink from the goblet, rubbing his penis with an ointment. Voodoo, she had called it. Voodoo had made him do whatever she wanted.

Tears came to his eyes. Tears of hopelessness and fear. He saw what he had become. He'd thought he loved Cassandra, that she loved him. It had never been love, never. It had all been about control. Cassandra had controlled him completely, making him do--oh, what he had done. All the horror came spewing up and he vomited until the dry heaves shaking his body was the only thing that remained.

He wanted to purge himself of all that was Cassandra.

He wanted to die.

He curled up in a tight ball and cried, hugging himself, rocking back and forth, tears streaming down his face. What he had done to that poor girl, that poor frightened girl. He should have been stronger, resisted. Even if Cassandra had forced him, he was to blame,

He remembered something that his father used to say. *"Even if bad things happen to you, you have the choice. You don't have to let them make you bad."* He had a choice. He had done some bad things, but he didn't have to let them make him bad. He had a choice. Suddenly, he remembered the nail file and scrabbled frantically in the dirt until he found it. The sharp edges cut into the palm of his hand. He found the link in the chain and started filing. More than ever he was determined to escape.

He was sitting up when Stanos entered.

Stanos smiled. "We are feeling better?"

Wade nodded. "I have returned to normal."

"Good. The mistress will be pleased to hear it." Stanos bent down to unlock the shackle.

"Don't bother. I'm not going with you. Never again!"

Stanos stared intently at Wade, then went out, and locked the door. Night came. Wade sat in the darkness, waiting. Cassandra opened the door and entered. She carried a lantern.

"Stanos says you won't come."

Wade shook his head. "Never again. I would rather die than let you touch me. I would rather die than ever hurt another human being."

She put the lantern down, knelt and grabbed his chin in her fingers, holding his head still, staring into his eyes, trying to hypnotize him. He kept the image of Sue's bloody body in his mind, and she finally looked away. She rose to her feet and stood looking down at him.

"I could bend you to my will," she said, "as I have done before."

"Maybe," said Wade, afraid, remembering what he had become, her willing and obedient slave.

"But I think I like you better this way. I am going to keep you alive a good long time to serve me as I choose." He stared up defiantly, although he knew that it was no more than useless bravado. "And when you finally die, you will become one of my get, tied to me like Panther or Wolf. Once you are a vampire, you will do my complete biding, willingly. You will have no choice. I will bring other Sues here for you to kill and feast on. We will hunt other campers in the woods. You will fall on them and drink their blood as Panther drank your friend's. You think you can resist me, but you can't resist the hunger. You won't be able to; you will kill. Over and over again, you will kill, and I shall watch you and enjoy what I have made you."

She touched him, and he batted her hand away. "Stanos, put the rest of the manacles on him."

It took both Stanos and Cassandra to fasten them but Wade finally lay helpless, chained hand and foot.

Cassandra touched him as she had done so often before, and he felt himself responding. She laughed. "Maybe tomorrow night, you will be more willing." She picked up her lantern. She and Stanos left, leaving Wade crying in shame in the darkness. He wanted to die, but that wouldn't end his suffering. That would only begin it.

~ * ~

Donovan swore as he put down the binoculars. Stanos' van was gone. He had left sometime during the day while Donovan slept. Donovan looked down at the cabin--quiet--still--deserted. Two nights of watching, and he had yet to see anything.

He urged himself to be patient. Maybe tonight Cassandra would take her get and go hunting. He was sure she had get. That would explain the two bite marks on the mauled campers and the report of the two kidnappers.

He thought of trying to sneak into the lair while Stanos was away, but he doubted he could get in and out of the well-protected lair undetected. Instead, he decided to drive into the town and see what he could learn. Two nights ago, when he arrived, Danvers had been closed up tight; everyone was home, asleep behind locked doors. He hadn't stopped, but continued up the mountain.

Fifty years ago, he'd spent a lot of time here, watching from a small cave overlooking the lair. He'd expected Cassandra to escape. Hoped she would, so he'd have an excuse to hunt her down and kill her, but Cassandra had accepted her exile.

Exile! Meager punishment for the murder of Amanda and Clare. If Valentine was right, and Stefan had his way, even that would come to an end soon.

Donovan prepared to leave the cool darkness of the cave for the bright sun. A long duster over the Pendleton shirt and jeans, gloves to protect his hands, dark glasses and a Stetson pulled low to protect his face and eyes. Last, he tied a bandana across his face like a bandit.

Keeping to the shadows of the deep woods as much as possible, he hiked down to where he had left the car. It was quiet in the woods; the occasional sound of his hiking boots slipping on the steep trail the only noise in the drowsy heat of afternoon. He forced himself to keep moving, fighting the sun's lethargy that left him feeling dull and heavy.

He reached the protective shelter of the car with relief.

The road down the mountain was gravel, narrow and twisting, full of ruts and potholes. He drove slowly, trying to avoid as many of the bumps as he could. The heavy car had extra heavy-duty shocks, but still he was jostled from side to side.

It was about 4:30 p.m. when Donovan drove past the city limits sign. To call Danvers a city was a gross exaggeration. There wasn't much. A fire house, a couple of old and decaying churches, a bar. Donovan parked in front of the minuscule brick post office, a genuine relic. He untied the bandana from around his neck and dropped it onto the seat. He didn't want to look like a bank robber. Despite his Stetson and sunglasses, he cringed at the sun's brightness when he opened the car door. He hurried into the relative safety of the building.

The clerk eyed him suspiciously. Donovan took off his hat and sunglasses. "Didn't mean to startle you," he said, sending soothing thoughts. The woman relaxed a little. "The name's Donovan Reed. You are?"

"Betsy. I'm the postmistress." Now she smiled. "What can I do for you?"

"I'm looking for a friend, and I don't know if I am even going the right direction."

"What's your friend's name, if he's in the area, I'll know him."

Just the fact that he was asking questions would get back to Stanos. Small towns were like that. But Donovan couldn't find out anything without asking. He had two choices, one was to use his power to erase the memory of his questions or he could let Stanos, and thereby Cassandra, know he was asking about them. Let them wonder, after all these years of silence, what he was doing.

"Stanos. His name is Stanos Asai."

"You just missed him. He was in here not more than an hour ago for his mail. And boy, was he upset."

"About what?" Donovan asked, encouraging her to answer. "You can tell me."

"He's expecting a package. Been expecting it for several days now. It seems important. Of course, I don't know what it might be. It comes from the same company, once a month, but this is a special shipment." Betsy eyed him. "Are you one of those scientists?"

"What do you mean?"

"I'm sorry if I said anything wrong. Some of us speculate that he's a scientist working on a secret project. That's why he doesn't want anyone snooping around. Then there are those packages, from that medical supply company."

Donovan grinned. “Sorry. I don’t know if he’s working on a secret project or not. I’m not a scientist.”

Betsy looked as though she didn’t believe him.

“Can you tell me how to find his place?” Donovan asked, deciding to keep up the appearance that he didn’t know where he was going.

“He won’t like you coming. He’s a real hermit. Lived here almost forever. Even before I became postmistress. Don’t like people, like I said, although he’s friendly enough with me. Kind of old-fashioned and polite. He won’t like it, your going up there. Took a shotgun to some folks awhile back when they got too close.”

“I’ll be careful.”

“You know, in all these years, you’re the first one who has come looking for him. Well, if you’re set on going, go through town until you cross the bridge. On the right, right after the bridge, is a road. Got no sign, but it’s just right across the bridge. Turn and go up it. It’s a dirt road, not in too good shape, especially up at the top. There are a couple of turn-offs, but you keep to the right. Stanos’ place is about twenty-five miles back up in the hills. Believe me, you’ll think there can’t be anything up that far. Oh, a few camping spots. Hunters during season. Right now its mushroom hunters.”

“Mushroom hunters?”

“Yep. In a good day they can make a couple hundred dollars.”

Donovan thanked Betsy, donned his hat and glasses, and hurried out to the car.

He checked his gas gauge and then pulled up beside the tiny hardware store with a single gas pump. A man came out smiling. “Can I help you?”

“I think I’d better get a full tank of gas. From what Betsy says, I’ve got a long way to go, and I don’t want to run out of gas, not where I’m going.”

"And where is that?"

"Out to visit Stanos Asai."

The man looked at him in surprise. "That's a long way out. The guy ain't too friendly." He pulled the hose out if its rack and stuck the nozzle in the tank. "What you want with him?"

"I'm a distant relative."

"Didn't think he had any relatives, although a few nights ago I saw him with a couple of guys in that van of his. At least I think I did. Where they came from, I sure don't know. No one's been up to his place in a long time. Like I said, he ain't too friendly."

The pump clicked off. Donovan handed the man enough money to cover the gasoline. "Thanks. And thanks for the information."

Donovan stopped at the grocery store, thinking that maybe Stanos had done some grocery shopping. He didn't see Stanos' car, but he went in anyway.

"I was wondering if you had seen Stanos Asai today. Betsy said he was in town."

"Don't know the name."

"Older man, very old-fashioned, polite."

"Oh, you mean the Liver Man."

"Liver Man?"

"Yeah, he always buys liver, protein shakes, spinach, iron capsules. I figure he's got reoccurring anemia."

"How come?"

"Oh, it seems to go in spurts, sometimes he goes for weeks, then nothing for a long time."

"He's been buying lots of liver lately?"

"Yep. Last couple of weeks. He just stocked up."

"Do you know where he was going?"

"Back up the mountain, I think."

"Thanks." Donovan left, pondering the meaning of the fact that Stanos was buying liver. He wondered if the kidnapped girl could still be alive.

Outside, he noticed a phone booth and decided he'd better call the clinic while he had a chance. He dialed the number, then turned his back to the sun and shut his eyes against the glare.

Sandy answered. "I'm glad you called. You may have a newborn up in Yakima. Police found a body, bite marks, lots of blood. I've got Weber & Kleine Security checking the police report. We should have a clue by tomorrow whether it is one of our kind or just another brutal murderer."

If it was a newborn, the sooner he got to it the better, but Donovan didn't want to leave, not now. He decided to wait for the police report and hope it was a false alarm. "I'll call tomorrow and see if we know anything definite. How's everything? How's Thom doing?"

"Everything is fine, including Thom and Rat. Don't you think I can run the clinic without you?"

"I know you can. It's just that I like to imagine I'm needed, sometimes."

"Have you found out anything?"

"Not really. I think Cassandra may be keeping her victims alive for a while, playing with them."

"That's cruel."

"So is killing them. I've got to go. I want to get back before sunset."

"You be careful."

"I will."

Donovan hung up. He drove out of town, crossed the bridge and turned right. The road was partially paved for the first couple hundred feet, then it turned into gravel, well-groomed for the first couple of miles, but as signs of habitation faded and he climbed higher, the road worsened.

Donovan came around a corner, put on his brakes as he saw the car parked half in the road. It was jacked up, a tire lying on its side. Donovan stopped his car and got out.

The mountain blocked the sun, leaving the road in deep, comfortable shadow.

Donovan called, but got no answer. He checked the vehicle, but found it empty. Walking around the car, he discovered another flat. Where could the man have gone? It had been at least five miles since he had seen a house, and he would have noticed a man walking down the road. A large bucket of wild mushrooms set beside the trunk, drying out, but not too dry, so it hadn't been there for long.

Donovan began to get a sick feeling in the pit of his stomach. Stanos had passed this way within the last hour. Stanos, whose blood supply hadn't come. It would be easy to offer the man a lift to a phone. And once there--

Donovan got back in his car, drove around the parked vehicle, and continued up the road. He had planned to just watch, but now he knew he had to act or another innocent was going to die.

Eleven

As Donovan arrived at the cabin, he felt the true sunset. The moment when the sun slipped beyond the rim of the world, not just out of sight behind the mountains. His strength returned with the coming of the night. He was alive again, but then so was Cassandra and, if what he suspected was true, so were her get. A light shone in the window of the log cabin. Stanos' van was parked under a roughly constructed lean-to. Deceptive. Donovan knew the lair was underground and would be strongly protected from intruders. There was no way to sneak in. A frontal attack was in order. He couldn't wait for help, not if he wanted to save a man's life.

He got out of the car, walked to the front door, and knocked loudly. Waiting a few moments, he knocked again. Again he knocked, beginning to wonder what he would do if no one answered.

The door opened a crack. "What do you want?" a voice demanded.

"I want to see Cassandra." Donovan pushed the door open, despite Stanos' attempts to hold it closed, and entered the cabin. "You will tell your mistress that Donovan is here. You will tell her now," he commanded.

"I remember you, sir," Stanos said.

Donovan felt the man's hostility, but chose to ignore it. "Cassandra, please."

Stanos gave a slight bow. "Come this way, sir."

Donovan followed Stanos into what appeared to be a small bedroom. He detected no heart beating nor smelled the scent of living blood in the cabin. The human must be below. Stanos opened a secret panel, unlocked a door, descended the stairs, and unlocked another gate. "Wait here, while I lock the doors and gate." Donovan waited as Stanos climbed the stairs and came back down. It was then Donovan saw the small gun in Stanos' hand. Stanos fired. The bullet stuck Donovan's side. Donovan screamed. His body flamed in agony as the silver bullet burned his flesh.

Donovan tried to reach Stanos, but he collapsed to his knees. Stanos stood above him, gun pointed, clearly frightened by what he had done. Then Donovan heard running footsteps and Cassandra's voice, "What happened?"

"I have protected you, mistress."

"Donovan!" Cassandra bent over him. The bullet was still in his body, the pain so intense he wished he could pass out, but that was not to be. "Donovan, you don't know how long I've wished to see you this way, helpless." She grinned.

"Over a hundred years," he said, between gritted teeth.

Two men picked him up and carried him down the hallway. One black, one white. Cassandra's get. He'd been right. It didn't seem to matter. Only the pain mattered--the continuing agony as the silver poison spread through his system.

He heard Cassandra say, "Bring him in here." He was dragged along. "There, put the manacles on him." He had no strength to resist as they manhandled him into the manacles. His legs didn't want to support him; he hung with the weight of his body against the manacles, the metal cutting into his flesh. He raised his head and saw himself reflected hundreds of times in mirrors, each of him smaller and smaller until he disappeared into nothingness. Behind him, reflected in the mirror, was Cassandra. He slowly twisted his body until he was looking at her. He managed to lock his knees and ease the pressure on his wrists.

Cassandra unbuttoned his duster, his shirt, and pulled out his shirttails so she could examine the wound. “It’s still in there,” she announced. Donovan could have told her that.

He heard a hurt animal moaning and realized he was the animal.

Cassandra stood in front of him, hands on her hips, staring at him. “I should leave the bullet in you.”

Donovan knew if she did, he would be dead in no more than twenty-four hours from silver poisoning. He hung helpless, waiting for her to decide his fate.

Finally she did. “Wolf, Panther, get that coat off of him and his shirt. Unchain one wrist at a time; he still has strength. Stanos, find me a knife and something to pry out the bullet with.” She examined the wound more closely. “It’s in too far for me to dig out without cutting away most of your side. I’m going to try driving it straight through and out the back. Stanos, find me a spike or something like that and a hammer.”

“Did I do wrong, mistress?” Stanos asked.

“No, Stanos, I think you did very well. This could work very much to our advantage. Now, go.”

The other two, Wolf and Panther, she had called them, undressed him, one arm at a time, then re-chained him. Stanos returned, and Cassandra laid the tools out on the table, examining them.

Picking up a long spike and a hammer, she rammed the spike into the open hole of the wound. Donovan screamed and tried to escape the torture. The three men pulled his feet out from under him. Holding onto his legs and knees, they pulled him tight against the chains, so he couldn't move. Cassandra rammed the spike in deeper. His body quivered, but he couldn't jerk. Finally the spike touched the bullet. He groaned. She probed around until she thought she had the spike positioned then she hit the spike with the hammer, driving the bullet deeper into his flesh. He screamed. That was all that was left to him, screaming. She continued to force the bullet through his flesh until it rested just under the skin. She picked up the knife, cut an X in his flesh, and with one last hit of the hammer drove the bullet free. She pulled the spike out. He felt its shaft as it was dragged through his body.

The men let him go. He hung with no strength in his legs to support himself. She lifted his head and looked into his eyes. "Why are you here? Did the Directors send you?"

Donovan didn't answer; couldn't answer. His throat didn't seem to work.

"Stanos, go milk our new guest and bring me a cup of his blood." She looked at Donovan's tainted blood on her hands. "Watch him," she told Wolf and Panther. "I'm going to get cleaned up."

Donovan closed his eyes. His wound was healing. The oozing blood slowed, but not completely. Flesh that would have normally started to heal was burnt and blistered, as though acid had been poured into the wound. He no longer had the burning agony of the silver eating into his flesh, spreading its poison, but his whole side was aflame with pain. That pain was accompanied by the clamoring of his awakened hunger.

Cassandra returned and ordered Wolf and Panther to leave.

"What am I going to do with you, Donovan, now that I have you?" she asked, coming close, touching him. "Why are you here?"

Donovan didn't answer.

Stanos entered. "Mistress." He put a tray on the table. Donovan could smell fresh blood. "The boys want to know if they can have him now. They are complaining that they are hungry."

"They're always hungry. No, they may not have him. Milk him and give them a cup, enough to cut their hunger. We may have to ration our supplies, if we don't get more blood tomorrow." She turned to Donovan. "You wouldn't know anything about that, would you?" Then she turned back to Stanos. "If the boys complain, tell them tomorrow we will hunt."

"Yes, mistress."

"You may go now. I'll call if I need you."

She waited until Stanos left, then picked up the goblet and walked slowly toward Donovan. She stood in front of him, taking sips from the glass and smiling. "Now, why are you here?"

When he didn't answer, she came forward and held the goblet to his lips, giving him a generous swallow. His body absorbed the blood and cried out for more.

"Did the Directors send you?" she asked again.

"Yes," he managed to croak.

"Liar. I have friends; they would have warned me if the Directors were moving against me. I think you came on your own. The question remains, who else knows that you planned to come up here? And what did you expect to find?" She held the cup to his lips again, and he swallowed eagerly. He would have finished the blood, but she pulled away the goblet. She stood a few feet from him, sipping and watching him.

The blood restored him; his vision cleared somewhat. He took a good look at Cassandra. She had changed into a black negligee, all lace and sheer fabric that revealed more of her figure than it hid. Her skin glowed white against the black.

Black hair hung loose about her shoulders. Her face had only the most artful traces of make-up.

The seductress or the young bride attempting to please her beloved. She became aware of his look.

"Perhaps you truly just missed me and wished to see me again." She put the cup down on the table and returned to him, her arms going around his neck, pulling his head down, until her lips found his, kissing him fervently. Her hands began to stroke his body. They had been lovers once. Her fingers followed a familiar path, touching him where he had not been touched in a long time. "Donovan," she whispered, her voice full of pain and longing. "I still love you. Please."

He thought for a moment of playing along, convincing her that he loved her as well, getting her to release him, then escaping. He knew he was in trouble here. She couldn't afford to let him go. Cassandra had nothing to lose by killing him, shoot him and blame it on Stanos.

This was the woman who had killed Amanda and Clare. He couldn't pretend to love her.

Cassandra seemed to sense his decision and pulled away herself. "You know, Sir Alfred liked boys better than women. Young, beautiful boys. This viewing stand was his idea. He liked to awaken to find his first treat of the day waiting for him. Eager and ready. I too learned to appreciate young, beautiful boys. Sir Alfred liked to have the boys do me, while he was doing them. His lovemaking was nothing like yours. He wasn't gentle or kind or loving."

"You didn't want gentle, kind, or loving. You liked to be hurt. You wanted me to hurt you. I just couldn't do it. I'm not like that."

"No, you aren't. Maybe that's why I still love you." She sighed. "Now, answer my questions. Who knows you are here? And why did you come?"

"I came because you are getting sloppy. Those three boys. That waitress. Now the mushroom hunter. If I can see it, how long before the Directors see it?"

"And you told whom?"

"Several people. Give it up. Let me go."

"I should've left the bullet in you."

"Kill me and you really will be in trouble. You know it."

"Why are you intent on destroying me? Why can't you just leave me alone to enjoy myself?"

"You killed Amanda."

"Amanda, it's always Amanda." Cassandra's face contorted in rage. "It always was Amanda. I never had a chance with you, even from the beginning. You couldn't love me because you loved her. Well, she's dead. I killed her fifty years ago." She knelt before him, her arms around his legs. Her eyes were full of tears, as she looked up pleadingly. "Couldn't you forgive me?"

"I can never forgive you. Not in fifty years. Not in one hundred and fifty."

Her body shuddered as though he had physically hit her. After a long time, she stood and wiped the tears from her eyes.

"I should have killed you, not Amanda." Her voice was cold. A shiver ran down Donovan's spine. "But I'm not going to kill you. That would be too easy. I'm going to keep you alive, wishing you were dead, until you do my bidding. You will be my sexual plaything as I was yours. Yes, I was yours just as much as I was Brandon's and Sir Alfred's. Did you know that Sir Alfred didn't die in an accident? I killed him. I was tired of being his whore. I've had fifty years alone to think and plan. I've created somewhere rather special. I call it my punishment room. I've never really had an opportunity to try it out. Now I think I will. Stanos," she yelled, "bring Wolf and Panther."

The blood had given him some strength, but not enough to overcome two vampires. He struggled as they dragged him from the room. Cassandra hit his wounded side. The pain redoubled and the resistance went out of him. They pulled him along the corridor to a locked room. She unlocked the door, and they dragged him inside. She hung a lantern over a hook in the wall.

Someone was in there, someone alive. The light shone on a face. The third boy--the missing one. Wade, that was his name. Still alive. He was chained spread eagle. He stared up at Cassandra, bravely fighting his fear.

She handed the key ring to Stanos, who unchained the boy and dragged him to his feet. She sniffed the air. "Take him, Stanos, clean him up. Oh, and feed him, I'll want him strong tonight."

The boy glared at her.

She touched the boy's face. He jerked back. "You think you can resist me, that you can say no. You won't be able to. Chain him to my bed. I will use him later." Stanos dragged the boy out of the room.

Cassandra turned her attention back to Donovan. "Now him." Wolf and Panther wrestled Donovan to the ground, fastening the manacles around his wrists. "To experience the full effects of what I have planned, you need to be naked."

She pulled off his boots and pants, while Wolf and Panther held him down and laughed. The chains were attached to his ankles.

"Now, Donovan, I want you to truly appreciate this. Look up." Donovan did and saw a hole in the ceiling and the stars beyond. She went to the wall and pulled a lever. A grill closed over the opening. She pulled two more levers and two more grills closed. "If it were the full sun, it would kill you. But it's not full sun, just a small bit. Here and there, burning your flesh.

Killing you by inches. Oh, and the next day will be worse, because you will know then just how painful it can be. After that, we will talk. I think you will be more willing to do my bidding, to be my abject slave." She left him, taking his clothes, the fur blankets, and the lantern, locking the door behind her, leaving him alone in the dark in an empty prison.

~ * ~

Wade had awakened at the first agonizing scream. It wasn't repeated, so he began to think he hadn't heard it. It was dark, and he was uncomfortable, needing to use the bathroom. He had almost decided to start yelling for Stanos, when the screaming started again. It went on for a long time before there was silence again. What was happening?

Wade waited. Chained hand and foot, cold and uncomfortable. Finally, no longer able to contain himself, he soiled his clothes like a baby. That made him cry in shame, but not wanting to attract attention, he made no sound.

He was no judge of time, but the moon appeared, making a dim circle that slowly moved toward him across the floor.

The door opened and Cassandra entered. She ordered Stanos to unchain him and take him away. Wade glanced at the man Wolf and Panther held.

He was bare-chested with a terrible wound in his side. No doubt this man was the source of the screams Wade had heard.

Stanos took Wade by the arm and led him out of the room.

"Who's that man?" Wade asked Stanos, as they walked down the corridor.

"His name is Donovan."

"What happened to him?"

"I shot him."

"You should take him to a doctor," said Wade, before realizing what a stupid statement that was. "Why did you shoot him?"

"He's the reason she's trapped here. Now, hurry up."

Wade was only too eager to comply, to get the smelly pants off. He washed his body, towel dried, dressed, then ate a quick meal. Stanos stood over him glaring.

"Let's go," Stanos said, grabbing his arm. "The mistress wants you ready and waiting."

A sudden fear filled Wade. He wanted to resist, but remembered the screams and the man, and went obediently. Stanos chained him to Cassandra's bed and left him alone to wait.

He had half-expected to be chained in the alcove as he had so often, but he saw blood splatters on the mirror and carpet, a lot of blood. The wounded man. The man Stanos had shot.

He heard Cassandra in the parlor and stiffened, waiting for her appearance, but she didn't come in. Instead he heard her talking. After a few moments, Wade realized that she was talking to Stanos.

"What am I going to do?" she asked.

"Kill him, mistress," Stanos said. "He deserves to die for what he did to you, the pain he has caused."

"I can't kill him. He's too well protected. He's sired too many offspring. They will know he is dead, and they will come for me. I have to keep him alive, but I can't let him go. I've got to know exactly who he told and what he told them."

"People know he came here?"

"Yes. He said so, but he wouldn't say who. He said it was because we've been sloppy, attracting too much attention. He said the Directors will figure it out soon. I've got to know whether he has been talking to the Directors and whether he has proof or just suspicions. But that shouldn't be a problem after tomorrow. I think he will be more than willing to cooperate."

"Perhaps Stefan could help?"

"He's too much of a coward to do anything active. But he will, I think, find it to his advantage to do what he can. He's not fond of Donovan. I'll call him. At least, he can tell me if Donovan has been talking to the Directors. But we must solve the problem ourselves."

"What if we hid him somewhere, kept him alive, but later, when suspicion has passed, we could kill him?"

"Yes, but where can we hide him? They're certain to come looking for him."

"Why not where he is now? I could wall up the doorway and no one would suspect the room exists. We could arrange a way to lower food to him."

"We will have to clean up our mess. It'll mean getting rid of Wolf and Panther. We'll invite the Directors to come. They won't find anything, no Donovan, no get, only me, proclaiming my innocence. What else are they going to do but believe me?"

"And the man?"

"Donovan was right, we've been sloppy. I think it would be best if he thought he spent the night in his broken-down car and you came along in the morning. Maybe driving Donovan's car. No, I will drive Donovan's car. He will say he saw Donovan pass him without stopping to help. Then you can come along and help the man. Tell him how Donovan spent the night and left early to go--somewhere. We will have to think of something plausible."

"An excellent idea. You know how snoopy the people in town are. They will talk. It'll add credibility to our story. What about the boy?"

"He has such a beautiful body. There must be something special done with him."

Wade started to tremble.

"I know. We'll leave him to Donovan. When Donovan gets hungry enough, he'll kill him." She laughed. "So much for

Donovan's high morals. He'll drink human blood just as quickly as the next one."

Cassandra entered the bedchamber. She looked surprised to see Wade. "I'd forgotten you," she said. She walked over to the bed and stared down at Wade. He stared back at her, trying not to let his fear show. She sighed. "Sorry Wade, I don't feel like it any more tonight. Stanos, take him back, put him in with Donovan. Oh, Wade, I wouldn't get too close, he's rather hungry."

Stanos unchained him, and Wade quickly rolled off the bed and reach for his pants.

"Tomorrow, Wade, tomorrow," Cassandra called after him. "I will give you my full attention."

Wade trembled as he followed Stanos out of the room.

~ * ~

Donovan lay in the darkness, grateful for it, for the night. The day was not far off and with it would come the sun. Donovan stared up at the ceiling. The grillwork hid the stars, but it would not hide the sunlight. He didn't need to wait until morning to know what it would feel like when the sun touched his naked body. He yanked on the chains, hoping to free one of the rings embedded in the floor. He didn't have the strength. The wound in his side ached abominably, but now that the silver bullet had been removed, his system was no longer being poisoned. It would heal in time. If he had the time and blood. His need for blood hammered at his senses. He gritted his teeth and tried to shove it out of his mind.

He thought about the boy. Donovan didn't understand why Wade wasn't dead. Then he realized Cassandra had said it. Sir Alfred had liked young boys. She had developed a taste. Despite the fear, the gauntness, Wade was good looking. She had kept him alive as her plaything. The thought made Donovan sick to his stomach. What confused him was why she hadn't bound the boy to her. There were bite marks. By now, he shouldn't be able to resist. He should be her willing slave.

The door opened. In the light from the corridor, Donovan saw the boy shoved into the room. As the door was shut and locked again, the boy moved to the far side of the chamber and squatted.

"Did she hurt you, Wade?" Donovan asked.

"How do you know my name?"

"I read about you in the papers. They were looking for you."

"But they aren't any more, are they?"

"No. They gave up the search," Donovan answered truthfully.

"Mike, did they find Mike?"

"Yes. They found him."

"He was dead, wasn't he?"

"Yes."

"Like his brother. His throat torn out? I keep seeing Josh and I imagine Mike the same way, Panther tearing him apart. I hear Mike's screams, over and over in my mind, and I see Panther coming back into the firelight, licking his fingers."

Donovan had read the autopsy report. He decided to lie. "No, it wasn't as bad as Josh. Panther, that's the black one, isn't it?"

"Yes."

"He just drained him dry. It's like going to sleep. Not painful."

"Yes, I know. You just get weak and tired."

"Have they been feeding off you?"

"Yes, mostly just Cassandra. But not since Sue." His voice faltered.

"What happened?" Donovan asked gently.

The boy didn't answer. Donovan didn't press him.

"How long?" Wade asked.

"How long?" Donovan asked, not sure what Wade meant.

"How long have I been here?"

"About three weeks." If Donovan had only known that Cassandra would keep this boy alive. Three weeks in hell. But he'd expected Cassandra to indulged herself and dispose of the body quickly. He never thought that the boy might still be alive after all this time. "I'm sorry."

"It's not your fault. You're a vampire too, aren't you?"

"Yes."

"Stanos says you are responsible for Cassandra being here. He hates you."

"I suppose he's right. In a way I'm responsible. Cassandra killed someone I loved very much."

"And they sentenced her to live here for seventy-five years."

"Yes. How did you know that?"

"Stanos told me. He likes to talk a lot about Cassandra. How do you know her?"

"I met her after the Civil War."

"After Brandon. She dressed up for me once and told me that was the way she looked when she became a vampire. She told me about Brandon and how he used her when he gambled, giving her to the winner. How he would have her walk around naked. I figured that's why she liked to keep me naked, to get back at Brandon for what he did to her."

"I think you're right. A lot of bad things happened to Cassandra that made her the way she is."

"My dad says that even if bad things happen to you, you have the choice. You don't have to let them make you bad."

"Your father is a smart man."

"I've done some bad things, but I don't have to let them make me keep doing bad things."

He said it with such determination Donovan wondered what bad thing he had done.

"Why did Cassandra kill your friend?" Wade asked.

"She was jealous of Amanda. She thought if she killed Amanda, she could make me love her, that she could have Amanda's position, her power. But Cassandra isn't Amanda."

"Was Amanda a vampire too?"

"Yes." Suddenly Donovan didn't want to think about Amanda any more. "You mentioned Sue? Is she still alive?"

"No. I killed her." Wade's voice was flat and dead as he spoke. "Cassandra made me. I raped her and drank her blood. They raped her too and drank her blood. Panther and Wolf." Wade's voice broke with a sob. "I told Cassandra I wouldn't, that I didn't want to be a vampire, that I wouldn't hurt Sue. I really meant it, but she, Cassandra, did things to me. She said it was Voodoo. She made me drink something and she rubbed some cream on my, well you know, and it made me want to do it bad. I couldn't help myself. Cassandra made me, but I shouldn't have, I should have resisted more, but she made me believe that I loved her and needed her."

"It's not your fault, Wade. Cassandra did a bad thing to you, she made you do a bad thing, but like your father said, you have a choice. You don't have to be bad. Did you drink Cassandra's blood?"

Wade nodded his head, then thinking that Donovan couldn't see in the dark. "Yes."

"How many times?"

"I don't know."

"Three times?"

"Yes. More."

Donovan was silent. With all the opportunities to bind the boy to her, why hadn't Cassandra made the boy her servant? Could it be a ruse? Could Wade be play-acting? Donovan didn't think so.

Wade said, "When I remembered what I did to Sue, I wanted to die, but Cassandra says that when I do, I will become like Panther and Wolf, a vampire, and I will have to do her bidding. I couldn't stand that. I want to die, but not if it means I'm going to be a vampire." There was terror in his voice. "Tonight she said she is going to have you kill me."

"What?" Donovan demanded. "When did she say that?"

"When she was talking to Stanos. I was in the bedroom and I overheard."

"Could you tell me exactly what she said? It could be important."

Wade was silent for a moment, obviously trying to remember what had been said. "Stanos wanted to kill you, but Cassandra said they couldn't." Wade repeated what he had overheard. "I'm sorry it's so confused. I really didn't understand it. Then Stanos asked what she was going to do about me. She said she wanted to do something special with me. She was going to put me in here with you, and that when you got hungry enough, you would kill me. Will you kill me? She said you're hungry." Donovan heard Wade swallow hard.

"Of course not." Donovan laughed, trying to lighten the tension, but it sounded forced. He stopped. "No, I won't." As he spoke the words, he knew they were a lie. If Cassandra walled him in with this boy, eventually Donovan would grow so hungry, he wouldn't be able to resist. He might not kill at first, but take enough blood, even over a long time, and he would kill the boy. "Yes, I'm hungry. When we lose blood, we get hungry. When Stanos shot me, I lost a lot of blood."

"I know, I saw. Are you still bleeding?"

"No. We heal fast. I would have to lose a lot more blood or go for a very long time before I got hungry enough to touch you."

Wade looked at him as though he knew he was lying.

"What's the matter?" Donovan asked.

"That's not true. Vampires have to feed every night or almost every night."

"I see. Do you know how old Panther is?"

"He was Cassandra's favorite before me. He's very jealous of me."

"A newborn. Newborn vampires need a lot of blood. When you get older, you don't need as much. Besides, you could sort of call me a vegetarian vampire. I don't drink human blood."

"You don't?"

"No. I drink mostly cow's blood. Sometimes I hunt for my food, like rabbit. After I became a vampire, I was afraid of hurting humans so I went into the mountains and lived alone. That was all I had to drink, animal blood. Not all vampires are like that. Cassandra obviously isn't. But I am. I won't hurt you. You don't have to worry now. I'm chained up tight so I can't do anything to you."

Wade nodded slowly and relaxed a little.

"And about you becoming a vampire when you die. Despite what Cassandra said, it isn't a sure thing. There are very few people who can become vampires. It's a genetic thing, like having blue eyes, only it's very rare, sort of like an inherited disease. Only about 5% of the population can become vampires. It isn't likely that you are one of the 5%."

"You mean if I die--"

"You just die like most other people."

"And if I don't?"

"I won't lie to you. There's a chance. But I will give you my word, that I will do everything in my power to protect you from that happening." He laughed. "Although chained like this, it doesn't seem to be much I can do."

"If you weren't chained?"

"What?"

Wade crept closer, holding himself alert, in case Donovan made a move toward him. “I’ve been working on one of the links of the chain. I have a file. I’ve managed to cut it part way.”

“I tried breaking the chains earlier. It didn’t work.”

“Maybe I could file it some more.”

“It’s almost sunrise. Let’s get some sleep. Later you can work on it.”

Donovan felt the sun rise above the rim of the earth. He knew there was no way he could fight it this morning. He slipped helplessly into oblivion. At least he wouldn’t be lying awake, watching and waiting.

Twelve

When Wade first woke, he thought he had slept through the day because it was so dark. Looking up, he realized the opening in the roof was covered by grates. The sun shone through the holes in the grates to make a pattern of light spots across the floor.

He tried opening the shutters, but he wasn't strong enough to pull the metal levers. The first time he was free of his chain, and now the way out was blocked.

Wade looked at the man. He appeared dead. Maybe he was dead. No, vampires didn't die.

He appeared about Wade's father's age, light brown hair, instead of dark. Last night, his voice had sounded nice in the darkness. It had felt good to have someone to talk to, someone who understood. Wade hadn't felt as though Donovan thought he was a kid. He had listened when Wade talked, and made no demands. And was honest. At least he hadn't avoided answering any of Wade's questions. Wade hoped Donovan was right about it being a slim possibility that he would become a vampire. That was Wade's worst fear.

Well, one thing Wade knew for certain--this man was Cassandra's enemy, so he would be a good person to have on Wade's side.

He felt around the loose soil until he uncovered the nail file and went back to work on the link. As he sawed, he changed the position of the file to use all surfaces evenly. The diamond powder had worn off in spots, and it was metal against metal.

Donovan woke with a scream. Wade jumped back against the wall. The man struggled to move his feet, within the confines of his chains. He half sat up and stared at the pattern of light on the floor.

"What's the matter?" Wade asked. "Is it your wound?" The wound was a gaping, oozing hole.

Donovan shook his head and lay back down. "Vampires are allergic to sunlight." Wade looked at the bright spots on the floor.

"What's going to happen?" he asked in a whisper.

"I'm not going to burst into flames, if that's what you're thinking. You know how it is when you have been out in the sun too long, and you get a sunburn." Wade nodded. "Ever had one where you were burnt so bad you blistered?" Wade nodded again. "Well, instead of it taking hours to burn, we burn in minutes. That's what happened. My foot was in the sun too long." Wade looked down at the foot. There was a round quarter-sized burn, red and blistered. "If I was out in the sunlight all day, I might die. Sun poisoning. Cassandra's idea is just small spots of sunlight, not enough to kill me, but enough to give me a lot of pain."

The sun drew closer to Donovan's foot and he moved it, which only postponed the inevitable. The pattern of sunlight dots was broad enough that there was no way Donovan could escape.

Wade went back to filing. If he could cut through the link, then Donovan could get out of the sun's reach. But Wade wouldn't be through the link before the sun reached Donovan.

"Maybe you can break the link," said Wade.

Donovan positioned the weakened link against the floor ring and pulled. Nothing. Wade pulled as well. The link wouldn't break.

The sun touched Donovan's leg. The skin reddened. He gritted his teeth. Wade put his hand out, casting a shadow. Donovan gave a shuddering sigh.

If Cassandra hadn't removed the blankets, but the cell was empty. Wade did the only thing he could. He stood and placed himself between Donovan and the sunlight. He couldn't block all the spots, but a lot of them. When one spot or a group got too bad, he would shift. It exposed another part of Donovan's skin, but at least it gave a few minutes of relief from the intense pain, before the sun burned that area red and blistered.

Donovan moaned and whimpered, but he did not let himself scream again.

Wade had always welcomed the sun. It had warmed his chilled body. Now it seemed to take forever to cross the floor and start to climb the wall. When the last spot moved beyond, Donovan's body was shaking as though it were chilled or maybe feverish. Wade had managed to protect most of his torso, but his arms and legs had multiple burns, many of them very deep, blistered wounds.

Wade sat down and picked up the file and began working on the link. It wasn't too long until sunset. Then, Wade shivered, he would be taken to Cassandra.

The door unlocked, Stanos entered.

"Come," he said, as he had on all the previous nights, and Wade went with him.

~ * ~

Stanos fed him and brought him to Cassandra's room, as he had on other nights. As he fastened the manacles around Wade's wrists, he said, "You will please the mistress. You will be ready for her when she awakens. You will think only of her."

Stanos adjusted the lights and crept from the room.

Wade looked around. The blood had been cleaned off the mirrors. An attempt had been made to clean the carpet, but the stains still showed faintly. Wade knew he should be thinking of Cassandra, getting ready for her. He remembered all the other nights, how her touch had aroused him, how it had made him feel, how as he stood waiting for her to awaken, he would harden in anticipation. This time it didn't happen. Those other times, he had been afraid too, but this time it was different.

He could see the bed, see Cassandra asleep. Almost instinctually he knew when she woke. He felt her eyes on him. She didn't say anything, didn't move, only looked at him until he was almost certain that she was still asleep. Then her eyes flashed red in the darkness.

She was out of the bed, approaching him, naked as always. Before he would have been afraid of displeasing her by not being ready. Now it gladdened him that he felt no response. Yet he was afraid of her anger.

"Wade, my beautiful boy," she whispered, her fingers touching him. "I have missed you." The fingers brushed down his body, through his pubic hair, caressing him. She pressed her naked body against his. Her fingers stroked the length of his penis. It remained flaccid in her hand. She moved in front of him until she was staring him directly in the eye. "Wade," she said softly. "You remember everything we have done. How much you love me! How much you want me! Remember now, how my touch made you feel, how you wanted to please me, to touch me. Don't you want to touch me now?"

"No."

"You can't deny me," her voice seductive. "You can no longer resist. You remember my touch, you want my touch. You need my touch. You remember."

"I remember Sue," he said coldly. That was what he kept seeing as Cassandra talked.

"You are mine. You must obey only my words, only my voice. You are mine, you cannot resist me." Her face darkened with anger.

Whatever had been there was gone. Her words meant nothing to him. She slapped him. His cheek stung with the force of the blow. "I'm sorry, my love." She stroked the abused cheek. "I didn't mean to hurt you, not my beautiful boy. It's his fault. I will make him undo what he has done to you."

She turned and left him. He heard her enter the dressing room, get dressed, and then she left the bedroom. Wade wondered who she thought had done what to him.

~ * ~

Thom looked at himself in the mirror. Something was different. He stared at his face. With abrupt shock, he realized what was missing. His fangs were gone. He no longer looked like a monster. He grinned broadly. No fangs.

Whistling he walked out into the living room. Sandy was there. She had just put the bottle of blood on the table.

"Good evening, Thom."

Thom started to speak, but there was a sudden pain and his fangs extended.

"Damn," he said. "They were gone and now they're back."

Sandy laughed. "Don't worry. It happens. This is the adolescent stage."

"Adolescent?"

"Yeah, remember when you were a teenager and something was always popping up at the most embarrassing moments."

He sure did remember those awkward and often embarrassing times. "How much longer?" He heard the petulant whine in his voice.

She poured him a glass of blood. "Each vampire is different. You will learn to control them, just like you did your raging hormones. Try thinking about something other than your fangs. That often helps. The smell of blood almost always triggers them, even in the most experienced vampires."

He looked at her over the rim of the glass as he drank. "Your fangs aren't showing."

"Lots of practice. When I decided to become a nurse, I figured I would be around blood a lot and showing fangs could be very inconvenient."

"I hadn't thought about that."

"I was highly motivated. I always wanted to be a nurse."

"How did you become a vampire?"

"I was one of Amanda's girls, a prostitute in San Francisco. In 1849, it didn't matter that I wasn't particularly pretty, anything female was priceless. A heady time for someone like me. Donovan was with Amanda back then. Anyway, I got consumption. Not much could be done for it. No modern medicines. Amanda took care of me until I died. No one expected me to survive the change, sort of surprised us all when I did. Since both Amanda and Donovan had been using me as a blood source, I'm a spawn."

Thom was surprised. He had assumed that she was a sire like Donovan or a second like Valentine.

"Where's Valentine?" he asked.

"She left this afternoon for San Francisco on business. She'll be back tomorrow night."

"That's another question. How can she be up and about during the day?"

"The older you get the easier it is, but most of all it is a matter of training again. Even you would wake up if the threat or pain were great enough. Your survival instinct. Not all vampires bother to go through the training process; it's rather painful. We use an electric shock as an alarm clock. But for someone like Donovan or me, being seen only after dark would be too suspicious."

"It's all so complicated."

"Yes it is. It isn't easy being a vampire, but then it isn't easy being a normal human, either. We just get along the best we can."

"It isn't at all like I pictured it! It isn't how anyone pictures it! Look at *Dracula* and look at all the vampire movies. I'm no handsome vampire cutting a dashing figure in evening clothes and a black cape. I'd look plain silly in a black cape. Instead of seducing women and drinking their blood, I exist on cow's blood, bottled and pasteurized like bottled milk. You're a nurse, Donovan's a doctor, Valentine's a dress designer. Not one of you wears black or dresses like a vampire. It's so ordinary, mundane. Not only that, I'm a part of a conglomerate, a corporation. Where's the romance of being a vampire?" He sighed. "At least there aren't any vampire hunters out there looking to kill me. Or are there?"

"No. Not that there wouldn't be if someone could prove our existence. Times have changed. Some of the older ones tell of when people believed, truly believed, in us, when they hated and feared us. When Bram Stoker made "Dracula" and "vampires" a household word, he did our kind a great service. He fictionalized us. The movies, the new books, all that helps to change us into creatures of fantasy and illusion. It's our protection, our coloring. It is interesting that people want to believe we are real and yet they don't. To them we remain fantasy. It is that fantasy that keeps us safe."

"Have you ever thought of coming out of the closet and letting the world know that vampires are real?"

"We think about it, but the time isn't right. Maybe someday, but not now. We'd be hunted and either killed out of fear or enslaved. We'd become the objects of experiments, lab animals, as scientists tried to wring out the secret of our long life and mental powers to satisfy the craving of the masses. It would bring chaos and destruction, not only to the vampire community, but the whole world. It's better that we remain a secret, safely hidden in plain sight."

"I suppose you're right. Have you heard from Donovan?"

"Last night. He had nothing to report. I'm expecting him to call tonight sometime. We thought we had a newborn in Yakima. It turned out to be just a brutal human murderer. They've arrested the man."

Thom remembered Valentine's talking about some vampires liking to kill. "Have you ever killed anyone? I mean after the first kill?"

"Yes. We are killers by instinct. We take great pains to put a civilized-ritualistic face to our killing, but we do kill."

Thom shook his head. Was he truly a killer? The potential was there--the question was could he do it? Or maybe the question was could he stop the beast within from doing it?

Maybe being a vampire wasn't so mundane after all. By definition, could a group of killers truly be mundane?

After Sandy left, Thom sat, sipping the blood and mulling over what he had become. If he had a choice, would he have chosen to become a vampire? He didn't think so. But the choice wasn't his. He tried to reassure himself that it was better than lying dead in a cold grave.

~ * ~

Sunset brought Donovan renewed strength, but it also brought ravenous hunger. Donovan was glad that Stanos had taken Wade away; the smell of a living human would only have increased his hunger. Still, he worried about the boy and what Cassandra was doing to him.

Cassandra entered, carrying a lantern, which she hung on a hook beside the door.

"Where's Wade?" Donovan asked. "What did you do to him?"

"That was the question I came to ask you."

Donovan stared up at her in puzzlement.

"He was mine. When I looked at him, he desired me. I was all he could think of. All he wanted was to please me and to make love to me. Now, he doesn't even respond when I touch him. All he says is he remembers Sue. What did you do to him?" She screamed the last part. "What did you do?"

"Nothing. I swear to you, I did nothing."

"I don't believe you. You must have done something."

She looked at Donovan's body. The burns covered his arms and legs but not his torso. Frowning, she glanced up at the grillwork. It was still in place. "It was Wade, wasn't it? He stood between you and the sun. You made him do it, didn't you? Just like you told him not to respond to me. You are making him behave the way he is. You are going to make it right! You will make him love me again, you will!" Now she sounded like a little girl pouting.

"I don't know what you are talking about. I didn't do anything. Yes, he tried to protect me from the sun, but I didn't make him."

"And you didn't spoil him?

Donovan began piecing parts together. "You had him made, didn't you? It has something to do with Sue, the girl you had Stanos kidnap from Portland. Tell me what happened?"

"He was mine, he would have done anything for me, anything. Then afterward, I don't know."

"Why didn't you kill him?"

"I was going to, but I was afraid I'd lose him and I didn't want to. After that night, he was sick, but he didn't die."

"He remembers killing Sue. Somehow that broke your hold over him. I don't think there's anything you can do to get him back."

"You could make him mine again."

"I don't think it would work. He doesn't trust me. He doesn't trust any of us."

"What am I going to do?"

"Let him go." It was against the cardinal rule, but Donovan didn't want to see the boy suffer any more.

"I can't."

"It won't do you any good to keep him, he'll only hate you. He told me that you plan to wall us in here together, that you want me to kill him for you." Cassandra said nothing. "He will become mine then, and hate you all the more."

Cassandra shook her head. "I would rather have him hating me, than be without him."

"Cassandra, listen to me. We can still make this all right. I'll forget what happened. What are the Directors going to do anyway? So your servant shot me. I'm alive. You have been poaching a few humans. Most of the Directors do the same. Yes, you attracted some attention to yourself, but you did let that mushroom hunter go, didn't you?"

"Yes. He only remembers that he slept in his car all night and had a rather fabulous dream of making love to a beautiful woman. He saw you drive by and will swear that you left last night. Stanos will swear. I will swear."

"Let me go. I can't do you any harm."

"No." Cassandra shook her head.

Donovan caught her eye. “You can let me go,” he commanded, using his own power. She blinked once, twice, then she shook her head.

“I promised to take the boys on one last hunt. I will have Wade brought back here. You will make him love me again. Do you understand? If you do that, maybe then I will let you go. Maybe.”

She left him.

~ * ~

Cassandra came back and went into the dressing room. When she returned she was dressed in black--dressed for hunting.

She unchained Wade and, taking hold of his arm, dragged him back to the prison. The door was unlocked, but then Donovan was still chained, so it didn’t matter.

She pointed to Donovan’s body. “Why did you do that?”

Wade knew that she meant protecting Donovan from the sun.

“I didn’t want to see him hurt.”

“I see.” She began removing her belt. “You have been a very bad boy. Lean against the wall.” Wade turned obediently around and did as she commanded. She yanked his pants down around his ankles. “I am going to have to spank the bad boy.”

“No.” Wade heard Donovan’s cry as the belt struck its first blow. He jerked and gasped in pain, then held himself steady for the next blow. After the fourth, a little cry escaped his lips. Donovan was struggling against his chains, begging Cassandra to stop. She didn’t. Wade counted the blows. Each time his cry was a little louder. Eight hard blows with the belt buckle end. Tears streamed down his face. He didn’t think his legs would support him much longer. Then she was close to him, rubbing her hand over his abused flesh.

"I've broken the skin. You're bleeding." She licked her bloody fingers. "Maybe, Donovan, Wade will let you lick his ass." She laughed. She leaned close to Wade's ear. "If you won't give me pleasure one way, I will get it another."

Then she was gone, the door locking behind her. Wade crumbled to his knees and curled up into a tight ball of pain and agony.

"Damn it," said Donovan. "Are you all right?"

Between gulping sobs, Wade managed a yes.

Cassandra had left the lantern. Wade could see Donovan's face, see the concern. He noticed a trickle of blood running down Donovan's arm and saw the red broken abrasion where Donovan had tried to pull his hand free of the manacle. Donovan had tried to stop Cassandra. It didn't matter that he had failed, Donovan had tried.

Gradually, the stinging pain subsided, but the soreness didn't go away. The tears stopped. Wade had been spanked before as a child. His mother had a wooden paddle for when he had been exceptionally bad, which had been maybe twice. But he had never been beaten with a belt, although a friend of his said his dad used a belt. God, it hurt. He would never beat his child, Wade swore.

After a time, he crawled over, found the nail file, and began to file. He had to lay flat on his stomach; he couldn't sit down.

Donovan lay perfectly still, but Wade sensed a tension about him and when he looked up, he saw Donovan's fangs were showing. Wade started to inch away.

"No, keep filing. I won't hurt you. It's just the smell of fresh blood. I can't help the fangs, but don't let them frighten you."

"How do you kill a vampire?" Wade asked, as he went back to filing.

"Vampires aren't easy to kill."

"But how?"

"A wooden stake through the heart only works sometimes. It's got to hit the heart just right to burst it. So it isn't reliable. The best thing is to chop the head off."

Wade nodded. "Cassandra said that was how Brandon died."

"Sun can kill us, but it takes a while, a day or two. Shooting usually doesn't work unless you have silver bullets. That's what Stanos shot me with, a silver bullet. If it had been an ordinary bullet, it would be healed by now. But silver poisons us. Shoot us in a vital organ or with enough silver bullets or just leave the bullet in and we will die. It takes a lot to kill a vampire."

"What happens when I die, if I'm going to become a vampire?"

"It will seem like you lose consciousness for a moment. You die, but it doesn't seem like you do, because almost immediately your body begins to respond and you wake up. You can't move at first. Your heart doesn't pump blood so you appear dead. The first thing you want and need is blood. If there is another vampire there, they will cut a vein and let you suck. You don't have fangs then. Those come later."

Wade was silent as he filed, thinking. "Could you kill me?"

"What do you mean?"

"I thought if I became a vampire, I would kill myself, but it's kind of hard to cut off your own head."

"We vampires have a strong survival instinct. I don't think you could kill yourself."

"That's what I was afraid of. If I become a vampire, will you kill me, before I can do anything? Will you promise to kill me, please? I couldn't bear being a vampire. You said last night that you would protect me."

"I meant keep you alive."

"I thought that was what you meant. Now, I want you to promise me that if I die or when I die that if I become a vampire, you'll kill me."

Donovan was silent for a long time. "I don't make promises lightly. But neither do you, I think. All right. I promise to keep you safe and if you become a vampire to kill you, if necessary."

"Thank you." Wade went back to filing,then the blade broke. He tried to file with the piece, but it was too hard to grip. Finally, he threw it down in disgust and felt tears coming. He brushed them away.

"Sorry," he said. "I don't think I'm going to be able to do any more."

"That's all right. We'll just have to think of something else."

"At least, Cassandra probably won't be back tonight, if she went hunting," said Wade.

"She said she was going hunting."

"When was that?" Then Wade knew whom the person was that she had blamed. "What did she think you did to me?"

"She thought I hypnotized you into resisting her. I didn't. I told her so."

"What happened to me, do you know? Why did I change?"

"I'm not sure. We vampires do have a power, a power to hypnotize, to control people. Most of the time, it's little simple things. Someone sees us, so we tell them to forget and they do. Remember, you mentioned Cassandra talking about returning a man to his car."

Wade nodded.

"That was a man whose car had broken down a short way from here. Stanos picked him up. They were going to use him like they used Sue, for blood. My coming scared her. Cassandra hypnotized the man into believing he spent the night in his car. He won't remember being here."

"That isn't what she did to me!"

"No. She wanted to control you completely. Over time she convinced you that you loved her."

"I would have done anything for her."

"I think what you did, what you remember doing to that girl, broke her spell and now, this is the part I don't really understand, she can't hypnotize you anymore."

"You really think so?"

"She tried real hard tonight. I think if she could have reestablished control, she would have."

Wade sighed. "You mean I'm safe. Maybe she'll let me go."

"Cassandra doesn't let go very easy. I think tonight you had a sample of what it is going to be like. I'm sorry."

Wade nodded.

Donovan sat up. "Well, let's see if maybe you filed enough for me to break the chain." He positioned the chain and pulled, pulled hard. Wade tried to help. Donovan let out a frustrated groan.

"What's wrong?" Wade asked.

"You're too close."

"What do you mean?"

"The smell of you is driving me crazy. God, I thought I was stronger than that. Look, I'm afraid for you, so just stay out of my reach." Wade inched back. He watched Donovan pull at the chain. "Damn. I'm too weak."

"If you were stronger, do you think you could break the chain?"

"Yes."

Wade's heart hammered in his chest. "If you had blood, would you be stronger?"

"Yes."

"Then you can have some of mine."

"No, I couldn't," Donovan said.

"It's all right. No one has fed on me in days," Wade said.

"No."

"What are we going to do? Cassandra's going to seal us in here tomorrow or the next day, and we really will be trapped. And tomorrow you're going to get burned by the sun again, even if I do try to protect you. I will, you know, no matter what she does to me afterward. But if we can break the chain, at least you can avoid the sun, and maybe we can escape."

"Let me think."

Wade knew Donovan must agree. It was the only answer.

"All right," Donovan said at last. "I'm afraid I may lose control and take too much. What I think we can do is this--I'll move as far as the chains allow and you sit just out of reach, then give me your wrist. You can pull back if you think I've taken too much."

Wade nodded. Donovan maneuvered his body so that the chains were pulled tight. Wade inched his wrist close until Donovan's fangs could sink into the flesh. The pain was sharp, but not great. Wade felt a sense of euphoria that he had come to associate with Cassandra feeding on him, but without the sexual overtones that went with her feeding. He sat for a long time. Then Donovan's fangs released their grip, his tongue licked the wounds closed, congealing the blood, and he lay back.

"Thank you," he whispered. He looked at Wade with concern. "I didn't take too much, did I?"

Wade shook his head. "I don't think so. No, I'll be fine."

Donovan lay with his eyes closed for a while, then he got up, positioned the chain, and pulled. The link snapped. The broken chain whipped around, almost hitting Wade. He jumped back and grinned. "We did it."

"Yes, we did." Donovan held his hand up for quiet. He stood motionless, listening.

Wade waited too. Had anyone heard the chain break? Was Cassandra back from the hunt? Had Stanos heard? They waited what seemed an eternity, but no one came. The door stayed locked.

"Now, we have to work on the other chain," said Donovan at last.

Wade felt a pang of disappointment. They didn't have the file or the days it had taken him to file through the chain.

Donovan bent to examine the ring that held the other chain. "I think I can work this ring loose." He gathered the chain in his hands and pulled on the ring. Nothing happened. He changed positions and pulled again. "This is going to take awhile. Why don't you try to get some sleep? I'll work on this."

Wade was tired. He curled up on his side, for he was still very sore. But for the first time, he felt hope. There was a chance.

Thirteen

Donovan positioned himself and gave the chain two hard yanks, followed by a long steady pull, another two yanks, then he changed position, working his way around the ring set into the rock floor. He hoped to loosen the ring's pin and eventually pull it free. A rhythm quickly developed. It was mindless work. He looked at Wade, who lay sleeping, a deep, quiet, too quiet sleep.

He was afraid he'd taken too much blood. His body's craving for the precious liquid had been so intense, it had been difficult to pull back. He had hoped the boy would stop him, but Wade hadn't. Donovan had felt Wade's willingness to sacrifice himself, to give all. The boy couldn't stop him, so Donovan had forced himself to stop. He hoped in time.

He knew all the psychological reasons behind Wade's willingness. The Patty Hearst syndrome. The tendency to begin to identify with your captor. But Wade had broken Cassandra's control, though not totally. It was as though he had managed to break the part created by her vampire powers and the pleasure and pain of sex, without breaking psychological hold of a captor over a victim. His willingness to obey her order, to stand and let her beat him until he bled. Not that part.

Donovan had to get the boy out of here, and soon. He'd seen Cassandra's face as she whipped him. The pleasure was sexual. She'd do it again. She'd find an excuse to whip him. The question was whether or not she would draw the pleasure out, beating him many times, but never enough to kill him. Or would she lose control completely and once started be unable to stop until her victim was dead. Not much of a choice.

He stopped pulling and grabbed the ring, trying to feel if there was any give. It stood firm against the pull of his hand, though he thought he could see small cracks in the rock, cracks that he hadn't noticed before. He went back to work.

Wade's blood had given him back his strength. He would've had to drain Wade to satisfy his hunger completely, but he had taken enough. The burns had begun to fade. His bullet wound hurt every time he pulled on the chain, but it too was healing. He yanked, then gave a long pull, shifted positions. The chains rattled. He stopped and listened. He would have sensed one of the vampires, but he wasn't so sure he would have warning of Stanos' approach. So he held himself ready, listening, as he worked.

Yes, the captor and the victim theory explain a lot, but it didn't explain Wade's willingness to give his life's blood and possibly his life to Donovan, who was not his captor. Stories from the German concentration camps and the internment camps of Vietnam told of prisoners risking all for another prisoner. That made sense. It explained why Wade had formed a bond with Donovan, why he was willing to risk possible death. It explained why he had protected Donovan from the burning sun and vowed he would do so again. It was possibly a clue to why Sue's death had affected Wade so strongly, strong enough to break Cassandra's hold. Wade had identified with her as well. He would've done anything to protect her, but what he had done was kill her.

Maybe Donovan was making it all too complicated. Maybe the reason Wade hadn't pulled his hand away, lay in a much simpler motive. Feeding was always a sensual experience for a vampire, which was why they often fed during sex. It was a sensual experience for the victim as well. As addictive to the victim as it was to the vampire. Wade had said it. Cassandra had fed on him regularly, almost nightly, but she hadn't for days. Like any addict, he had begun to crave a fix, crave the feeling that came with feeding.

Donovan stopped. Had he heard something? He waited. When he heard nothing more, he went back to work. Here he was thinking about Wade's cravings, not his own. From the moment Cassandra touched that goblet to his lips, that particular monster had awakened. He tried to deny it, hide behind the overwhelming hunger of his wounded body, but he craved the taste of human blood. Wade's blood. His physical need for blood had eased, but not the desire for one more taste. Cow's blood took care of his physical needs, but never the other, darker need. It was a battle he had fought many times, a battle he had fought and won, but each time, it seemed harder. There were vampires who regularly visited prostitutes, paying for sex and a little blood, taking what they wanted, leaving the victim only with the memory of great sex and a generous tip. Maybe that was the answer. Maybe he should just give up the fight and indulge himself. But it was an addiction and like any addiction it could lead to excesses. Too many vampires were like Cassandra. In the last fifty years, how many victims like Wade had she held captive, controlled, manipulated, and used until they were all used up?

Something about Wade made him different. He had broken Cassandra's hold over him. Donovan doubted any of her other victims had done that, not considering Cassandra's reaction. They had gone eagerly to their fate, passionately in love with their destroyer. But there was more to it than that. Cassandra was obsessed with Wade. She had made him then, in a move totally out of character, had not killed him. Her reaction was intense when she believed Donovan had done something to Wade to turn him against her. Obsession was evident in her refusal to let him go, declaring that she would rather have him hate her than lose him. She meant it. In her limited capacity, Donovan thought she loved Wade, but it was a sick love.

As a psychologist, Donovan thought he understood Cassandra, understood the abuse she had suffered at Brandon's hands and what it had done to the frail, vulnerable child she had been. Understood the effect of all those years with Sir Alfred controlling her, letting her indulge every sick whim.

He had called her insane fifty years ago. Now, she was truly insane. She was falling apart before his eyes, and there was nothing he could do to help her. She had to want to be helped; she had to recognize she had a problem, before there could be any real improvement.

He felt dawn approach. Cassandra hadn't returned, so they were probably safe for the day. If she kept to the pattern, Stanos would fetch Wade before sunset.

He had to keep that from happening.

Even if Donovan didn't manage to break loose the ring, he thought he could take Stanos by surprise. If Wade refused to move, Stanos would be forced to walk past Donovan. Thinking Donovan was still chained and helpless, he wouldn't expect an attack.

What if Stanos had the gun? He wouldn't hesitate to shoot.

Even if Stanos wasn't armed, it didn't necessarily mean freedom, if Stanos didn't have the key to unlock the remaining fetters.

In that case, Cassandra would have the advantage. She could take Wade, and Donovan wouldn't be able to stop her.

Donovan yanked on the chain in frustration. He let go and tried the ring with his hand. It seemed to give a little. The cracks were more pronounced. He was making progress.

There was one other thing he could do. He had told Cassandra he didn't think he could use his power to influence Wade, but that wasn't true, especially after last night. Wade trusted him. He could use his power to put Wade back under Cassandra's spell. Make him believe that he loved her. It might keep Cassandra from beating the boy again.

Donovan had a pretty good idea what would happen to Wade. He couldn't do it, not even if it meant saving the boy from death.

He went back to work, pacing himself against the dawn. After all the energy he had expended, he knew he wouldn't be able to resist the sun's siren song.

The sun rose, and with it his energy drained. Concerned that Stanos might enter while he slept, Donovan repositioned the broken chain to look as though it was still whole and let oblivion steal over him.

~ * ~

Donovan woke to the sound of pounding. The sun had passed its zenith, diminishing its power, but it had yet to reach where he lay. Wade crouched near the ring, hitting it with a stone. His face was intense with concentration, so intense, that when Donovan moved, he jumped.

"How we doing?" Donovan asked.

"Not good."

"Let me try." Donovan knelt and yanked the chain hard. The ring gave slightly, but was still firmly embedded.

"Do you need more blood to make you stronger?" Wade asked.

"It wouldn't help. Until sunset, I'm weak, no matter what."

"I had this silly idea, but it wouldn't work."

"Tell me, even if you think it's silly."

"I thought if I could climb out of here, I could go for help."

"What do you mean?"

Wade pointed upward. "I used to think if I wasn't chained, I could climb out the opening. I planned to tear the blanket or use my pants for a rope. But if I climbed on your shoulders, I think I could reach the hole. The problem is we would have to open the shutters."

Donovan looked upward. It could work, and Wade would be away from Cassandra. He would be safe. "Let's do it."

"I can't open the shutters. I tried. I'm not strong enough. Besides if we opened the shutters, it would let in more sunlight."

There were three metal levers on the wall, connected to the three shutters. Donovan couldn't reach them, not still chained, but the length of free chain could. "What if we put the chain over the three levers, you pull one end and I the other, they might go down."

Wade considered it for a moment. "It might work, but how would you close them?"

"I won't have to."

"But the sun."

"It's direct sun that's the threat, and I can move around to stay out of its path."

Wade shook his head. "I can't. Cassandra would punish you, if she finds me gone."

"I'm not worried. Stanos will come for you before sunset. I'll overpower him, get the key, and escape."

"Then I should stay to help you."

Donovan smiled. "It takes a lot to kill a vampire, but it wouldn't take a lot to kill you. If I have to protect you, it could keep me from doing what I have to do. I want to get you out of here. Find a good hiding place and stay there. Don't come back here, not tonight. Tomorrow during the day, noon, you can check then."

"I could go for help."

"No. It's miles from nowhere, you'll get lost."

"I won't. My dad and I have camped up here for years. I know my way around. He taught me a lot about surviving in the woods. There's a campground not far from here. There are bound to be campers or a ranger."

Donovan's mind whirled. He wanted Wade out of there, safe, that was all he had been thinking about. Not about the consequences, what happened after, if Wade escaped. Donovan was certain that Cassandra hadn't planted the usual restraints. If she had, Wade wouldn't have been able to talk to him as he had. So far Donovan hadn't attempted to mesmerize the boy. He'd been afraid to break the frail trust that was between them, but he couldn't risk letting the boy go, without blocking the truth.

He took Wade's hands in his, looked deeply into his eyes. "Listen very carefully," he said, exerting his mental force. His body and mind remembered Wade's blood, remembered the link that was between them, and he used the knowledge to establish a connection. "Listen to me. It's very important." Wade listened, his mental resistance down. Donovan knew he could do as Cassandra asked, give her back Wade, at least for a time, or he could free him. It wasn't really a choice. "When you are out of here, if you start talking about vampires, people will think you are crazy and you aren't. They will lock you up and not let you be with your parents. You don't want that?" Wade shook his head no. "You must never talk about vampires. You must not speak the word vampire. In fact you won't be able to speak the word vampire. You will remember Cassandra, but not that she was a vampire. You won't remember that I am a vampire. Once you leave here, you will forget all about vampires. They are just a silly superstition. They aren't real. They don't exist. Do you understand me?" Wade nodded. "What have I told you?"

"I won't tell anyone there are vampires. I promise."

"Good." Donovan patted Wade's cheek, breaking the spell. "Remember what I said."

Wade grinned. "I don't want people to think I'm crazy, so I'm not going to talk about vampires."

"That's right." At least, Wade hadn't resisted this small use of Donovan's power, but then, Donovan's suggestion hadn't gone against any of Wade's beliefs. Yes, people would think he was crazy if he talked about vampires, so he shouldn't talk about vampires.

They placed the length of chain over the levers and pulled down. Slowly the levers descended, then suddenly, resistance diminished and the shutters popped open. Donovan cringed at the bright sunlight flooding the chamber.

Wade looked at him in concern. "This won't work. Help me shut them."

"No, I'll be fine. It's just a little bright, that's all. Don't worry. It isn't that long until sundown. Now, up on my shoulders." He leaned back against the wall, made a cup out of his hands for Wade to step on, and Wade scrambled up, planting his feet on Donovan's shoulders, his hands resting on the ceiling for support. "Ready?" Donovan asked.

"Ready."

Donovan slowly edged toward the hole until he felt the burning kiss of the sun as he stepped into the circle of light.

"Stop there," Wade said.

Then the pressure on his shoulders was gone and he stepped back against the wall into the blessed relief of the shadow. He watched Wade's legs disappear through the hole.

"Are you all right?" Wade called down.

"I may look like a lobster in a few places, but I'm fine. Go on now, find a safe place to hide and don't come out. Once I've freed myself and taken care of Cassandra, I'll come looking for you. If I don't find you, I'll leave you a sign by the hole, something for you to find tomorrow that will let you know everything is all right. Then I'll meet you..." Donovan debated about setting a meeting place. The lookout cave would be too hard for Wade to find. "I'll meet you back here at the hole an hour before sunset tomorrow."

"Be careful."

"See you either later tonight or tomorrow," Donovan said. He crouched and started working on the ring. *I'll see you or I'll be dead*, he thought.

~ * ~

Wade looked around. He stood on a wide flat rock, cleared of all brush. To his left, the windowless back of the cabin, was half hidden in trees. He oriented himself with the sun to get his bearings. As he looked north, over the tree-filled valley, he recognized the rock spire with its one tall tree. He had used that as a landmark many times. He even knew where he was standing. He and his dad called it Table Top. Below, he caught glimpses of the stream that ran by the camp. He could almost point to the camp site. It wasn't that far.

Donovan had told him to find a place to hide. Wade had no illusions about Donovan's chances, especially if he couldn't break free. Even if Donovan did, it was four against one--three vampires and one old man with a gun and silver bullets. Donovan just wanted Wade away from Cassandra, hidden, safe.

There was no place to hide up here, too exposed. Wade moved toward the cabin. The rocky surface hurt his feet, but since he went barefoot a lot, the soles of his feet were pretty tough. He ignored the discomfort.

He worked his way around the cabin to the front and peered cautiously around the corner. Just another mountain cabin. A couple of windows. A chair on the front porch. An empty lean-to off to one side.

Wade tried to think where to hide. If Donovan didn't stop her, Cassandra would come looking for him and the darkness wouldn't bother her. Wade trembled at the thought of what she would do to him if she found him. It almost made him run back and climb down the hole.

He leaned against the wall, letting the sun warm him and tried to think. He stared out over the valley. It took him a while to realize what he was staring at. A thin wisp of smoke, a cook fire. Someone was camping down there.

Someone who could help.

He started down the road, though he knew he couldn't keep following it. Cassandra or Stanos would expect that. But climbing down from Table Top would be too difficult, so he would follow the road until he found an easier way into the valley, then cut northwest until he found the stream and follow it to the campsite. He didn't think it was the same one where he, Mike and Josh had camped; this one was further downstream, closer to the trail head.

He kept to the soft grass along the side of the road, wishing he had his boots.

He told himself that it wasn't far, that he should be there before dark.

Whoever was there would help him. They would call the park ranger and the police.

They would come and rescue Donovan.

Wade winced as a sharp rock cut the sole of his foot.

~ * ~

Donovan kept working at the ring, but the bright sun weakened him. It was too painfully to look at so he kept his eyes closed as much as he could. He pulled and he yanked. His shoulders and arms hurt from the burn he got lifting Wade to the hole. Beside that, the reflective sun was giving him a gentle burn all over. By nightfall, he would be as red as a proverbial lobster. Painful, but not life threatening. More blood and the burn would fade away. He didn't think he would have the chance. Stanos would arrive and he still would be chained.

Had it been wise to get Wade out of here? When Cassandra found him missing, she would go hunting for the boy and if she caught him--Donovan didn't want to think about what she would do.

He pulled on the ring, but each pull was getting weaker. The sun slowly drained his strength, but he kept on. It was the only chance he had.

The ring slipped out of the rock so unexpectedly that he was thrown off balance and fell backward. Free! He crawled across the floor, and then used the wall for support to climb his way to the levers. It took almost more strength than he had left, to push the first lever up, closing a set of shutters. He leaned against the wall trying to regain his strength. The second lever refused to budge, then broke free and closed the second set. The sunlight diminished considerably. Finally, he pushed up the last lever and the last shutter closed. He breathed a sigh of relief. The chamber wasn't dark, but the sun had been reduced to spots on the floor, which he could easily avoid.

He found a relatively comfortable piece of wall to lean against and let his mind float as his body regained strength. He watched the pattern of light play across of the dirt floor. It was rather a pretty design, now that he could admire it from safety. All too clearly he remembered the agonizing pain the day before. Finally, the spots of sunlight started to crawl up the wall. If Stanos was coming, it would be soon.

Stanos didn't have vampire eyes. It would take him a moment to realize that Donovan wasn't chained to the floor, and in that moment, Donovan must attack and overpower the man. He waited with the patience of a hunter stalking his prey until he heard the key in the lock.

The door opened and Donovan sprang.

Stanos was holding the gun, but he was too surprised to fire. Donovan grabbed the weapon out of his hands and threw it across the room. With his last strength, he dragged Stanos inside and let his teeth sink into Stanos' throat.

Stanos struggled, but Donovan held on, drinking Stanos' hot blood quickly. The hunger that he had fought so long to control became a raging, uncontrollable beast. Stanos' struggles slowed, then ceased, and Donovan kept on. He couldn't make himself stop. He wanted to be filled with this warm sweet, salty blood. Filled to the top.

"Stanos!" It was Cassandra's voice.

Donovan looked up with Stanos' life-blood dripping from his chin.

Cassandra moved, not toward him as Donovan expected, but across the room. It took him a second to realize she was going after Stanos' gun. In that moment of inaction, she reached it and picked it up. Donovan held Stanos in front of him, expecting her to fire.

She didn't.

They stared at each other, circling as two animals about to attack, not taking their eyes from each other.

"Is he dead?" she asked.

Donovan, surprised by the question, looked down at the limp body. He didn't know. Had he killed Stanos? He shook his head. He hadn't killed a human since those horrible days after the Alamo. All these years and he hadn't killed. He hadn't lost control.

"Pick him up," she ordered, motioning with the gun.

Donovan obeyed her order. The old man hung limp in his arms. Donovan could detect no heartbeat, see no breath.

"Take him to my bedroom." Donovan carried Stanos out of the chamber and through the corridor, aware of Cassandra following, gun aimed at his unprotected back.

He gently put Stanos on the bed and looked up at Cassandra. "I'm sorry. I lost control. I didn't plan..." his voice trailed off.

She stared past him to the body on the bed. Donovan thought of rushing her, but then her attention returned to him. "I want you to go manacle yourself."

Donovan didn't move. The gun fired. The bullet hit the floor between his feet. "Do you remember you taught me to shoot? Now move."

Donovan went. He stepped on the platform.

The chains still dangled from his wrists and ankles. She tossed him the keys and he unlocked the fetters. Reaching up, he fastened one of the manacles around his wrist, then the other. She came close, pressing the gun against his side. He closed his eyes, expecting her to shoot, but she merely tugged on his wrists to make sure the manacles were properly fastened. Then she dropped the gun and went to the old man lying on the bed. She sat next to him, smoothed his hair, found a handkerchief and wiped the blood from his neck. Her eyes never left him.

"Stanos, you mustn't leave me. Please, you mustn't leave me." She took the small knife from the nightstand and cut her wrist, letting the blood drip down onto Stanos' lips.

They waited to see if the old man would survive the change. Donovan knew long before she did that he would not. She didn't want to believe. She kept pleading with Stanos not to leave her.

Finally, she started to cry.

She cried for a long time. Donovan hadn't thought her capable of such emotion. Why should he be surprised? This man had been part of her life for over sixty years, longer than any other person in her life. He thought about how he would feel when Yolanda died, and she wasn't bound to him as his servant.

Donovan let her cry. He knew the emotional release was good for her. Besides he was afraid of what Cassandra would do when she finally noticed him, standing naked and helpless. Would she pick up the gun and kill him? Or would she rage at him in anger? Or want him to hold her and comfort her? Even though Donovan was a trained counselor, he had no clue which way she would go.

What she did, he didn't expect. She simply got up, folded Stanos hands neatly on his chest, straightened his legs and body, gently shut the staring eyes, kissed his forehead, and walked out of the room without even looking at Donovan. She had laid the body out as was proper, except she hadn't wiped her blood from his lips, the lips that had never opened to receive her gift of life. That never would.

She was gone a long time. When she returned, there was a calmness about her that truly frightened him.

"Where's Wade?" she asked. "Where have you hidden him? None of the perimeter exits have been breached, so he must be hiding here, but I can't find him."

When Donovan didn't answer, she picked the gun, pressed the barrel against the palm of his hand and shot. The bullet passed through his hand and hit a mirror behind him, cracking it as Donovan's scream of agony echoed around the room.

"Where is Wade?"

"Leave him alone, Cassandra. Just let him go." His fear for Wade mounted, fear that she would find him and what she would do.

She tried to put the barrel of the gun next to his left hand, but he fought her, kicking her away. She felt backward, knocking over the table, sending the lamp and statuary crashing to the floor. She aimed and fired. This time the bullet passed through the fleshy part of his right arm and hit the mirror, which shattered, pieces falling to the floor.

Cassandra got to her feet and approached him. "Where is Wade?" she asked. Her tone was reasonable. There was no anger in her voice.

"I won't tell you where that boy is."

She stared up at him for a long moment, then turned and left Donovan hanging in agony, his own blood dripping down. At least the bullets had gone through, they weren't still in his flesh, eating away at it. But Cassandra had wanted it that way. She hadn't been trying to kill him, just hurt him, punish him. Not even that, just make him tell her where Wade was.

It was very quiet, too quiet. He tried to sense Cassandra or her get, but he couldn't. He was alone. Cassandra was gone.

Fourteen

Valentine woke Thom with a kiss. His arms went around her, pulling her down on the bed with him.

"Did you miss me?" she asked.

"No," he lied, and they both knew it.

He smiled at her. "Look, Ma, no fangs."

"So I see, but I bet I can make them come back." She nuzzled his neck as her hand fondled something lower. His fangs erupted, just as she had predicted. He used those fangs to nip her sweet flesh and lap the warm blood.

"Thom, you're going to get blood on my blouse," she complained.

"Then take your blouse off."

"You do it."

"With pleasure." He unbuttoned the blouse and slipped it from her shoulders, returning his mouth to the little wound. She arched against him with a moan of pleasure. Suddenly he was in a hurry. He tore off his pajamas. Just as quickly Valentine divested herself of the rest of her clothes. They came together like the clash of two cymbals. Hard, sharp, loud. Valentine reached her moment of release before his own, crying out. Thom felt her satisfaction echo through him. He slowed a bit, setting a slightly slower pace as he continued to thrust himself deep within her. So the urgency had been Valentine's, not his. He could see how this emotional echo thing could be useful. He turned his attentions to projecting his own needs and desires, and soon Valentine was moving in tune with him. Together they climbed the peaks of pleasure. Valentine's fangs sank into his neck as he climaxed, intensifying the moment until it was almost unbearable.

He thought of Donovan's warning. Yes, he would enjoy every moment of this beautiful, passionate woman, creating memories to treasure through his long future. He thought of Valentine seducing him so long ago. Then he had meant nothing to her except a source of blood. What did he mean to her now?

"What's the matter?" she asked, picking up on his mood.

"Donovan said you don't love me, that love is a human term and I am no longer human. In the Haight Ashbury, did I mean anything more to you than a food source? Do I mean anything more now?"

"Sex is one of the easiest, most enjoyable ways of acquiring blood. Passion clouds the thinking and makes it easier for us to influence the donor's mind. In any city, you can find a prostitute and pay her to let you do what you want. It is also easier to pass unnoticed if you use many partners rather than just a few. Each time you are with a person makes it a little bit harder to make them forget, but forget they must. Vampires have one cardinal rule that we all live by. No one can know of our existence unless under our complete control. Only if you bind a human to you as your servant, can they know your true identity.

"Binding them makes you are responsible for their lives from that moment until they die. It's a great responsibility, holding another's soul, becoming their total reason for living. It's not something you do lightly. It's marriage with no chance for divorce. You can't free them. You can only kill them. That's why you tend to cultivate a, how should I say it, rather cavalier attitude toward humans. They tend to be nothing more than blood donors. You choose someone you find attractive, pleasant, but it can't be anything more, you can't let it be.

"Between vampires it's different. There is no hiding, no lies. But vampire blood doesn't satisfy like living human blood, not over the long term. While I may have a vampire lover, I still seek human donors, donors that I usually have sex with. Vampires can't afford to be jealous or to love, not like humans. Even with other vampires, we don't love. Our lives are too long. Can you imagine being married for three hundred years? We tend to choose short-term liaisons. But I do like you, Thom, very much. Shall I show you how much?"

Without waiting for a reply, she kissed him. He let go of his doubts and settled for enjoying the moment. Afterward, Valentine took Thom upstairs, handed him a newspaper, and told him to go sit in the common room.

He looked at the newspaper. "What is this for?"

"To hide behind. I want you to practice being around humans and not letting your fangs show."

He did as he was told. There were four people sitting in front of the TV watching a sitcom, and an old woman sitting alone in the corner. A rich scent filled the air, a scent that made him hungry. He felt the pain as his fangs erupted and hurriedly took a seat, putting the newspaper in front of his face. He peered over the top, his eyes drawn to the cluster of humans. He could smell them--hear their hearts beating. He tried to look away, but he was mesmerized. Fantasies played through his mind, fantasies in which necks played a prominent role, necks, blood, and sex. Not only were his fangs out, but he was getting an erection. He wanted to jump up and run back to his room and hide.

It was too soon for this.

He wasn't ready. He couldn't handle it.

No, he chided himself, he must learn to handle it. He stayed where he was, forcing himself to watch TV, to try to think of something other than the warm, enticing bodies across the room.

Valentine came in, smiled knowingly at the newspaper positioned in front of his face, walked over to the old woman and sat next to her, taking a frail hand in her own.

"Have you seen Amanda?" the frail voice asked.

"No, Yolanda, I haven't."

"I wonder where she is. Will you help me find her?" she asked, her voice pleading.

Amanda? Yolanda? Was this really Amanda's servant that Valentine had told him about? It must be. All these years and she was still looking for Amanda. What had Valentine said about servants? You can't free them; you can only kill them. He would never make a servant, never. It was too cruel.

He noticed his fangs had retracted. He lowered the paper, still watching Yolanda and Valentine.

Sandy came in and gave the TV watchers a warning that it would soon be time to return to their rooms for the night.

"Have you heard from Donovan?" Valentine asked Sandy.

"No, and I'm worried. He said he would call last night. He didn't. And he hasn't called tonight. That isn't like him."

"No, it isn't." Worry marred Valentine's beautiful face. "If he doesn't call soon, I'll go looking for him."

The look of relief on Sandy's face told Thom just how worried she had been. Well, if Valentine was going, Thom decided, so would he. He owed it to Donovan.

~ * ~

Wade moved slowly on cut and bruised feet, but he wouldn't let the pain stop him. He was almost there, had to be almost there. He had found the stream before dark and made his way down it, sometimes walking in the water. The cold helped his feet, numbing them for a while, making him forget the pain of the cuts with a different kind of pain.

He stopped to rest, sitting on a rock, although that too was painful, for he was still sore from the beating. He could smell smoke, close now. He tried to look for the glow of a fire ahead. Yes, there it was. Not far off, but to his poor sore feet, it seemed like miles. He thought of calling out. Maybe whoever it was would hear him and come to investigate, but he didn't, because he was afraid that Cassandra, Panther, and Wolf were waiting in the darkness. He kept quiet and, gathering his courage, made his way closer.

He could see the fire between the trees, when he was grabbed from behind, a hand going over his mouth, cutting off his scream. Cassandra's voice was soft in his ear. "Don't struggle."

But he did. He thrashed about, but as before, Cassandra's strength made him feel like a small child.

"Do you hear something?" a voice from the campfire. A female voice.

"Just an animal," a deep male voice answered.

Cassandra whispered in his ear. "Stop struggling or I will sic Wolf and Panther on them. Such a nice family, two kids, a boy and a girl."

Wade stopped struggling. The image of Panther and Wolf falling on the woman whose voice he had heard was too real.

"You'll come with me quietly, without making a sound."

Wade nodded against the hand over his mouth. The hand went away. The other was like iron around his wrist as it had been that first night, as she dragged him behind her. Tears blinded him, tears of pain, tears of despair. Finally, he could walk no more and fell to the ground helplessly. She picked him up and carried him easily.

They entered a small glade filled with soft grasses and ferns. The moon had risen, shining down, lighting this place. Gently she laid him down and bent to examine his feet.

"My poor Wade. They must hurt something terrible, so cut, so bruised. That's how I found you, you know. I tracked you by the smell of your sweet blood."

"Where's Donovan?" Wade was afraid to ask, but he had to know.

"He's chained up."

Wade closed his eyes against the pain. Donovan hadn't been able to break free. "Is he all right?"

"Do you mean is he still alive? Yes, he's alive. You care about him, don't you?"

"Yes, I do."

"I once cared about him, too. I loved him. I worshiped his body as I worship yours now. It's a beautiful night, isn't it?"

Wade just stared at Cassandra. "I guess so."

"No, listen, listen to the stillness. See how the moonlight ripples, making everything glow. It's warm tonight, isn't it?"

"Yes," said Wade. "Where are Wolf and Panther?" Wade was worried that they had attacked the campers, despite what Cassandra told him.

"They're dead. I killed them today as they slept. I cut off their heads and drank their blood."

Wade gagged at the thought.

"Donovan was right. The Directors told me I could have no more get, so I won't."

She got up and walked away from him. He followed her with his eyes, but even in the bright moonlight he couldn't tell what she was doing. Finally, she returned, walking toward him, eyes glowing red, dressed in white. Then he realized she wasn't dressed in white, it was her pale white skin and she was naked.

She stood before him, arms outstretched as though she could absorb the moonlight into her very being, then, Wade thought, maybe she could.

She knelt beside him and touched him softly. He stiffened.

"Don't be afraid. I'm not going to hurt you." She picked up his wrist, licked it, then he felt the sharp bite of her fangs, and the pleasure rolling through him as she sucked. Her other hand stroked his body, gently, slowly. She stopped sucking, licked the wound closed and lay down beside him, her naked body close to his, her head on his shoulder.

"Feel the beauty of the moonlight, let it fill you, Wade."

She took her time, biting him and lapping gently, softly, then stopping. Touching him, stroking him, arousing him slowly, until he no longer had any will, any resistance. Finally, she mounted him. She gave him her own wrist to suck, and he did. She continued to take from him, biting and drinking. The moon was no longer shining into the glade when she finished, when she licked the last wound in his neck closed. Wade lay unresisting as she stroked his body. He had no more to give her, no more strength, no more blood. In the back of his mind, he wondered if she had taken too much, if he would die. It didn't seem to matter.

After a while she got up. He thought she was probably getting dressed, but when she returned she was still naked. She took one of his wrists and tied it to his ankle, then picked him up and threw him over one of her shoulders, slipping her head and arm through the circle his bound wrist and foot made, wearing him like one of those sash things that beauty queens wear. She walked off through the woods, Wade hanging limp and unresisting over her shoulder. She started to hum, a pleasant tune, but not one that Wade knew. Maybe she had learned it a hundred years ago.

Cassandra carried Wade into her bedroom and gently laid him at the foot of the bed, cut him free, and then took the restraints attached to the bed's end posts and fastened them to his wrists. Wade didn't resist. He had no strength to resist. He saw Donovan, saw the dried blood that had run down his arm. Donovan's eyes were open, full of concern for Wade. Wade grinned. Donovan was alive. He had been hurt, but he was still alive. A great sense of relief filled Wade. They both were alive. Cassandra pulled pillows from her bed and placed them carefully under Wade's body and brought the fur blanket to wrap around him. She tended his feet, bathed them and wrapped them in clean cloths. Wade couldn't seem to keep his eyes open. He slept.

~ * ~

Wade knew that he had slept the whole day through for Cassandra and Donovan were both awake when he woke.

Cassandra wouldn't even look in Donovan's direction. When he tried to talk to her, she didn't seem to hear him. It was as though Donovan had ceased to exist for her. She went away and brought back food for Wade, soup which she fed him a spoonful at a time, talking to him as one would talk to a child.

When she asked him if there was anything more he wanted, he asked to go to the bathroom, but she told him no, he mustn't walk on his poor feet. She brought him an old-fashioned chamber pot and helped him use it as though she were a nurse helping a sick patient. It was then that Wade saw Stanos body lying on the bed.

"What happened?" he asked.

She looked at him without comprehension.

"What happened to Stanos?"

"I think he is sleeping," Cassandra said, vaguely. "I'll get you more soup."

When she left the room, Wade looked at Donovan. "You're wounded. Are you all right?"

"The bullets went through. She didn't want to kill me."

"What happened to Stanos?"

"I lost control." Regret and grief filled Donovan's voice. "I haven't killed in a very long time. I didn't mean to. I was just so hungry, I couldn't stop. Then Cassandra arrived. She got to the gun first. But what happened to you?"

"I saw the smoke from a campfire and thought I could make it down there and get help. But I guess these feet weren't made for walking that far. She caught me just before I got there. I could see the fire, hear their voices. She told me she would send Panther and Wolf to kill them if I didn't go with her. So I went. Later she told me she had killed Panther and Wolf." He paused for a moment. "We had sex in a moonlit glade. It was unreal. She was so gentle, almost loving. I thought she would be angry, that she would hurt me, but she didn't." When he saw Donovan's look, he added, "It wasn't the same as before. I don't think she was controlling me, it felt different."

"Listen, Wade, be very careful. Don't trust her. She's, well..."

"...Insane? I've known that for a long time."

"Yes, but she has lost touch with reality. There's no way to predict how she'll respond to anything. Or what will happened when she lets herself recognize that Stanos is dead."

Cassandra returned with more soup, which she fed Wade. Then she wandered into the dressing room. When she finally emerged she was dressed in the burgundy ball gown. She shook Stanos. "Wake up, Stanos, I need you to button my dress." She shook him again and stared down at him puzzled. "Stanos always buttons my dress."

"Perhaps I could button it for you," Donovan suggested. She didn't even look his direction.

Wade said, "Let me button the dress. You know I know how."

She smiled, came around the bed and stood with her back to him.

"Cassandra, I can't button you while I'm in restraints."

She turned and obediently unfastened the restraints. Wade tried to stand, but the pain was too great. He sat on the end of the bed, taking the pressure off his injured feet.

"Are you all right?" Cassandra asked, full of concern.

Wade gave her a smile. "Turn around. I will button your dress."

She did as he bid her and he buttoned the dress.

She spun, sending the full skirt billowing. "Am I beautiful?"

"Yes, you are, but you have forgotten those white gloves."

She hurried back into the dressing room. Wade tried to stand, but collapsed back on the bed, sending Donovan a look that said he was sorry.

"It's ok, you're doing fine and so am I."

Cassandra came back smoothing her gloves. "You could dance with me. Oh, no, your poor feet. You can't dance."

"Donovan could, if you unchained him," Wade suggested.

"I'll ask Stanos. He'll dance with me. He's a good dancer." She went around the bed and shook him. When he didn't respond, she shook him harder. "What's the matter with Stanos?"

Wade looked at Donovan questioningly, but Donovan didn't have any answers.

"He's an old man," said Wade finally. "Old men like to sleep." Cassandra looked at him suspiciously. She looked back down at the body.

"He's not asleep. He's dead," She said in a flat monotone.

"He was an old man," Wade said. "He must have died in his sleep."

"Who will be my servant?"

"I will," said Wade.

"You can't be my servant; you're my lover."

"But I buttoned your dress for you. I can be your servant."

She considered the matter for a moment. "No, you are my lover. I must have a servant."

"Perhaps Donovan could be your servant?"

"I remember Donovan. He can't be my servant. He was my lover, but he betrayed me. You won't betray me, will you, Wade?"

Wade shook his head.

"I'd better take care of Stanos' body. I'm sorry he's dead."

"He was very old. Humans die," said Wade.

Cassandra nodded vaguely, picked up the body and carried it out of the room.

"What do we do now?" Wade asked.

"Do you know where she keeps the manacle key?"

"Actually, they don't need a key, but you have to have two free hands to trip the release switch."

It wasn't far across the room, but Wade couldn't even take one step. He let himself down off the bed and started to crawl across the floor like a baby. He reached the platform and forced himself to stand, gritting his teeth against the pain. He felt for the release catches, his fingers fumbling. He had never done it, only seen Cassandra reach up, but never with a clear view. The pain from his feet made him want to throw up. His head spun dizzily, his eyes couldn't seem to focus. Things were getting black around the edges. He was going to faint, but he couldn't, he couldn't let himself. Cassandra would be back soon. He had to free Donovan. His fingers found two spots on the manacle's edge that gave. He pushed them, nothing happened.

"Try pushing them together, at the same time," said Donovan.

Wade did as he was told.

Then he felt Donovan's arm go around him, supporting him, as the blackness engulfed him.

"Wade, wake up, Wade." Wade struggled to the surface of consciousness.

Donovan was holding him. Wade knew he needed to do something, but he wasn't sure what.

"Unlock the other manacle," said Donovan. "Reach up and find the releases."

Wade's arms felt as if they were made of concrete, so heavy, so useless, as he tried to raise them, to do as Donovan asked.

"What are you doing?" It was Cassandra's voice. "I told you not to stand." She was pulling him away from Donovan, picking him up. He tried to struggle, but he had no strength. "Naughty boy," she said, laying him face down on the bed. "If you won't listen to Cassandra, I have to protect you." Wade felt her fasten one of the restraints around his wrist.

"Don't, please don't."

"Shh, my love." She stroked his hair back out of his eyes, then reach across him to chain his other wrist. "I will take care of you." Her hand stroked down his back, touching his buttocks. "Who did this to you? Who hurt you?"

Her fingers gently touched the wounds of her beating.

"You did," said Wade.

"I would never hurt Wade, never hurt his beautiful body. Why are you saying these terrible things? Who told you to say these lies?"

"It's the truth. You beat me with your belt."

Donovan's voice was low and urgent. "Stop, Wade."

But Wade didn't care. "You beat me with a belt for helping Donovan. You hurt me."

Wade turned his head so he could see Cassandra's face. She was shaking her head. "No, I would never hurt my Wade."

She crumpled into tears, bending to kiss the flesh she had beaten, her tears moistening his back.

Wade was suddenly sorry. "It's all right," he said softly. "They don't hurt any more."

"It's all Donovan's fault. He made me beat you. He forced me to hurt my beautiful Wade." She got up from the bed.

"Cassandra," Wade called her, suddenly afraid. She didn't answer. He pulled against the restraints, but they were tightly fastened. He raised his head, trying to see where Cassandra had gone, what she was doing, but she was out of his narrow field of vision.

Then Wade saw her. She walked toward Donovan, who was struggling to free himself from the remaining manacle. He couldn't. He needed to press both edges of the manacle in two spots, and he couldn't do it one-handed. Cassandra carried the wide leather belt she had used to beat him.

"Cassandra, come here," Wade called. "I need you. Please come here." She turned and looked at him. "Please. I need you, I want you."

She walked over to the bed. "I have to punish Donovan."

"No. You don't."

She nodded her head up and down.

"No. I want you to make love to me now. To give me pleasure. Remember how I undressed you, how I undid the buttons? Please, I want to do it again. Release me so can undress you, so we can make love. Now!" The thought made Wade queasy, but he would do anything to keep Cassandra from beating Donovan.

Cassandra smiled. "When I am through."

She turned and walked back to Donovan, brought the belt up, and started to beat Donovan.

Wade struggled against the restraints. He called out to her, but she was no longer listening. Donovan tried to grab the belt with his free hand, but he couldn't quite seem to get a grip on it. Tears of pain and anguish filled Wade's eyes until he could no longer see Cassandra beating Donovan.

Fifteen

Donovan raised his hand to protect himself, the belt buckle hit his wrist, cutting the flesh. Cassandra's face was a contorted vision of uncontrolled rage. He tried to grab the belt, but she yanked it out of his hand and brought it down again, hard. This time it hit his back. He groaned in pain, tried to twist away, but he was trapped. The buckle cut into his flesh, and he felt blood running down his back.

"What's going on here?" A woman's voice but not Cassandra's.

Donovan twisted until he could see the doorway. Valentine. Relief surged through him.

Cassandra hit him again. She hadn't even heard Valentine; she was so wrapped up in her fury.

Donovan took the blow, and the next, as Valentine rushed forward. Thom followed her.

Valentine grabbed Cassandra's arm. Cassandra turned, a spitting ball of fury, and attacked. Valentine was thrown to the floor by the viciousness, lost beneath the mound of burgundy fabric. Cassandra's hoop skirt flipped up, revealing pantaloons. It was almost funny, except for the animal growls issuing from Cassandra's throat.

Thom tried to pull Cassandra off Valentine, but she shook free. The next time Thom reached for her, she had her teeth clamped into Valentine's flesh, and she couldn't be pulled loose. Thom encircled Cassandra's waist with his arms, locking them by grabbing his forearms, then he pulled. Valentine screamed as Cassandra took a piece of flesh with her. Cassandra struggled in Thom's arms.

Donovan reached out and grabbed one of Cassandra's flailing arms and pulled her and Thom toward him. She struggled, but Donovan's freed hand was the uninjured one, so his grip was firm.

Valentine rose to her feet, her eyes flashing in anger, fangs bared. She started toward Cassandra.

"Valentine," Donovan commanded her. "Get me out of this manacle." She looked at him, uncomprehending for a moment, then she mounted the platform.

"A key?"

Cassandra was screaming obscenities now.

"You don't need one. There's a release catch on the manacle--two, one on either side-- both hands, press the edges together."

"Do it," Thom urged. He had braced himself against the wall and was tightening his grip around Cassandra, pulling her hard against his body. The hoop skirt flipped upward, blinding them both.

Valentine unfastened the manacle. Donovan freed, suddenly found himself pulled off the platform by the fury of Cassandra's struggles. Valentine grabbed Cassandra's other arm. The fact that she was securely held didn't stop Cassandra from struggling.

Valentine looked at Donovan. "What do you suggest we do with her now?"

"There's a room down the hall we can lock her in."

"We saw it."

They dragged and pushed Cassandra, who was screaming insanely, calling for Wade. Finally, they shoved her into the prison room and locked the door. She beat against it, screaming obscenities and shouting what she was going to do to them, especially if they hurt her Wade.

Donovan hurried back into the bedroom and removed the restraints from Wade's wrists. Wade grabbed him, clinging, crying, his body trembling in fear and shock. Donovan kept reassuring him over and over that he was all right.

Valentine grabbed Donovan's hand, examining the wound. "Upstairs, Thom, in the refrigerator, bring all the bags."

Donovan added, "Look around for a transfusion kit." Valentine looked at him strangely.

"What's a transfusion kit?" Thom asked.

"You know, needle, tubing, so you can give a person a transfusion."

"Do you need one?"

"No, but Wade does."

"Donovan?" Valentine asked as Thom left. Donovan ignored her.

He picked up the fur blanket and wrapped it around Wade's shivering body. "I'm all right," he told Wade. Wade eyed Valentine fearfully. Her fangs were still out and with the blood flowing from her wounded shoulder, she wasn't particularly a comforting sight.

"It's all right, Wade, these are my friends. They've come to rescue us. You remember Amanda. This is her daughter, Valentine." Valentine pulled on Donovan's arm. Again he ignored her. "Just lie there and rest. You're safe. Cassandra is locked up. She can't hurt you or me any more." Donovan exerted a bit of mental pressure. "Just go to sleep. It's safe now." Wade's eyelids closed. His shivering lessened. Donovan watched him for a moment to be sure he was asleep, then he followed Valentine out of the room and shut the door.

"What's going on here? And who is that?" Valentine demanded.

"Well, I have a question for you. What are you doing here?"

"I got worried and tired of waiting."

"You haven't by any chance seen a pair of pants around here, have you?"

Valentine stamped her foot in frustration.

Ignoring the fact that he was nude, Donovan sank down onto the sofa. "Can't this wait?" he pleaded.

Valentine frowned, but nodded.

Thom returned, carrying the bags in a cooking pot. Donovan grabbed one and bit into it, drained it, and took a second.

Valentine motioned Thom over to lick the blood from her neck and seal the wound. "No use wasting good blood," Valentine commented as Thom nuzzled her neck, obviously enjoying the duty.

Donovan took a third. He decided that Wade needed the sleep more than the transfusion, so he put a couple of bags aside for him.

When Thom was finished, he and Valentine turned to examine Donovan.

"What happened to you?" Thom asked, eyeing the wounds.

Donovan sighed. From the look on Valentine's face, he knew he wouldn't be able to put it off much longer. He pointed to his side. "This is where Stanos shot me with a silver bullet when I arrived. Cassandra removed the bullet. The sunburns are fading pretty rapidly." He pointed to the red patches on his arms and legs. "The room where we locked Cassandra has a sunroof. And the last two--" The wounds in his hand and arm were still open and painful. "Cassandra shot me after I killed Stanos and helped Wade escape."

"And why, pray tell, was she beating you when we arrived?" Valentine asked.

"She was upset because she blamed me for the fact that she had beaten Wade with a belt. Wade said she killed her two get, but you'd better check."

Valentine crossed her arms. "Not until you tell me who Wade is and why you told him about Amanda."

"Wade is one of the three lost boys. I showed you the clipping."

"But that was..."

"...Three weeks ago. I know. We were locked up together and he asked me why Cassandra hated me, so I told him. He's had a rather rough time, but he's done everything he could to help me."

"She didn't make him?"

"That's a long story. Now, will you go check the rest of the place and find me a pair of pants."

Valentine listened to him this time, and she and Thom left.

~ * ~

Thom followed Valentine as they continued their search of the lair's empty rooms. One room with table and chairs looked every bit like a formal dining room. Did vampires dine? There were several storage rooms stuffed with furniture, boxes, all neatly arranged. A bedroom with two beds had an odd smell that made his fangs ache. Kicking something, he looked down and saw a dead rat. He jumped back with a grimace.

Another room was a torture chamber, with racks, chains, and whips. Again that smell, but now Thom thought he knew what it was--the smell of old blood.

Inside the last room off the hallway they found three bodies. An old man laid out carefully, hands folded, eyes closed.

The other two...Thom swallowed hard, wondering if vampires could vomit. These had been dumped, arms and legs akimbo. Their heads had been cut off. The black head had rolled across the room and lay face up, eyes staring, mouth opened in a snarl, fangs showing. By a strange twist of fate, the head of the white man lay near the black body, a black hand resting across it as though caressing it.

Valentine hardly gave the bodies a glance. Instead she began examining a contraption that looked like a small furnace.

"Good, she's got a crematorium," Valentine said, opening the door and peering inside. "There won't be any problem getting rid of the bodies."

"But-but..." Thom stammered. He had been about to say something about calling the police, but one didn't call the police, not if you were a vampire, not if the bodies were vampires. "Who are they? And what happened?"

"The old one, that's Stanos, Cassandra's servant. The other two, I have no idea, but obviously they were Cassandra's get and she killed them."

"Why?"

"Maybe Donovan knows. Did you see any clothes?"

"Yes, in that bedroom."

"Get him a pair of pants, and we'll go talk to Donovan."

~ * ~

Donovan leaned back against the sofa and took a fourth bag, sipping it more slowly. He could hear Cassandra raging, screaming and pounding on the door.

Thom and Valentine returned. Thom handed him a pair of pants. They weren't his, but they fit reasonably well. Donovan wondered what had happened to his boots. They were good boots.

"There are three bodies in one of the rooms. Stanos and two more," Valentine said.

"Black and white?"

Valentine nodded. Thom looked rather sick.

Donovan almost commented that it saved them having to kill Cassandra's get, but stopped himself in time, remembering that Thom was a get.

"What happened?" Valentine asked.

"According to Wade, she planned to keep me alive, wall me up in that room where we locked her, and then brazen it out with the Board of Directors. She killed her get to destroy the evidence."

"She's bonkers, isn't she?" Thom asked.

"That isn't the term I would have used, but she's bonkers." Donovan could have used the proper medical terms, in denial, having a dissociate episode, obsession, but bonkers would do.

"What do we do now?" Valentine asked.

"I want to get Wade back to the clinic as quickly as possible. Then I guess we inform the Directors and let them decide what to do about Cassandra."

"I'll stay and watch her," Valentine volunteered. "While I'm here, I'll do some cleaning up. She won't be coming back here, especially when the Directors hear that she tried to kill you."

"I'm not sure what the Directors will do. I do know that at the very least she needs medical treatment. Now, I'm going to wake Wade and give him the transfusion."

"Is it necessary?" Valentine asked.

"Yes. He's been pretty badly used. If he doesn't get some more blood into him, he could die."

"Oh, I suppose, you're right."

Thom was looking back and forth, questions in his eyes. Valentine smiled at him as she explained, "Cardinal rule: no one may know of the existence of vampires except under direct control of a vampire. Cassandra made him: he was to be her get. I can understand Donovan not wanting him to die and become Cassandra's get. He wants to wait until we can initiate him properly. You didn't ask me, but I would be willing to stand as a blood-mother, so would Sandy, that just needs one more. Edmund would do it, if you asked."

Donovan didn't tell Valentine there wasn't going to be an initiation. He was too tired to argue with her, and he knew there would be an argument.

~ * ~

Donovan looked down at Wade, watching the red flow of blood through the tube into the boy's arm. He looked so young as he lay curled almost in a fetal position with his thick, dark lashes fanned against pale cheeks and lips almost as pale.

"Thom, see if you can find some clothes for the boy and find me a shirt and my boots."

Thom left.

The screaming stopped abruptly.

"At last." Valentine sighed with relief.

Alarm coursed through Donovan. It was too quiet. He thought of the hole in the ceiling. "Did you see a gun around here? Cassandra's gun?"

"No."

"Let's find it."

Valentine picked up on Donovan's anxiety, and she quickly joined him in searching. Finally, Donovan found the gun lying on Cassandra's dressing table. He flipped the cylinder open. Silver bullets gleamed in three chambers. He closed the gun.

Thom came back into the room, carrying some clothes. He looked at Donovan, gun in hand, and stopped.

"In your search, you didn't find any shackles, did you?"

Thom nodded slowly. "Whips and chains, a real torture chamber."

"Get some."

"What are you going to do?" Thom asked.

"Make sure Cassandra doesn't escape."

Thom brought the chains, and the three of them approached the locked door. Donovan indicated for Thom to unlock it and step aside.

Standing in the center of the doorway, gun ready, Donovan pushed the door open.

The room was empty. From the grill in the ceiling dangled a rope of torn petticoats.

"Damn!" said Donovan.

"Come on, Thom! We're going hunting!" said Valentine.

"Be careful," Donovan said. "Keep Thom with you, Valentine. He won't recognize Cassandra's presence until too late."

Valentine nodded as they hurried toward the stairs.

Where would Cassandra go? Donovan wondered. He started to follow Valentine, but stopped at the bottom of the stairs and looked back down the corridor. Had Cassandra really escaped or was it only a trick to lure them outside the lair? He turned back, turned back to Wade, suddenly sure that she wouldn't leave without him.

Cassandra was bending over the boy, holding him in her arms. The needle had pulled free and blood was leaking slowly onto the carpet. Wade's eyes were open--dark, frightened eyes.

"Put the gun down," Cassandra said.

Donovan shook his head.

"I'll kill him if you don't."

"You'll lose him then. He's not going to survive the change."

"You don't know that."

"But you do. That's why you didn't kill him before."

She shook her head. "He's mine. And always will be."

Wade looked at Donovan, the fear melted away from his eyes. "Shoot, Donovan. Remember your promise."

"What promise?" Cassandra demanded.

"He promised to kill me rather than let me become a vampire like you. Do it, Donovan. Shoot. That gun has silver bullets. Kill me. Kill her. End it now," Wade pleaded.

Donovan laid the gun on the table, and Wade started to sob.

"Let him go, Cassandra," said Donovan. "If you love him, let him go."

Cassandra shook her head. "I need him."

"You can have me instead." He slowly went down on his knees in front of her. "I will be your abject slave. I will do everything you want. I will make love to you. I will forget Amanda and love only you. Let him go."

Cassandra's laugh was the cackle of a mad witch. "I don't want you anymore. I have what I want. I just came back for a few things. But I'm leaving now, with Wade."

Wade bit the arm that held him prisoner, struggling like an animal caught in a trap.

As her attention focused on Wade, Donovan grabbed the gun and leaped toward her. All three tumbled to the floor; Donovan pressed the gun against Cassandra's head.

"I'll kill you," Donovan hissed, "remember it has silver bullets." She stared up at him. His finger tightened on the trigger. At the last moment, he shifted the barrel of the gun and fired. Cassandra screamed as the bullet lodged in her shoulder.

"Now, you know just how it feels." He yanked her up and dragged her body into the bedroom and tossed her onto the bed, fastening the restraints around ankles and wrists. She whimpered in pain.

He looked down at her. He should have killed her when he had the chance. A part of him screamed in frustration, whining that was what he wanted--to kill her as she had killed Amanda and Clare. But he couldn't. Even now, after all she had done, he couldn't kill her.

He didn't understand himself. Maybe he still loved her? Or maybe he felt responsible for what she had become? Or maybe fifty years was just too long to carry a desire for revenge?

Still, watching her writhe in pain gave him a great deal of satisfaction. He knew he shouldn't feel pleasure at the suffering of another, but, well, if he couldn't kill her, he could at least enjoy a bit of revenge.

Donovan returned to Wade and picked him up.

Wade stared accusingly at him. "You didn't keep your promise."

"I promised to do everything in my power to keep you from becoming a vampire and to kill you *only* if you do become one. I said nothing about killing you before." He put his arms around the boy. "Don't worry, I'll keep you safe, I swear. I won't let her hurt you or anyone else again."

"I know." The trust was absolute. Donovan wondered if he could keep his promise.

Valentine and Thom came rushing in. "We heard a shot."

"Cassandra took a bullet to the shoulder. Thom, I want you to take Wade back to the clinic now."

"No," Wade protested. "Please, I don't want to go with him." He started to tremble in Donovan's arms, his eyes so filled with fear that it hurt Donovan to look at him.

"All right. We'll go together, but first I need to take care of Cassandra's wound."

"I can handle that," Valentine said. "If you're going, you should get out of here."

"Thom will stay with you."

"He should drive you."

Donovan shook his head. "I'm fine. Even if she is wounded, I'm not about to leave Cassandra here alone with you. I'll be back tomorrow night with transportation."

He helped get Wade dressed and then had Thom carry the boy upstairs. Wade protested, but Donovan insisted. The boy lay unresisting, but stiff in Thom's arms.

~ * ~

After Donovan left, Valentine and Thom searched the cabin, looking for surgical tools and bandages. She found a complete kit in the small bathroom.

They could hear Cassandra cursing and crying as they returned.

"It hurts," she moaned.

"I'm sure it does," Valentine said coldly. "Just as I'm sure Donovan's wounds hurt."

Cassandra's face and body mirrored the pain she was suffering. The wound was ugly, oozing blood, skin blistered.

"I thought we were supposed to heal quickly?" Thom said.

"Silver. Silver poisons a vampire. That much of the legends are true. As you can see, it doesn't kill us, at least not right away. If I were to leave the bullet in, eventually it would kill her. Hold her down, would you?" She picked up the long-handled tweezers and a gauze pad.

Thom held Cassandra, but she kept twisting away just as Valentine would start to probe for the bullet.

"Sit on her chest," Valentine ordered. "She may look small and frail, but she isn't. Besides, I understand she likes it rough."

Awkwardly, Thom climbed onto the bed and used the weight of his body to pin Cassandra. Valentine was right, she wasn't frail. Thom remembered her strength as she had struggled to escape. He stared into her dark eyes and saw madness.

Valentine dug for the bullet, totally ignoring Cassandra's screams, and finally pried it from the wound. She wiped the blood away and bandaged the shoulder.

"Silver contaminates the blood, not fit to drink, and licking the wound won't help it heal. Only time can heal a silver wound, time and blood." Valentine checked the restraints, making sure they were tight. "Was there any blood left?"

"I think one bag."

"Give it to her."

Thom found the bag, nipped the end, and let the red fluid dribble into Cassandra's mouth. Cassandra swallowed hungrily and, when the bag was flat and empty, asked for more.

"There's no more," Valentine said, turning away. She picked up the gun and handed it to Thom. "Do you think you can shoot her, if she tries to escape?"

The gun was heavy in his hand. Could he shoot? He wasn't sure.

"Aim for the head. A silver bullet in the brain is usually fatal. It would be better for all concerned if she died."

Thom stared at Valentine in shock. She meant her cold, harsh words. This was a Valentine he didn't recognize.

He handed the gun back to her. "You do it. I don't want anything to do with killing."

"You're as bad as Donovan. He should have killed her when he had the chance. But no, he's going to call the Board of Directors. They won't do anything." Valentine raised the gun and took aim at Cassandra.

"Go ahead, kill me!" Cassandra's dark eyes glowed with hatred.

Slowly, Valentine lowered the gun. She gave a harsh laugh. "I'm no better than Donovan. I look at her and I know I would be hurting Stefan. I hate what Stefan has become, but I remember the child I loved. I think of the others that carry her blood that I would be hurting. That's the difference between Cassandra and me. She wouldn't hesitate to kill."

Thom put his arms around Valentine, pulling her to him. "I prefer you to her any day. It's not a bad thing not to be able to kill."

She let him hold her, comfort her. "Are you hungry?" she asked.

"A little."

"I'd better go hunting. We're going to need blood. Can I trust you to watch her? Can I trust you to shoot her if she tries to escape?"

"Yeah, I'll shoot her, just don't expect me to try to kill her."

Valentine smiled. "I'm glad you aren't a killer, either. Oh, don't look into her eyes. She'll try to control you, and you might not be able to resist."

Thom remembered Valentine's vivid demonstration of a vampire's power.

After Valentine left, Thom put more logs on the fire and sat on the lounge with the gun on his lap.

He didn't look at Cassandra, but stared into the fire.

"What's your name?" she asked.

He almost answered her, until he realized that he wanted to answer, needed to answer. She was doing it, trying to make him respond. He said nothing.

"Come on, you can tell me!" The tone was almost a command. A part of him wanted to obey her. He wished that Valentine were here to protect him.

Suddenly, as if by a miracle, she was. She carried a scarf, which she used to gag Cassandra, then she placed a bag over her head.

"Now, you should be safe from her. I felt her trying to grab hold of you."

"I did too, and I didn't know what to do."

"When this is over, we'll work on some protection techniques. I wouldn't leave you, but we're going to need blood."

"I'll be all right." The words were meant to sound brave, but they didn't and Thom knew it.

Cassandra's curses were muffled by the gag and the bag over her head, still she twisted and pulled, trying to free herself.

"Determined bitch, isn't she," he said.

"You've got it. Bitch is right. I'll be back as soon as I can."

Thom was left alone with an insane woman and three dead bodies. Life had certainly changed since he died.

~ * ~

"Dinner's served," Valentine said, as she dropped a couple of burlap bags on the floor. Thom eyed them suspiciously when he saw one of the bags move.

Valentine disappeared and came back with a large porcelain bowl, a couple of cups, and a long knife. She reached into one the bags and pulled out a struggling animal.

A raccoon's cute face stared at him with bright, masked eyes. With a deft stroke, Valentine sliced the creature's throat and held it over the basin to catch the gushing blood. Thom swallowed hard and looked away, but the vision of the raccoon's face remained behind his closed eyes. The animal made pitiful sounds as its life drained away. Thom got up and left the room.

After awhile Valentine brought him a cup of blood. "Drink it."

Moments before the raccoon had been a living creature. Now it was dead. Its blood presented to him in a cup.

"I'm not hungry," Thom said, though his fangs ached and his body screamed for what the cup held.

"Don't be squeamish." Valentine thrust the glass into his hand. "Drink."

It was the command of his master. Even though he wanted to refuse, he found the cup raised to his lips and he drank. The blood was hot. Nothing like the bottled blood he normally drank. That was a flat, dull nothing compared to the rich, complex taste of the fresh hot blood.

"That's better," Valentine said. "When we get back, I'll have Donovan teach you to hunt. There's nothing quite like chasing down a deer and sinking your fangs deep into the throat."

Thom stared at Valentine. Gone was the sophisticated clothing designer, what was left was something feral. It scared him.

"I want you to try some of the meat." She took his hand and pulled him back into the other room. The raccoon was a limp carcass lying dead on the table. She took the knife and skinned the animal. Then she sliced off a sliver of flesh and held out to Thom.

"I thought we couldn't eat anything," Thom said, trying to postpone the moment. A drop of blood dripped from the meat.

"We are animals, predators. Blood, flesh it doesn't matter. Try it."

Thom started to shake his head, but opened his mouth. She would force him, if he refused. The meat did taste good, almost as good as the blood. He wanted to be disgusted, but the beast inside him demanded that he feed it more. He took another sliver. With precision, Valentine cut off more of the flesh and dropped it into the blood in the bowl. She fished out a piece, sucking and gnawing happily.

"I'd almost forgotten how good a fresh kill tastes," she said, almost humming with pleasure.

After her own hunger was satisfied, she removed the bag and gag from Cassandra and proceeded to feed her. Cassandra ate with a ferociousness and concentration that was frightening.

Thom took another sliver of meat, relishing the taste, despite all his previous inhibitions against raw meat. He might fool himself into believing he was in control, but his hunger was a thing apart, beyond reason, beyond control. It was his master and he its servant. He took another slice of meat to feed the hunger and sighed with resignation. He was a vampire; he and the blood hunger were one.

Valentine licked her fingers clean, checked Cassandra's restraints. "Come on, Thom, I need some help. I started the crematorium before I left, it should be hot enough now."

Unwilling, Thom followed Valentine.

The bodies were where they had left them. Valentine opened the furnace door, and hot air blasted Thom. Valentine picked up a head and casually tossed it into the flames. Thom shuddered.

"Help me with this body," she said, grabbing the headless corpse below the arms and dragging it toward the crematorium.

Thom couldn't move. He wanted to run, to hide. Valentine looked up at him. "Come on!" she ordered. Thom straightened his shoulders. He was a vampire. Whether he liked it or not, vampires were about death. What he had seen at the clinic, the civilized drinking blood from a bottle, never touching or being contaminated by it, that was an illusion. This was the reality. He'd better accept it, fast!

He grabbed the body by the ankles, helped Valentine swing it into the furnace, and gagged at the pungent smell of burning flesh.

He helped her with the other cadaver, but couldn't bring himself to pick up the head.

He was relieved when all three bodies were disposed of and the door shut.

"Who do you suppose those two were?" he asked.

"It doesn't matter. They're dead," Valentine said coldly.

But it did matter to Thom. He had just helped cremate three people, vampires, and didn't even know the names of two of them. Who would mourn them? It seemed only right that someone did.

~ * ~

Donovan drove through the night; Wade slept beside him. He kept glancing at the boy, worried about his condition, but he was more worried about what was going to happen to Wade. How was he going to protect the boy?

Maybe he should have killed Cassandra when he had the chance? No, he realized, with Cassandra alive, Wade would only be a get. If Cassandra was dead, Wade had the potential to become a new sire. The Board was sure to demand a culling. It was an old custom, dating from medieval times. When a vampire died, all those the vampire had blooded were gathered together and killed to see who would rise as a sire. If Cassandra was dead, the Board wouldn't risk losing a sire. Wade's fate would be sealed. Suddenly, Donovan was glad he hadn't killed her.

It was almost dawn when they arrived at the clinic. He gave Wade over to Rose's care and called Doc Herman to check the boy out.

Doc arrived, grumbling about the fate of all doctors to be awakened out of a dead sleep. "You couldn't handle this one?" He took a look at Donovan and then down at the boy. "What happened to you and him? What did you do to your hand?"

Donovan shoved his hand in his pocket out of sight. "It's nothing. Don't even think about it." He commanded and saw Doc Herman respond with a slight nod of acceptance. "I found the boy wandering in the woods. His feet are pretty badly cut up."

"They sure are. We'll need to report this. He's been abused."

Donovan turned to stare deep into the doctor's eyes. "I was thinking that it might be better to keep quiet about this for a few days, until I have a chance to check it out, find out what the situation really is, and let the boy recover some of his strength before putting him through the bureaucratic meat grinder."

"All right," the doctor agreed.

It was easy for Donovan to manipulate the man. Doc Herman had seen too many children returned to abusive parents by well-meaning government officials. It was one of his pet peeves.

"Maybe we can handle it without getting the police involved," Donovan said. "For now, let's keep Wade's presence between you and Rose and me." The doctor nodded. "Wade, I'm going to leave you in the care of Doc Herman and Rose. They'll take care of you. It's almost sunrise. Rose, open the shutters so Wade can look out and see the sunrise. I'm going to get some sleep. You will be safe here."

Wade nodded slowly.

"Don't worry. I won't be far away."

Sandy met him at the door to Wade's room. "You're too pale." She handed him a bottle, the blood was fresh and still warm. He let the sweet elixir flow over his tongue, replenishing his body.

"What happened?" She glanced at Wade through the open door.

"I'm going to called Edmund. Come listen in so I don't have to explain it twice."

They went down to his office. He called Edmund and told his story. "Cassandra's had a complete breakdown. I think it would be best if she was brought back here to the clinic for the time being."

"I agree."

"I'll bring her back tomorrow night."

"I'll let the Directors know."

"Thanks."

When Donovan hung up, Sandy said, "You didn't mention the boy. Who is he?"

"The missing boy from about a month ago. Wade Kain. He's had a really rough time."

"I bet he has."

"What I told Doc Herman goes for Edmund and Darkhour. I don't want them, or anyone, to know about the boy, at least for the time being. He needs time to recover his strength."

"You want the blood work done, don't you?"

Donovan sighed. "Yes. Get it started. We'll need to know our options. If we're bringing Cassandra back here, we'd better be sure that wherever we put her, she can't escape. She's insane, but that's done nothing to limit her intelligence. She's already escaped once. That time I had to shoot her. I don't want to have to do it again."

"I'll take care of the security. Is she violent?"

"Yes. She'll need restraint."

"Done."

"I'm going to take a shower."

"I wish you would. You smell!" she teased.

"Oh, thanks," he protested, smiling.

~ * ~

It was late afternoon when Donovan rose and got dressed. His wounds were healing nicely. He wrapped a bandage around his hand, not for protection, but to keep what was obviously a bullet hole from raising questions. He went to check on Wade.

He found the boy under heavy sedation, wrapped up warm against the chill. Sandy stood by him, taking his pulse.

"How's he doing?" Donovan asked.

"We've pumped blood into him, and vitamins. He was anemic, although not as bad as I would have expected. His feet are cut up and bruised, some infection, so Doc ordered him a round of antibiotics."

Donovan looked down at the sleeping boy. "Why the heavy sedation?"

"There was a slight problem. He asked Rose if she was a vampire."

Donovan frowned. "He said the word vampire?"

Sandy nodded. "Rose was rather surprised. Fortunately, the doctor had left so no one else heard him. What's going on?" she demanded.

Wade shouldn't have been able to ask about vampires. He shouldn't have been able to say the word. Donovan's frown deepened. "Thanks," he said. "I'll take care of the problem."

"Then it is a problem?"

"Hell, yes," Donovan snarled. "I planted the command myself."

"I just assumed Cassandra hadn't bothered to do it. She figured it didn't matter, since he was going to end up dead. So why didn't your command work?"

"I'm not sure. Maybe because he was Cassandra's, not mine. Or maybe it has something to do with the fact that he broke her hold over him."

"She exchanged blood with him, everything?"

"Yes. She planned to make him her get. She had the poor boy believing he loved her and would do anything for her. Then he told her he didn't want to be a vampire. She forced him to participate in the rape and murder of that girl they kidnapped. She almost killed him, but she was terrified that he wouldn't survive the change, so she stopped just short of death. I'm not sure how, but somehow that night broke her hold over him. The fact that he can now resist her has made him even more attractive to her. She's obsessed with him."

"Perhaps the best thing to do would be to initiate him as a second."

Donovan shook his head. "I told this boy I would protect him from becoming what he fears most, a vampire. I promised I would do everything in my power to keep it from happening. And I gave my word that if he changed, I would kill him, because he would rather be dead than live as a vampire. Sandy, I can't do it, I can't kill him."

Sandy frowned. "He knows too much about us. You can't keep him sedated forever."

"It won't hurt him for a few days, give his body time to heal and give me a chance to figure a way out of this mess. Do me a favor? Stick to the story that Cassandra hadn't bothered with any prohibitions. I don't want anyone to know that I gave him a command and it didn't work.

"All right," Sandy said hesitantly.

"Don't worry. I'll handle it, somehow. Did you get the van loaded?"

"Yes. Do you want me to go with you?"

"No. Valentine, Thom, and I can handle it."

As Donovan drove through the growing darkness, his thoughts were on Wade. The boy had ignored a command that Donovan had planted. Did that mean Wade had developed the will to resist not just Cassandra, but Donovan as well? Wade was no longer under Cassandra's control, which made him a threat. Donovan had seen it in Sandy's eyes, the fear. If the Board ever learned what had happened, out of that same fear, they would order Wade's immediate execution. He had rescued Wade from Cassandra, now the question was, could he keep Wade safe from the other vampires? More important, could he keep the other vampires safe from Wade?

Sixteen

Cassandra glared at Donovan, hatred in her eyes.

"What have you done with my Wade?" she demanded.

"He's safe, safe from you, Cassandra, and he isn't *your* Wade."

"Liar! Liar! He loves me. He only loves me. He wants to be with me. Bring him to me." She pulled against the restraints, struggled as he slipped the needle into her arm, forcing the strong sedative into her bloodstream. "I'll kill you, Donovan, I promise I will kill you!" Cassandra's scream faded as the drug took effect.

"Come on, let's do this," Donovan said to Valentine. "That drug isn't going to last long." He and Valentine undid the manacles and strapped Cassandra's unresisting body into a straightjacket.

"You'd think she wouldn't have any voice left," Valentine said. "She screamed the whole time you were gone. Pleaded with me to bring her Wade. Says she can't live without him. I'm not sure she can."

Valentine, Thom and Donovan transferred Cassandra to the gurney and strapped her down.

"I cleaned up the three bodies," Valentine continued. "She had a small crematorium."

Donovan nodded.

"What should we do about all her stuff?"

Donovan decided. "I'll make arrangements to have it brought to the clinic. We may as well make her as comfortable as possible. I don't think she's going anywhere soon. It might help her to be surrounded by familiar things."

"Knowing how you feel about her," Valentine said, "perhaps another place could be found, someone else to be responsible for her."

Donovan shook his head. "There is no other place equipped to handle a mentally disturbed vampire. Besides I'm partially to blame for what she became. Maybe this time I can help her."

Valentine put her hand on his shoulder. "You're a fool. She'll just be a constant reminder."

"Yes. But I'll lose Yolanda soon. Then who will I have but Cassandra to remind me? Let's get her into the van. Thom, you drive. I'll need to monitor the IV drip. I don't want her coming around on the way back to the clinic. Valentine, you can follow us in your car."

~ * ~

Thom concentrated on the road. Even sedated, Cassandra moaned and cried out for Wade. He was tired of hearing her voice. After what she had done, he had expected to hate her, but he felt sorry for her.

When they passed through Danvers, Donovan said, "Help me remember I need to establish a reason for Stanos' disappearance."

"What do you mean?"

"We need to give the townspeople a reasonable answer for why Stanos just disappeared." Donovan smiled. "It shouldn't be too hard. According to Betsy, the postmistress, some of them believe that Stanos is a scientist working on a secret project. When we come to clean up the lair and seal it, I'll stop in and leave a change of address and implant the hint that Stanos made a breakthrough in his research and has been moved to a more secure facility. If I tell Betsy, the whole town will know. A good lesson for you, Thom. You can't just walk away. In this day and age, people will start questioning, looking for you, and expecting to find you. That's why Valentine is arranging to die in a car crash."

"How does that work?"

"A staged accident outside a small town where the coroner happens to be a servant. He will certify the death and see to the supposed cremation of the body. Valentine ends and someone new begins."

"How did you explain about my missing body?" Thom asked, suddenly curious.

"Didn't. It will remain one of those unsolved mysteries. Let people believe that space aliens or body snatchers got it. Oh, and help me remember to report my car missing. Cassandra abandoned it somewhere to support her story that I left of my own free will." Donovan laughed. "I guess I'd better start making a list instead of asking you to help me remember things."

"How's Wade?" Thom asked.

"Physically getting better, but I don't know about mentally. No matter what happens, he has suffered a major trauma. He didn't deserve what happened to him. He was an innocent boy, and now he's caught up in this mess."

"What's going to happen to him? Valentine talked about making him a second. Doesn't he have a choice?"

"I hope so. I really hope so." Donovan fell silent.

The rest of the drive continued in silence. Thom was thinking about choice. Valentine hadn't given him any choice. When she had exchanged blood with him, she had only been concerned with her own pleasure, not with what might happen to him in the future. He could rationalize that it had been the drugs, the prevailing attitude of freedom, the lack of concern for the future, but in truth, she had condemned him to an existence without asking. Without even thinking to ask him. At that moment, he thought he hated her.

"Those two men, who were they?" Thom asked.

"She called them Panther and Wolf," Donovan replied.

"Surely their names weren't Panther and Wolf."

"I suppose not."

"You don't care, do you?" Thom accused.

Donovan looked at him, surprise written across his face. "I guess I don't. As far as anyone knew, they were already dead. Maybe last year, maybe ten years, who knows? It doesn't matter."

"It matters to me," Thom said bitterly.

Donovan was silent for a long time. "I've kept a file of clippings of all the incidents from that area where I suspected Cassandra might be involved. You're welcome to look at that. It might provide you a clue."

"Thanks. It doesn't seem right that no one will mourn them. They were her get and she just cut off their heads." The horror that Thom had suppressed welled up, and he gripped the steering wheel tightly to keep his hands from trembling.

"Valentine isn't like that," Donovan said softly.

"I know." But did he really know? Did he really know anything about Valentine?

"Cassandra came from the South," Donovan said. "She was born and bred within the context of slavery, where people accepted the idea of one person owning another one. They're probably better off dead, knowing Cassandra's idea of get. She robbed them of their free will and their ability to think. They were no more human than a dog is human. She treated them with just as much respect, putting them down when they no longer could be of use to her."

"I don't think I like being a vampire," Thom whispered, as he turned into the clinic's driveway.

Donovan directed him around the side of the clinic to the garage.

"Damn!" Donovan said, at the sight of the two men who appeared at the clinic entrance.

"What's the matter?" Thom asked.

"It's nothing," Donovan said, shaking himself a little. "Just someone I would rather not see."

Donovan climbed out of the van. "Hello, Stefan, Edmund," he called out in greeting.

There was something familiar about the older, heavyset man. Edmund, Sir Edmund Horn. Thom remembered him from the night Donovan found him, at least Thom thought he did. That night was a bit hazy.

Donovan walked across the garage to meet them. "I didn't expect to see you here, Stefan."

"The Directors sent me to investigate what happened," Stefan said self-importantly.

So that's Stefan, Thom thought. He had met Cassandra and wasn't too impressed with her. Now, he was going to have a chance to meet Stefan. He looked at the man critically, remembering what Valentine had said about him, the man Valentine had raised as her son, whom Cassandra had taken away as her fledgling. The man who had admired Hitler. The man with a cruel streak.

Stefan was tall, well dressed with a broad, boyish face, which most women would find extremely attractive. He certainly didn't look like a monster. But maybe it was what Valentine had said about Stefan or maybe it was the air of self-confidence or rather self-absorption that Thom had often found in men with good looks and power, but Thom felt an instant dislike.

Valentine parked her car next to the van, got out, and walked toward the men. Thom knew her well enough by now to know that she wasn't pleased. The slight frown, the brisk movements. No. She wasn't pleased. "Couldn't the Chairman of the Board have found someone a bit more impartial?" she asked, then without waiting for an answer she turned to the older man. "Hello, Edmund." She gave the large man a warm hug.

Thom hesitated a moment and then got out of the van. He wondered if there was some protocol that he was supposed to follow when he met other vampires. Valentine had never mentioned any, but that didn't mean there wasn't one.

Valentine grabbed his arm and pulled him forward.

"This is my get, Thom Barber. This is Sir Edmund Horn and Stefan Wolkmir."

Thom reached out to shake Sir Edmund's hand. "I understand I have you to thank for my good looks."

Edmund smiled. "I'm glad to see that it turned out so well."

Stefan was eyeing Thom speculatively. "I don't remember you getting approval from the Board for a get, Valentine." Stefan's tone sounded critical.

Thom felt his fangs descend. He really didn't like this man.

"He's a happy accident," Valentine said.

Stefan noticed Thom's fangs and stiffened. His lip curled back away from his own fangs.

Thom just stared at the man, not knowing what to do.

Donovan stepped between them. "Excuse Thom, Stefan. He's a newborn. His fangs just retracted. Come on, Thom, help me get Cassandra out of the van." Thom hurried to the back of the vehicle. Evidently it was a grave insult to show fangs when being introduced to another vampire.

They wrestled the gurney from the van. Cassandra slept, under the continuing influence of the sedative dripping from the IV.

Stefan stared at Cassandra. "Was this really necessary?" he asked, pointing to the straightjacket.

"Yes," Valentine said. "I've been with her for the last day. It's necessary."

Thom pushed the gurney through the doors and found Rose and Sandy waiting. They took charge and wheeled the gurney to the elevator.

"Let Rose and Sandy get Cassandra situated," Donovan said. "Until then we can talk in my office." Donovan turned and walked down the corridor. Edmund and Stefan followed. Valentine hesitated for a moment, then set off determinedly after them. Thom trailed along.

"I'm sorry about the faux pas with the fangs," Thom whispered to Valentine. "I suppose it's really bad form to show your fangs when you meet someone?"

"Not particularly good form, it's sort of considered a challenge, especially between males. Don't worry about it though. My fangs ache when I'm around Stefan, he's such a conceited prick. And to think I raised him! I just hope he doesn't cause problems for Donovan."

Or for me, thought Thom.

~ * ~

Donovan took the chair behind his desk and motioned Edmund and Stefan to be seated. Valentine followed, taking a chair as though she had every right to be there. She looked at Stefan, giving him a cool, hard smile. Thom leaned against the wall, trying to be inconspicuous.

"What do you want to know, Stefan? Anything to help." Donovan smiled, but knew it was patently false.

"Why did you invade another vampire's lair?"

Donovan picked up the thick folder of clippings and slid it across the desk. "Cassandra has been getting careless lately. There were lost teenagers three weeks ago, boys who had gone camping on their own. She left two mutilated bodies practically on her own doorstep. When autopsy reports showed two different bite mark patterns, I began to wonder who was hunting with her. Then there was a young woman kidnapped in Portland. The police had a drawing of a suspect that looked very much like Stanos. Before I went to the Board with my concerns, I thought it wise to check the situation out. I planned to just watch for a few days to see if she was hunting with anyone, then Stanos kidnapped a mushroom hunter. Too many people knew Stanos had been on the road. Suspicion was bound to fall on him, and if it did, then someone might connect him to the picture of the suspect in the kidnapping. I went to talk to Cassandra, and Stanos shot me before I could."

"Reasonable," Edmund said, nodding his satisfaction.

"Is that why you killed Stanos, because he shot you?" Stefan asked.

Donovan shook his head sadly. "No. I didn't intend to kill him. I was starving and lost control."

"You? Lost control?" Stefan tone was derisive.

"Stanos shot me with a silver bullet. Afterward, Cassandra left me chained in the sun, a clever device, a hole in the ceiling with shutters to keep out most of the sun, but not all. Enough to cause a great deal of pain, but not death." Donovan didn't want to talk about Wade, but he knew he couldn't avoid it, not with Cassandra yelling for Wade. "Cassandra had kept one of the boys alive. Wade used his own body to provide me some protection and helped to free me from the chains. By the time, Stanos arrived my need was acute."

"Why didn't you use the boy as a food source?"

"I did. It wasn't enough.

"So where is he now?" Stefan asked.

Donovan thought of lying and saying that Wade had died from the abuse, but just the way Stefan asked the question, he suspected that Stefan already knew.

"Upstairs, in a private room. Do you have any idea what she did to that boy? Cassandra kept him chained like an animal when she wasn't using him." He let his anger and disgust ring through his words. "Her sexual perversions include whips and chains. She took a belt to him, beating him until he bled, because he dared to use his body to protect me from the sun. It was much more than just feeding off him, although she did that, too."

"So that's why you think she's crazy, because she likes a little pain with her pleasure?"

Donovan stared open-mouthed at Stefan for a moment, then he smiled. "No. You and I both know what she's like as a lover. But it's more than, as you say, a little pain with her pleasure. She has taken it to extreme cruelty. That alone is not enough to say she is crazy. She is having a disassociate episode, unable to accept the reality of Stanos's death."

"For which you are to blame!" Stefan said.

"That couldn't be helped," Edmund said soothingly. "Under the circumstance you or I might have lost control as well."

"I don't think keeping Donovan chained and trying to whip him to death is particularly rational, do you?" Valentine asked Stefan. "I spent yesterday with her. I can tell you she isn't in her right mind."

"She is no longer able to control her impulses," Donovan said. "She isn't behaving rationally. She is a danger to herself."

Sandy knocked and entered. "You can see her now. She's coming out of the sedative."

Cassandra lay in the hospital bed, restraints around wrists and ankles. She glared up at Donovan with hatred.

"I'll kill you, kill you, kill you." The refrain went on, a litany of hatred.

She saw Stefan. For a moment, there was a return of normalcy.

"Stefan, you have to help me find Wade. Donovan has taken him away and hidden him from me. You have to help me. Wade is my lover. He loves me, only me," Cassandra cried. "Please bring him now. I need him, don't you see? I need him, and Donovan took him away from me. Donovan did it to hurt me. Tell him that he must bring Wade back. He must make Wade mine again, he must!" As she talked her voice rose until she was screaming.

Edmund looked at Donovan. "I think your presence is upsetting her. Why don't you leave and let me examine her?"

"I'll be in my office."

Edmund looked at Stefan, who shook his head. "I was sent by the Board to investigate what happened and to report to them."

"All right stay," Edmund said.

Donovan stopped to check on Wade. He held the boy's hand. Wade was heavy sedated, but still every little sound caused his body to jerk. Far too long he had lived in fear. Donovan wondered what he was going to do. How he was going to keep his promise?

~ * ~

Valentine and Thom had joined Donovan in his office, waiting. To Donovan, it seemed like a very long time.

"The new identities arrived," Valentine said.

"That's good," muttered Donovan, thinking of Wade.

"My name is still Thom," Thom said. "Thom Russo. Has a nice ring, don't you think?"

"Yes, nice ring," Donovan answered. He heard footsteps hurrying down the corridor.

Rose burst into the room. “Come quick. Stefan’s ordered Wade given to Cassandra.”

Donovan raced down the hall. Rose running after him, “I’m sorry. Edmund asked me about Wade’s condition and I told him.”

Valentine and Thom hurried after them.

Donovan burst into Wade’s room to find Sandy standing beside Wade’s bedside facing down Stefan.

“He’s too sick to be moved,” she said.

“He’s only sedated. You will move him downstairs now.”

“No!” Donovan said.

Stefan turned to look at him. “Both Edmund and I agree that having this boy near her, may calm Cassandra. She’s very agitated.”

“She’s never going near Wade again!”

Stefan’s eyes narrowed. “So there’s truth to her claim that you stole him from her?”

“I didn’t steal him. But she’s never going to get her filthy hands on this boy again. She’s already done him enough harm.”

“He’s hers. You had no right to interfere.”

“He is not hers.”

“Edmund and I both agree.” He turned to Sandy. “You will move him now. You may consider that an order.”

“No, she will not!” Donovan said.

“I represent the Board of Directors. It is my decision.”

“Then I demand an immediate hearing by the full Board of Directors.”

“Are you sure you want that? You invaded Cassandra’s lair, killed her servant, and tried to steal her property.”

“How can you say that,” Valentine cried out. “What about the fact that she had Donovan shot? Then tortured him? When we arrived, she was beating him.”

"Clearly, her long isolation has affected her mind. Who wouldn't be affected? I'm sure all she needs is to return to the society of her own kind."

Donovan was filled with horror at the thought that Stefan might release Cassandra. "She has had a complete mental breakdown," Donovan said. "Did you ask her about Stanos? She is in denial. She needs care, proper care."

"By you?" Stefan sneered.

"I happen to be the only one qualified to treat her. Edmund is a medical doctor, not a psychologist. We will let the Board of Directors decide what is best for all concerned."

"Tomorrow night. I will call the other Board members." Stefan marched out of the room.

"I knew he was going to be trouble," Valentine said.

Seventeen

Edmund found Donovan sitting at Wade's bedside, holding his hand. "Stefan's contacted the other Directors. The meeting is set for tomorrow night at midnight."

"Thanks," Donovan said.

"This the boy?"

"Yes."

"I'm sorry about what she did to him, but it would really be better to do as she wants and give her the boy."

"*No*!" It came out explosive. Wade whimpered in his sleep. Donovan soothed him. "He saved my life. I promised I would protect him. I'm not going to give him back to her."

"But she's made him. He's hers. Stefan has a point. There are those who would frown on you getting between a vampire and what is theirs."

"He isn't hers."

"What do you mean, he isn't hers? She made him?"

"Oh, yes. She made him all right. Do you know what she did to him? She used sex and torture to strip away everything that he was. She always was good at that. She made him give himself to her completely. He was to be her get, under her complete domination. She made him kill for her. Then she didn't bring him across."

"I don't approve of her methods, but what is done is done. He is already Cassandra's."

"He *was* hers. Not any more."

"What? What did you do?"

Donovan grinned. "I did nothing. He broke her control over him on his own."

"That's impossible."

"At least three bites; three exchanges of blood. He broke it after the third exchange. Actually, there was a fourth exchange, which had no effect. He's not hers. He's not anyone's."

"Are you sure?"

Donovan nodded. "Fascinating, isn't it?"

"Worth some study. You haven't had a blood exchange with him?"

"No, although he willingly gave me his blood to help us escape."

"You didn't do anything? No coercion?"

Donovan shook his head.

Edmund frowned. "If what you say is true, it complicates matters. I had thought he could replace Stanos as her servant or be brought across as her get."

"It won't work."

"Valentine mentioned making him a second."

Donovan shook his head. "The boy doesn't deserve to die."

"There's a chance he won't die. We haven't finished checking his blood or his genealogy."

"Edmund, I gave this boy my word that I would protect him from becoming what he fears most, a vampire. I made a promise that if he became a vampire, I would kill him. He would rather be dead than a vampire. Edmund, you've got to help me. He deserves to be free of us to live his life."

Edmund frowned. "He knows about us. After what Cassandra did to him, it won't be simple to mesmerize him into forgetting. If he does have the ability to resist Cassandra, then he might have the power to resist other vampires. We couldn't be sure of controlling him. The only solution is for him to become a vampire. Certainly not as Cassandra's get, but as a second. I would be willing to stand as one of his birth parents."

"I have to try to give this boy back his life. I have to. I think I can make him forget. There are brainwashing techniques--medications--human techniques that I can use to ensure that he forgets about us. I need you to back me on this. No initiation. I want him to have the choice. I want him free of us. Free to live his life. I'm asking this as a favor."

"I don't know. It's risky business."

"If it doesn't work, then we can consider the alternative. He saved my life, Edmund. That should count for something."

"All right. I'll support you, at least for the present. If what you say is true, I want to study him."

"What's your opinion of Cassandra's condition?"

"I'm not a psychologist. Sometimes she seems rational enough, but she denies that Stanos is dead and she's clearly obsessed with the boy and with killing you."

~ * ~

"It's a mockery, a complete shame," Valentine said. "They are literally putting you on trial."

Donovan smiled. "Don't they say, *The Truth shall set you free*?" Just as long as it set Wade free, Donovan would be satisfied. No, somehow he had to stop the others from accepting Stefan's opinion that all Cassandra needed was a little freedom.

He glanced at the clock. Midnight. "Let's go."

Six members of the Darkhour Board waited for Donovan in the large counseling room where they held group sessions. Don Diego, Board Chairman, sat in the middle of the long conference table. He was a Californian from the time that

California had belonged to Mexico, a courtly man, with a slow, lilting speech and a relaxed manner that did little to mask his autocratic nature. Next to him sat Stefan, as though Diego's proximity would convey Stefan more importance than he actually possessed. Fatima sat next to Stefan. Her dark exotic beauty was just beginning to show signs of age. She had ruled the harems of Sultans for over one hundred and fifty years, before venturing beyond their walls. Once freed, she embraced the modern world with great gusto. She joined Darkhour after the London Conference.

On the other side of Don Diego sat Judith. She was the newest member to the Board and one of the youngest sires. She was one of the heirs culled after Roderick's death during World War I. Roderick, in essence, had been Donovan's brother, having the same sire as Donovan. When Charles died at the Alamo, those he had blooded but not changed were culled. Roderick and Madelin survived to claim Charles' land and wealth as heirs and to start new bloodlines. Roderick and Madelin were part of the original Darkhour sires. Donovan wished Roderick were sitting on the Board. He could guess which way Roderick would vote. He had never gotten to know Judith well.

Next to her was Earl. Donovan thought he could count on Earl's support, since he was Donovan's cousin. Orphaned as a young child, Donovan had discovered Earl almost starving after the Civil War and sent him to Amanda to raise. He, along with Valentine, had been part of the first group of second generations.

At the end of the table sat Edmund.

Donovan repeated the story he had already told to Stefan and Edmund. He carefully described what he saw as Cassandra's mental problems, falling back into physiological jargon and his doctor's role.

Stefan spoke up. "If I had been isolated for as long as Cassandra, I too would be feeling the effects. I think that she only needs to have others of her kind around her."

"She is a risk to herself and to us," Donovan said. "She has become increasingly careless. Her recent actions have drawn too much attention and in her current mental state, I doubt she is capable of taking adequate precautions to protect herself and us."

Edmund spoke, "I agree with Donovan on this point. At this time her actions are not rational nor is she thinking clearly."

"But if Donovan had not stolen what was hers," Stefan said, "she wouldn't be in this state. You and I agreed, Edmund, she would improve if she had this Wade with her. Donovan refused. He is keeping what is rightfully hers from her. Cassandra wants the boy back."

"I refused to release the boy to her, because he is not hers," Donovan stated quietly.

"Of course he is," Stefan exclaimed. "You, yourself, said that she had him for over three weeks. She says that he loves her."

"He broke her hold after three blood exchanges."

"That's impossible!" exclaimed Don Diego.

"But true."

"You must have done something to the boy to counteract her influence," Fatima said.

"He had already broken the hold before I arrived. He refused to become a vampire and he denied her. I did nothing to influence him."

"No exchange of blood?" Fatima asked.

"No exchange of blood, although he freely offered his blood at one point. Just as he made every effort to protect me from the sun and to help me escape."

"The boy is here?" Don Diego asked.

"He is."

"Then we should be able to learn the truth of Donovan's statement. Have the boy brought here!" Don Diego ordered.

"No," Donovan protested. "He's too weak. Cassandra kept him chained like an animal, torturing him. Her brand of torture includes sexual abuse and physical pain. He is still recovering from the beating she gave him and his feet were cut to shreds when he tried to escape."

Stefan spoke, "You can't expect us to just take your word for it. No, I want both the boy and Cassandra brought here."

"Cassandra is violent," Donovan protested, again.

"I have seen Cassandra this evening," Stefan said. "She seems calm and rational to me."

Don Diego looked at the other Directors, who all nodded their agreement.

With resignation, Donovan stood. "I will have Rose and Sandy bring them."

~ * ~

"How you feeling, Wade?" Rose asked.

"Better. Where's Donovan? He hasn't been to see me." Wade was worried.

"He has. You were asleep when he was here, and he didn't want to disturb you because you needed your rest. Wade, do you feel up to talking to some people about what happened?"

"No." Wade shut his eyes. He didn't want to think about Cassandra, about what had happened to him. He just wanted to go home and see his parents.

Rose took his hand in hers. "I know you don't want to talk about it, but this is really important. This is sort of a trial, a hearing, to determine if what Donovan did was right."

"Of course, it was right," Wade said hotly. "He couldn't help himself when he killed Stanos."

"Well, they won't believe him unless they can talk to you."

"All right." Wade knew he had to help Donovan.

Rose helped Wade into a robe, shifted him to a wheel chair without putting too much pressure on his sore feet, and wheeled him down to the conference room.

"Are these people, are they vampires?"

"Yes. But don't worry, they won't hurt you."

Wade bit his lip to keep himself from begging Rose to take him back to his room.

On one side of the room sat six people. Vampires, Wade reminded himself, but they looked perfectly human. Four men and two women. On the other side of the room sat Donovan, Valentine and Thom.

Rose stopped the wheelchair in front of the table and rested her hand on Wade's shoulder. He took comfort from her touch.

The man at the end of the table brought his chair over and sat next to Wade. He was an older man, kind of old-fashion-looking, with a nice face.

"Hello, Wade, my name is Edmund. Do you mind if I ask you some questions?"

Wade shook his head. Edmund asked about what happened when Wade first met Cassandra. Wade found tears rolling down his cheeks as he talked about Josh and Mike.

"And Cassandra took you back to her lair?"

"Yes."

"Did Cassandra drink your blood?"

"Almost every night."

"Did you drink her blood?"

Wade nodded.

"More than once? More than three times?"

"Yes. She made me, just like she made me love her. She hypnotized me. She made me believe things that weren't true."

"I see. When did you realize that she hypnotized you?"

"After she told me to be jealous of Panther."

"Panther?"

"He was her favorite before me. She spent the night with him and told me to think only of her and to be jealous of Panther and what he was doing to her. I did. I hated him. In the morning, I realized what she had done to me. I swore I wouldn't let her do it me again, but she did. Then she made me rape and kill Sue. She used Voodoo because I told her I wouldn't hurt Sue and I didn't want to be a vampire."

"Was this before or after Donovan arrived?"

"Before."

"Did you drink Donovan's blood?"

"No, sir."

"Did he drink yours?"

"Yes. Once."

"Did he ask you to help him?"

"No. He tried to protect me, but he couldn't do much. She had him chained up. But he tried."

"So why did you help him?"

"Because he was her enemy and I thought if he escaped, he would take me with him."

"You wanted to leave Cassandra?"

"Yes."

"You're lying!" Cassandra interrupted.

Wade looked up in horror as the other nurse, Sandy, wheeled Cassandra in.

"You love me," Cassandra said. "You want to be with me."

"No." Wade forced himself to look directly at Cassandra.

"Donovan made you say that. You love me. Only me."

"Did Donovan tell you to say that?" Edmund asked.

"No!" Wade said. He felt Cassandra's eyes boring into him, demanding his surrender, trying to breach his defenses. He remembered Sue. He remembered Josh. He remembered that

Donovan had told him that she no longer had any power over him.

"I'm not yours, Cassandra, and I never will be again."

Cassandra looked at Donovan, her eyes gleamed with hatred, and before anyone could react, she rushed him, screaming. "You did this. I'll kill you. I'll kill you." The strength of her charge carried them onto the floor, her hands finding Donovan's throat.

Wade tried to go to Donovan's aid, but Rose held him back. Others grabbed Cassandra and tried to pull her off Donovan, but she gripped him with fanatical strength.

Sandy took a hypodermic needle from her pocket, pulled off the protective cap, and stepped close to ram it into Cassandra's neck. Slowly, Cassandra collapsed into a heap. They pulled Cassandra off Donovan and manhandled her limp body into the wheel chair.

Donovan just lay there. Had she killed him? Wade wondered. Then Donovan groaned and sat up.

Sandy started to push Cassandra's wheel chair from the room. "I'll get her back in restraints before she comes around and tries to kill someone else."

She wheeled Cassandra away.

Donovan came over to Wade and took his hand.

"Is it over?" Wade asked in a small voice. Donovan looked at the others. They looked stunned.

Edmund spoke. "I think that clearly answers the question of whether or not Cassandra is rational." He looked at Wade. "It is also clear that she no longer has any control over the boy. I theorize that her mental problems have limited her power to mesmerize and control humans. For our safety, we can't allow her freedom. I recommend that she stay here for care and treatment."

“Treatment?” one of the younger men laughed. Wade didn’t like the man’s laugh. It was cruel and harsh. “You think Donovan is going to treat her? Do you think she will allow him to treat her, the way she feels about him?”

“Until we can find someone qualified to help her,” Edmund said. “I will treat her under Donovan’s supervision and counsel, Stefan.”

Stefan. That was the one Stanos had talked about.

The man in the center spoke, “That sounds reasonable.”

“What about the boy?” The woman next to him asked. “It would be cruel to give him to Cassandra.”

Wade trembled. Would they order him given back to Cassandra? Donovan’s hand tightened around his.

“It might help her recovery,” Stefan said.

“Please,” Wade spoke up, his voice timid. “Please, don’t let her touch me again. I would rather be dead.”

“Since Cassandra has lost control of the boy, it wouldn’t work anyway,” Edmund said.

“I can make him forget,” Donovan said. “I can wipe it from his memory.”

The man in the center frowned. He seemed to be the leader of the group, the one who made the decision. “I don’t know. If he managed to break Cassandra’s hold, who is to say he couldn’t break yours? That he won’t remember?”

“There are ways, medicines--treatments--brainwashing--human ways that I can use to ensure that he forgets.”

“Perhaps it would be better to make him a vampire,” the dark-haired, dark-skinned woman said. “Do we know what his chances are of surviving the change?”

“Sixty-five percent,” Donovan said.

Wade looked at Donovan. “You said that it wasn’t likely that I would become a vampire when I died. You said.”

Donovan looked sad. "It would seem that you are part of the small percentage that possibly would survive."

"I don't want to be a vampire."

Wade looked at these people who were going to decide his fate. Who were thinking about making him a vampire? He turned to Donovan. "You promised."

"And I will keep my promise."

Wade struggled to stand, the pain in his feet shot up through his legs, into his heart and mind, and suddenly everything seemed so clear. So right.

"I understand to become a vampire, I must die first, is that right?"

The man in the center nodded.

"Then I would ask a favor. I would like to choose the manner of my death and who will carry it out. Would that be all right?"

The dark-haired woman said, "It's against custom, but maybe this time, we could make an exception."

"Then I want Donovan to kill me, and I want him to de--decap--cut off my head."

"Do you understand what you are saying?" the woman asked.

"Yes, I understand. I would rather be dead than become a monster like you. I don't want to kill, to drink blood. I don't want to be a vampire. I would rather die here and now."

~ * ~

"Hello," Donovan held out his hand. "I'm Doctor Reed."

The two people in front of him had hope in their eyes, but fear as well. Wade's father took Donovan's hand. "I'm Robert Kain and this is my wife, Gladys. Have you really found our son?"

"I hope so. This way." Donovan led Wade's parents to a small room with a one-way mirror; beyond in the larger room, sat Wade in a wheel chair. "Is that your son?"

"Yes," Robert said.

"Wade, oh, Wade." Gladys was crying tears of joy. "Please, I want to see him."

"We need to talk first. I know you want to see your son, to hold him, but this is important. Let's go back to my office where it's more comfortable."

"Is he all right?" Gladys demanded.

"Come, let's talk in my office." He showed them out of the room, Gladys' gaze clung to her son, until the door shut off her view.

Robert looked grim as he took a seat in Donovan's office. Gladys was crying. Donovan handed her a box of Kleenex before he took his seat.

"Let me start by telling you that physically Wade is doing pretty well. His feet were badly cut up, but they are healing well. Mentally, he's not doing as well. When he was first discovered and brought here, he couldn't tell us his name. He was almost catatonic. I'm sorry that it took so long, but it has just been in the last couple of weeks that we've made strides, that he could finally tell us his name. This won't be pleasant to hear, some of it is conjecture; I haven't been able to get him to talk about very much. After his friends were attacked by wolves, Wade escaped and made it to the road and was grateful when some hunters picked him up. He was badly traumatized by seeing Josh attacked and killed. He and Mike ran, but Mike was dragged down, and Wade heard him die. He thought he was safe, but the hunters turned out to be sexual deviates, a woman and two men. They held him prisoner, sexually abused him, tortured him. When he arrived here, he still had the markings of a bad beating. How he escaped, he doesn't remember, but the local farmer found him wandering down a road, his bare feet so cut up that he could barely take another step. The farmer brought him to the clinic. We're the closest medical facility around. I've been working with him and finally we had a breakthrough. He started to trust me and talk to me."

Gladys was still crying. Robert held her hand.

"I did some checking after you called," Robert said. "You are highly respected. Although I wasn't sure when I found out that you deal mostly with people who believe they are vampires."

"I assure you, I am well trained, not just in dealing with so-called vampires, although it has been a fascinating subject to study. In cases like your son's, the important thing is the connection between the patient and the doctor. Does the patient trust the doctor?"

"I was told that."

"I'd like to keep treating Wade, if you'll let me. It's probably too early to discuss that. I'll take you to see your son. He may or may not recognize you. There are gaps in his memory. Don't worry, they'll fill in, but don't try to make him remember. I will tell him that I have told you everything that you need to know, that he doesn't have to talk about it unless he wants to, that you won't ask him questions about what happened. It's important that he feel he has control, that he isn't a victim. Your son is a very courageous young man; they tried to make him believe that he couldn't resist them. And for a time, he believed it. He even talks about being in love with the woman; her name was Cassandra. But he broke free. One thing he told me, he said you would tell him, that when bad things happen to you, you have a choice. You don't have to let them make you bad. He feels he has done some bad things, but he doesn't want them to make him bad. It took courage to escape."

"The police, have they found the people who did it?"

Donovan shook his head. "Wade hasn't been able to remember where they took him. He probably never knew. The police have a general area, but a house-to-house search didn't turn up anything. We may never know."

"I want them found and brought to justice."

"That won't help Wade, your wanting revenge. He'll be fine if we give him time to heal. Children are very resilient. But you both will need to let it go yourselves. I suspect you will need some counseling, too. This isn't easy to deal with, but you will. Now, I haven't said anything about you to Wade, so let me go and prepare him and give you time to get yourselves under control. I know I have said a lot and it hasn't been easy to hear. But, believe me, in time you will all put it behind you. Take as much time as you need, then my nurse will show you the way."

Donovan walked down the hall and opened the door. Wade looked up and grinned. "Hi, Donovan."

Donovan sat. "Wade, your parents are here. Are you ready for that?"

"If you say I am, then I am."

"You trust me, don't you?"

"Of course, with my life."

"Yes, with your life." Donovan leaned back in his chair. He felt guilty. Sometimes he wondered during the dead of night, if what Cassandra had done to Wade was really any worse than what he had done. He had wiped much of Wade's memory and then rebuilt it. He made him forget. Made him forget that Cassandra was a vampire, made him forget that Donovan was a vampire, too, made him forget that Donovan had been there. He had robbed the boy of his memories and with them, how much of his soul and his strength? But the boy would live. He would live.

The door opened and Wade's parents entered. Donovan left quietly, leaving them to their family reunion.

~ * ~

Edmund leaned back in the chair and stuck his feet out in front of him. He and Donovan were sitting on the front porch of the clinic. "It's sure quiet up here," Edmund said.

"Peaceful."

"How is it going with Wade?"

"Fine. His parents were here last week. Nice people. I got Wade's father a job teaching at the local school. They will be moving here soon."

"He has forgotten?"

"Yes. The conditioning will hold."

"I'm sorry about them declaring Wade as Cassandra's heir. I know that it made it a lot harder without being able to do a blood exchange. But with the condition Cassandra's in, it just seemed like a good idea to have someone blooded that could be culled if something happens to her."

It was like a sword hanging over Wade's head. "Was it Stefan's idea?"

"Diego's actually. He thought it would insure that you took good care of Cassandra. Make sure nothing happened to her, so nothing would happen to Wade."

The decision still galled Donovan, but there was nothing he could do about it.

"So what did you think of my session with Cassandra?" Edmund asked. "She seemed much calmer today."

"It's a facade. She's still in denial and she's still obsessed with Wade." There were days when Donovan wished he had killed Cassandra when he had the chance, but he only had to think of Wade to be glad he hadn't.

~ * ~

Wade and Donovan sat in Donovan's office. "So how's the new school?"

"It's O.K. Different from the school in Portland, more like my old school where everyone knows everyone, including me. I guess I'm sort of a celebrity, but people have been really nice. They don't ask me too many questions."

Donovan grinned. "That's good. I told them not to. That's one of the perks of being the old doctor in a little town. So you tried out for the football team?"

"Yep. Not sure yet what position the coach will play me, but I like it. I'm glad you talked me into going back and finishing school."

"How are the nightmares?"

"I keep dreaming that I am having sex with a woman and I bite her neck. I have fangs and I know it has happened. I am a vampire. I don't know why it should be the thing I fear the most. There are no such things as vampires."

"That's right. Vampires aren't real. I've told you before. It was your mind giving a symbol to what was happening to you. You couldn't accept your helplessness, so your captors had to be more than human. They had to be evil, so they became vampires."

Wade nodded. "I do know one thing. I keep seeing you as my hero. You come to save me. When I remember you, I know I am safe."

"You are. I will keep you safe," said Donovan. *I will keep my promise to you,* he silently vowed.

Meet Linda Suzane

After thirty years of writing, Linda Suzane discovered what she was destined to write about when a character stepped out of a short story and demanded that she tell the tale of how he was first bitten by a vampire. What happened afterward was a magical experience that every writer hopes to have, where they find the characters taking over the story, when the story almost writes itself. 200,000 words, four books later, Linda had the first draft of the Darkhour Vampires. Seeing the first book in the series, *Captivity*, in print is just the beginning. Linda is already hard at work on the second book in the series, *Freedom*. To learn more about the Darkhour Vampires, visit www.darkhourvampires.com

When not working on her Darkhour Vampires, Linda enjoys reading and reviewing Vampire eBooks for Suite101.com Vampire eBook Authors:

http://www.suite101.com/welcome.cfm/vampire_ebook_authors

or working on her website www.e-Vampires.net and it's newsletter for readers and writers of Vampire/Shapeshifter fiction.

Linda lives on the beautiful Oregon coast with her husband, four domineering cats, and an office full of dragons. She has published two other eBooks. *The Murder Game,* a romantic mystery about a mystery game designer whose game goes murderously wrong, is available from www.playmurder.com *Eyes of Truth* is a fantasy mystery with just a touch of vampirism, available from www.twilighttimesbooks.com